MAX in the LAND of LIES

ALSO BY
Adam Gidwitz:

A Tale Dark & Grimm
In a Glass Grimmly
The Grimm Conclusion

The Inquisitor's Tale:
Or, The Three Magical Children and Their Holy Dog

Max in the House of Spies:
Operation Kinderspion, Book 1

The Unicorn Rescue Society series:

The Creature of the Pines

The Basque Dragon
WITH JESSE CASEY

Sasquatch and the Muckleshoot
WITH JOSEPH BRUCHAC

The Chupacabras of the Río Grande
WITH DAVID BOWLES

The Madre de Aguas of Cuba
WITH EMMA OTHEGUY

The Secret of the Himalayas
WITH HENA KHAN

TOP SECRET

OPERATION KINDERSPION

MAX in the LAND of LIES

Adam Gidwitz

DUTTON CHILDREN'S BOOKS

DUTTON CHILDREN'S BOOKS
An imprint of Penguin Random House LLC
1745 Broadway, New York, New York 10019

First published in the United States of America by Dutton Children's Books,
an imprint of Penguin Random House LLC, 2025

Visit us online at PenguinRandomHouse.com.

Library of Congress Cataloging-in-Publication Data is available.

ISBN 9780593112113
1 3 5 7 9 10 8 6 4 2

Printed in the United States of America

BVG

Edited by Julie Strauss-Gabel
Design by Anna Booth
Text set in Maxime Regular

To Erica, Ryan, and Tony

Who know my secrets and love me anyway

It is difficult to get a man to understand something when his salary depends upon his not understanding it.

— Upton Sinclair

Between the truth and my mother, I choose my mother.

— Albert Camus (sort of)

To understand the story that follows, you have to remember a few things. Including what happened in the previous volume, *Max in the House of Spies*:

Max, a brilliant Jewish boy, was sent away from home and from his parents to escape the Nazis. Living in England, he convinced British intelligence to train him as a spy so he could go back to Germany. Last we saw him, he was dropped into Germany by parachute, harnessed to Major Johnny Jameson—and Major Jameson died on impact with the ground.

So that's what you have to remember. But you also have to FORGET a few things. You have to forget everything you know about World War II, about Nazi Germany, and about the Holocaust. For example, you might know that starting in 1941, Nazi Germany and the Soviet Union went to war with each other. You might know that in 1942, the Nazis began to systematically murder all the Jewish people living in Europe. And you might know that in 1945, Nazi Germany was defeated and Adolf Hitler killed himself.

But no one knew any of that in the fall of 1940, when we resume our story.

What they knew was that Germany was winning the war, their economy was booming, and their experiment with Nazism was going very, very well indeed . . .

CHAPTER One

"You're just going to *leave* him there?"

Max walked away from the body of Major Johnny Jameson. The muscular paratrooper with a hero's mustache lay staring at the sky, black blood pooling beneath his head.

"Max!" said Stein, the dybbuk who'd been sitting on Max's left shoulder for over a year now. Stein had the affect of a vaudeville comedian and a hint of Yiddish in his speech. "Max, shouldn't you *do something* with the dead guy? Wrap him in his parachute and bury him or something?"

Max ignored Stein. There were lights along the edge of the field. Max headed that way.

"I don't want to be here!" moaned Berg, the kobold who'd been sitting on Max's right shoulder for over a year now. Berg spoke with an antique German accent and had the mopey demeanor of some Bavarian philosophy student. "We got on your shoulders in the first place to get *away* from Germany! Now we're *back*?!"

Max would have told his immortal hitchhikers to keep

quiet—since he was a spy who had just parachuted out of a British bomber into Nazi Germany, and he was *really* hoping to avoid attracting attention—but that was unnecessary, because he seemed to be the only human who could hear or see Stein and Berg.

At the moment, though, he wished he could neither hear nor see them.

He needed to *focus.*

He was on a mission.

Well, two missions.

Mission One: infiltrate the Funkhaus, the center of Nazi radio and propaganda. This was the mission his British spymasters knew about. It was why they'd sent him.

Mission Two: find his parents. Mission Two was forbidden. Max's spymaster and adopted uncle, Lieutenant Commander Ewen Montagu, had made him promise *not* to go looking for his parents. Max had promised. He had lied.

Two missions. One twelve-year-old Jewish boy in Nazi Germany. *What's the worst that could happen?* Max asked himself. That was a joke. He knew what could happen. What probably *would* happen.

Just focus. Take it one piece at a time. Like assembling a watch. That's what his papa would have told him.

First piece: Get to my apartment building. Without getting caught.

The lights at the edge of the field turned out to be a couple of houses. Good.

Max figured where there were houses, there had to be a road.

He was right. The road was long and thin and newly paved.

Max looked left and right. "Which way to Berlin?" he murmured.

Stein pointed down the road. "Berlin is that way."

"You're sure?" Max asked.

"Let me think . . ." said Stein. "I've lived in Germany since the Sixth Day of Creation, and while the pavement is new, this road has been here since at least 1640—"

"And it was an oxcart path since the 1300s," Berg put in.

"—so, yeah. I'm *pretty* sure," Stein concluded. "Any other dumb questions?"

CHAPTER
Two

As Max made his way down the paved country lane, Berg said to Stein, "I can't believe Max just left that dead man in the field."

"Yeah," agreed Stein, studying the side of Max's face in the moonlight. "And he doesn't even seem upset about it!"

This was not true. Max was very, *very* upset about the death of Major Johnny Jameson.

But he couldn't afford to think about it.

Back in Tring Park, Uncle Ewen had said: *You have to have a strange relationship with truth to live a fiction, Max. You have to* believe *the fiction you're living, and your mind needs to be totally and utterly free from the truth.* Except. *You cannot* lose *the truth. You must keep it buried, in a box under the stairs in the cellar of your brain. You might even struggle to find it some days. But if it's tossed out, if it's lost . . . then so are you.*

Max had shut Major Jameson in a box, carried the box down into the cellar of his brain, and shoved it into a dark hiding place under the stairs.

He just hoped the body's smell wouldn't haunt his dreams.

Hours later, Max was walking down the broad boulevard known as Friedrichstrasse. It was two in the morning, according to the clock on top of the newsstand. Max should have been tired. He'd walked through the countryside, then through the wealthy suburbs of Charlottenburg.

But he was in Berlin now, for the first time in more than a year.

His town. His dangerous, thrilling town. The streets were empty. The five-, six-, seven-story buildings were lit from below by yellow streetlamps. Silent. Waiting. In just a couple of hours the city would explode again into raucous life.

Flush with adrenaline and sleep deprivation and the recent trauma of being attached to a dead man, Max didn't care that he was a Jew in a nation of Nazis. He was back in the city of his birth, where he'd spent every minute of his life before leaving for England. He knew the streets, the alleys, the signs, the crosswalks, the buildings. He knew it all.

And the two police officers strolling down Friedrichstrasse. They looked like any Grüne Polizei in Berlin, wearing long green trench coats and military helmets.

Except these two cops were heading directly for Max.

"Oh no," said Stein.

"They're coming for you," said Berg.

Max stopped. He did not run, though he wanted to.

He forced himself to stand there, watching the cops approach.

And he threw his mind back to England.

Specifically, to a kangaroo.

Specifically, specifically, to Kathy Kangaroo.

Specifically, specifically, specifically, back to what Jean Leslie had said after he'd been attacked by Kathy Kangaroo: *No matter what someone is doing to you, no matter how strange or scary it is, stay calm. If you stay calm, you can think.*

Max tried to slow his racing heartbeat as the two cops got closer.

One was older, with a small, curly mustache and a belly so big it seemed to be leading him down the street. The other cop was lean, and young. Young enough that he probably should have been in the army. But he wasn't. Which worried Max.

Max glanced to his right. There was a garbage-strewn alley with a door at the end. *Think,* Max told himself. *Stay calm and think.*

The door would be locked.

There was a trashcan in the alley, which looked to be full.

Beer bottles were strewn across the alley's cobblestones.

Hmm, thought Max.

And then he thought, *Perfect.*

He started speaking very quickly to Stein and Berg. (Just as no one else could hear Stein and Berg, no one could hear or see that Max was talking to them. Max didn't understand it—it was metaphysical or something. But he was used to it now.)

"I need one of you to go to the alley . . ." he began.

"Oh, no, we're not helping you ever again!" Berg said, waving his hands. "The last time we helped you, you brought us back to this Nazi-infested hellhole!"

Max ignored him. ". . . find a beer bottle that still has some beer in it, pour it in your mouth . . ."

"Ew! No! Are you listening to me, Max?" continued Berg.

"And then you're going to spit it . . ."

Suddenly, Berg stopped objecting.

Max finished explaining his idea. Stein laughed. Berg was smirking.

"Okay, never mind," Berg announced. "This is my kind of plan." And he slipped off Max's shoulder and disappeared.

Just in time, because the Grüne Polizei, or Green Cops, were now just a few feet from Max. The older one with the curly mustache stopped. The younger one didn't.

He was smiling. It was not a friendly smile. He walked until he was just a few inches from Max. Uncomfortably close. Max had to look up as the young Green Cop looked down into Max's face. "Where do you think you're going?" The young cop's breath smelled of alcohol, and his teeth were stained brown, like he fell asleep with a bottle of schnapps glued to his lips.

Max swallowed. "I'm going to my uncle's." This was the story that Lieutenant Charles Chumley and Uncle Ewen had drilled into him before he'd left England.

The young cop's eyes narrowed. Slowly. "You're going to your uncle's at two in the morning?"

Max did not have an answer for that. Johnny Jameson was supposed to have helped Max hide somewhere until sunrise. The plan hadn't been for Max to be walking alone through the streets of Berlin in the middle of the night. But before Max could think of an explanation for why he was going to his uncle's at two a.m., the older cop said, "What happened to your chin?"

Max touched his chin. He could feel dried blood, and now that he was touching it, he realized it hurt. He thought back to when the navigator had kicked them out of the bomber. He hadn't remembered slamming his chin against the bomb bay door until just now. He thought back to Major Johnny Jameson, with his head cracked open, in a field. Max wondered when someone would find his body.

And when the authorities would come.

And when they would see that Major Johnny Jameson was wearing a double harness.

And when they would start to wonder where the other parachuter was.

"Kid?" said the older cop with the little mustache. "Hello?"

"I'm going to my uncle's because my father's been drinking," Max improvised.

Suddenly, the young cop's hands were on Max's jacket, grabbing his lapels. "So? What's wrong with a little drink?"

Max murmured, "My dad gets kinda rough when he drinks."

The young cop jerked Max closer to him. Right into the

cloud of his boozy breath. "*And . . . ?* If your father wants to smack you around, that's his right!" He thrust Max away, making Max's head snap forward.

The older cop spoke to Max: "Who is your uncle?"

Max rubbed the back of his neck. "Pastor Andreas Maas."

"Where does he live?"

"Kreuzberg."

The young cop snapped, "Let's see your papers."

Max hesitated.

Every German had to carry their papers with them at all times. To prove who they were. To prove that they weren't enemy agents.

Or Jews.

Max, of course, was both.

"You do have papers, don't you?" the young cop demanded.

"No . . ." said Max slowly.

The young cop eagerly began fumbling to unclasp the leather pouch on his belt where he kept his handcuffs. Until the older one said, "Of course he doesn't have papers, Dieter. How old are you, kid? Ten?"

"Twelve," said Max.

Every German aged fifteen and above had to carry their papers. Kids didn't have papers. Except Jewish kids. Which Max was pretending he wasn't.

Suddenly, there was a clatter of bottles from the alleyway. The older cop looked over his shoulder.

Max smiled to himself.

But the young cop—Dieter—must have seen Max smile, because suddenly he grabbed Max by the collar and he began twisting Max's shirt so it choked him.

"Oh no," said Stein. And then he called to Berg, "Hurry up!"

Dieter had pulled Max close to his face. "Running away from a beating . . . that's the problem with this country! My father used to beat me and thank God he did! That's how you know he loves you."

Stein said, "Uh . . . *no.*"

The young cop was still breathing booze into Max's face. "Maybe I should give you the beating your father thinks you deserve," Dieter snarled.

"Dieter . . ." the older policeman said. "Come on . . ."

The young cop raised a fist. His knuckles were scabbed, like he used them a lot.

Stein shouted at Berg, *"What are you waiting for?!"*

The scabbed fist was drawn back—when Max, as calmly as he could manage, said, "Excuse me, did you pee in your pants?"

"WHAT?" snapped Dieter, on the verge of letting his fist fly. He looked down—and then he shoved Max away from him. A large wet stain trailed down his pants, from his groin to his knee.

"Oh, Dieter," said the older cop. *"Again?"*

Dieter said, "I didn't! I don't know how that happened!"

"I'm going to have to report this, Dieter. Drinking on the

job. Wetting your pants. It's embarrassing!" The older cop looked at Max. Then he jerked his head. "Get to your uncle's. And get that chin looked at. You might need stitches."

Max gave the older cop a silent, grateful nod—and then hustled away.

Berg had climbed back onto Max's shoulder. The kobold was laughing. He had done just what Max had told him to: gone to the alley, found a beer bottle with some beer still in it, poured it in his mouth, and then spit it onto the Green Cop's pants. He crowed, "What a good plan, Max! You've still got it! And how about my timing, huh? That is some expert prank work, no?"

But Stein merely murmured as he wiped sweat from his immortal brow, "One encounter with the authorities down. An infinite number to go."

And Max? Max's heart was beating so fast it hurt.

CHAPTER Three

When Max reached his apartment building about an hour later, the first thing he noticed was the large glass shopwindow. WATCH REPAIR, it said.

Max suddenly felt like he was levitating. For a mad moment, he thought, *My father's shop is open! Uncle Ewen was* wrong*!*

But as soon as he thought it, he saw the words printed below WATCH REPAIR.

WATCHMAKER BALDUR PERSICKE. A TRUE GERMAN.

Max stopped levitating. In fact, now he felt like he was sinking into the sidewalk.

Who is Baldur Persicke? he thought, before remembering that Persicke was the name of the family living in his apartment now.

Isn't Jacob Bretzfeld a true German?

And if he's not here, where is he? And where is Mama?

The shop was on the first floor, its door on the left. On the right was the door that led to the apartments above. That door, as always, was coated with layers of thick green paint that reflected the yellow streetlights behind him.

Eight buzzers, eight black buttons, set in a brass frame.

A small card next to the bottom left buzzer read PERSICKE, in crisp, typewritten letters.

Not BRETZFELD.

"Tough luck, kid," said Stein.

Suddenly Max wanted to lie down in the field next to Major Johnny Jameson and die.

Instead, he reached out and pushed the buzzer next to the name Maas. The sharp electric buzz made him wince.

He waited.

He glanced over his shoulder.

If Pastor Andreas Maas did not open this door soon, surely some neighbor would see Max standing in the street. And report him to the Gestapo. The Gestapo was not like the Grüne Polizei. They were much, much worse.

Max was about to ring the bell again when the door opened, and Max exhaled in relie—

It was not Pastor Andreas Maas.

It was a girl, just about Max's age.

"Who are you?" the girl snarled. She had yellow hair and hazel eyes that were squinting angrily. "What the hell are you doing ringing the bell in the middle of the night?"

Max was so surprised he couldn't form a single sentence. "I . . . I thought . . ."

The girl's gaze was withering.

"I'm . . . looking for my uncle."

"Your uncle doesn't live here. Are you *drunk*?"

Who was this rude, foulmouthed girl?

"I'm looking for Pastor Andreas."

Suddenly, there was creaking on the stairs behind the girl, causing her to spin around. "Pastor! Some boy claiming to be your nephew is here! In the middle of the night! And your stupid buzzer is so loud it woke me up! What the devil is going on? He's got blood on his face! Should I call my father? Or maybe the Gestapo?"

Pastor Andreas reached over the girl's head and pulled the door wide open.

"That won't be necessary, Liesel."

Max hadn't seen the pastor in over a year. He looked almost the same. He was still very tall, with a long neck and eyes so circular they reminded you that no one actually has circles for eyes, except for maybe Pastor Andreas. The only difference was that his hair, which had once been black with gray patches, was now entirely white. "Hello, Max," he said. Then he looked down at the girl. "I'm sorry, Liesel, I didn't expect Max until the morning. I apologize for disturbing you."

Liesel sneered up at the pastor. "Everything about you *disturbs* me. Is he really your nephew? You never said you had a nephew."

"He is the grandson of my oldest brother. And why would I have mentioned my nephew to you, Liesel? We never talk."

"I don't talk to traitors like you," she shot back. And then she stomped through the echoey foyer of the building, past the mailboxes on the left, up the stairs—making far more noise than the buzzer—and disappeared from view.

An instant later they heard a door slam. On the second landing.

Where Max's family's apartment was.

"I guess my parents really aren't here," Max said to Pastor Andreas.

Andreas put a long finger to his lips and gestured for Max to follow him up the stairs.

CHAPTER Four

Pastor Andreas's apartment looked the same. To the right, a kitchen, with a round table and two chairs. To the left, a living room—Max noticed the standard issue People's Receiver wireless radio right away, and also a small bookshelf that was bending under the weight of books shoved sideways and straightways and every-which-ways into each available crevice and cranny. Beyond the living room was the bedroom. Straight ahead, facing the front door, was the toilet. Max pointed at it and, after a nod from Pastor Andreas, hustled inside and closed the door behind him.

He examined his chin. Blood had dried in a streak down his neck. He wet a hand towel and wiped it away, and then cleaned the cut as best he could. He wouldn't need stitches. He hoped.

Then he headed to the kitchen, where a kettle was on the stove and pumpernickel bread and butter on the table. Max gratefully smeared as much butter on the thick slice as he thought he could get away with and shoved it hungrily into his mouth. Pastor Andreas set down a mug of watery hot cocoa in front of Max, which Max used to wash down the bread.

Pastor Andreas smiled kindly at the boy.

Max wiped his mouth on his sleeve, and with no prologue whatsoever, said, "Where are my parents?"

Pastor Andreas frowned. "We should keep our voices down," he said quietly. "You met Liesel Persicke already. My new neighbor."

"You mean the little Nazi who looks like she bathes in lemon juice?" said Stein. "She was grumpier than *you*," he added, looking at Berg.

"And you know, for some reason," Berg replied, "that did not make me like her any more."

Pastor Andreas, of course, couldn't see or hear any of this. He went on in low tones: "Liesel isn't even the worst of them. Frau Persicke, her mother, is the worst. Definitely a Gestapo informant. She calls them if the mail carrier isn't here before four p.m. each day. I bet even the Gestapo hate her."

He smiled at Max. Pastor Andreas had a charming, lost demeanor that made you relax immediately.

But Max didn't relax.

Pastor Andreas noticed this and kept speaking: "There's also Liesel's little brother, Bert. He's all right, for now. But each day that goes by he swallows a little more of the Persickes' bitterness. It's heartbreaking. Baldur, the father, focuses on his work and ignores his family."

Watchmaker Baldur Persicke. A True German.

Max said, again: "Where are my parents?"

Pastor Andreas got up and poured a cup of watery cocoa for himself. "I was contacted through the Grüber group. The same people who helped get you out of Germany. They said you were coming back. I couldn't believe it. After all we did to get you out, why on earth would you comc *back*? Most Jews would *kill* to get out Germany right now. Heck, *I'd* kill to get out of Germany. Not literally, of course." He smiled apologetically. "I'm a pacifist. That's why Liesel calls me a traitor, you know. Because I'm against the war."

"Have you noticed that he's not answering Max's question?" Berg said.

"Yeah, we noticed," Stein replied.

Max looked right into Pastor Andreas's round eyes and spoke very slowly. "Pastor Andreas. Please. *Where are my parents?*"

The pastor sat down. The creases at the edges of his eyes stretched until they met the white hair at his temples.

"I don't know, Max."

"What happened to them?"

"It's a long story. Maybe you should sleep. Have you slept at all tonight? You need to sleep. A young body without sleep is like a—"

"Pastor Andreas." Max's voice was a little too loud.

"Call me 'uncle' now," said Andreas. "For the cover story. And *please*, keep your voice down. Liesel is probably standing on her bed right now, with her ear against the ceiling."

Max's voice was very quiet when he said: *"Tell me."*

Pastor Andreas sighed and looked into his cup of cocoa.

And then he told Max.

CHAPTER Five

"About a month after you left, a Nazi official came to your parents' apartment," Pastor Andreas said, still staring into his cup.

Max's fingers were interlocked like a cage. On his shoulders, Stein's and Berg's tiny hands were doing the same thing.

"This Nazi was interested in your father's talent with watches. He was recruiting workers for a factory that makes very small parts for rifles, pistols, and bombs. Fine machine work, they call it. Your father would be perfect, the official told your parents. And if he agreed to come work in the factory, he could start making money again. Not a lot, being Jewish, of course. Couldn't take money from the pockets of *true* Germans, he said. But some. And your parents could stay in the apartment. Otherwise, they would be evicted."

Max's fingers were pressing so hard into his flesh that he was hurting himself. He pressed harder.

"So your father started working at the Krupp fine machine parts factory, over in Spandau. But I guess it didn't go too well."

"His eyesight," Max said.

"So you knew? I didn't," said Andreas.

Max looked at his clenched hands. "That's why he likes the radio so much. He can listen and rest his eyes."

Pastor Andreas looked momentarily confused. "I thought the radio was *your* passion?" And then, comprehension dawned on him. Max loved working with radios because it was the one way he could help his father feel better.

Pastor Andreas went on: "Your father kept making mistakes at the new job, because of his eyesight. And the foreman at the factory . . . well, he was not kind."

Max could imagine.

"Your father didn't like to talk about it, but your mother told me that the factory foreman was shouting at him, calling him a 'filthy Jew' and worse, from the beginning of the day to the end. It wore him down."

Max closed his eyes and tried not to imagine a foreman screaming hate at his intelligent, talented, delicate papa.

"Your father was getting weaker, from the strain of the work. And then," Pastor Andreas said, "the SS showed up to take the wireless set."

"What?" Max exclaimed. "Our *radio*? Why?"

Andreas shrugged. "It's one of Dr. Goebbels's policies. I don't remember what his supposed justification is. But I'm sure it was really just another law designed to make your people miserable.

"So, late one night, three men in SS uniforms came. When your mother opened the door, they pushed their way in and grabbed your wireless."

Max put his head in his hands. He had made that radio set. Pieced it together from parts he special ordered from the local radio shop. Paid for it with pfennigs he'd hoarded over the years. Its sound was mellow, but rich. Just like his papa liked it. The woodwinds sounded like they were in the room with you. You could hear each pluck of pizzicato strings. Max could see his father now, sitting on the sofa, his eyes closed, his head back, a faint smile on his face. Listening to what Max had made.

"I heard shouting," Pastor Andreas said. "I rushed downstairs. Your mother was screaming at the SS men, hitting them, as they carried the set out into the street."

"Did they smash it?" Max asked.

"No. They put it in their truck and drove away."

Max thought he would have felt a little relief knowing the set was not smashed—but he didn't.

"Your father went to the factory the next day . . . and he didn't come back."

Max covered his eyes.

"He didn't come back that day, or the next, or the next. Your mother went to every police station, Gestapo post, and SS office she could find, begging them to tell her where your father was. And then, one day, she didn't come back either." Andreas shrugged his thin shoulders. "She never came back. And neither did he."

Max stared through his fingers at his empty plate. Brown crumbs made a constellation.

Outside the window, even though it was still dark, there were no stars in the sky.

Stein said, “I’m sorry, Max.”

Berg said, “Yes, so am I.”

After a while, the sounds of Berlin waking up filtered in from the street.

“You should lie down,” said Pastor Andreas. “You can use my bed.”

Max didn’t argue.

He allowed Pastor Andreas to lead him to the bedroom. To pull back the covers on the single bed. To turn off the lamp.

Max put his face into Pastor Andreas’s pillow and sobbed until the sun came up. Only then did he fall asleep.

CHAPTER Six

It was past noon when Max stepped out of the front door of the apartment building. He refused to look at the shopwindow, which bore the name BALDUR PERSICKE instead of JACOB BRETZFELD, and the words A TRUE GERMAN instead of the blank space that, apparently, every non-Jew had been reading as NOT A TRUE GERMAN.

Oranienstrasse was a midsized street, with lots of cars and delivery vans and a few horse carts for things like vegetables and newspapers. And people, plenty of people. It was the end of lunch hour, so women in workers' clothes hustled past and older shopkeepers sauntered by, consulting their pocket watches judiciously.

Max felt hollowed out inside. Like someone had taken a chisel and dug around, peeling out the wood that had made him solid, until the shavings were scattered on the Berlin sidewalk.

He had been trying not to believe, when Ewen told him his parents weren't here.

He had been trying not to believe, when he saw the shop-window with someone else's name on it.

Even when he had heard that jerk girl slam the door to *his* apartment as if it were her own, he had been trying not to believe.

They were living with Pastor Andreas, he'd told himself. Or they'd left word with Pastor Andreas so Max would know where to find them.

But Max believed now that they were gone.

The question was—*where?*

Max looked across the street. There was another five-story apartment building. On the second floor, in the window all the way to the right, was a small red sign. In black Gothic letters, it read, DEUTSCHLAND MEIN FADER UND MUTER IST.

Germany is my father and mother.

The sign made Max's heart jump in his chest.

"That's the sign," Max said to Berg and Stein.

"What sign?" said Berg.

"The red one," Stein replied.

"Yes, I see the *sign*, thank you. I am asking *what* is the sign a *sign* of? Why is it making Max so excited?"

"I dunno. He likes the font?"

Max set off, trying to walk as quickly as he could without looking like he was hurrying. He turned onto a small street called Manteuffelstrasse. It was narrow but bright, with charming old cobblestones. It was also the wrong way.

Max was doing just what Lieutenant Chumley had taught him, during their weeks of games at Tring Park. To check if you're being followed, go the wrong way, then suddenly—

Max stopped in front of the window of a stationery store, as if the fountain pens had caught his eye. He furtively glanced back the way he'd come, to see if someone had followed him down the street.

No one had.

He waited a minute.

He was alone on Manteuffelstrasse, save an elderly couple who had just emerged from their apartment building with empty grocery baskets. He waited, apparently gazing at the pens but actually watching the reflection in the plate glass shopwindow, until the couple had turned onto Oranienstrasse.

Then he headed for the canal.

"Stein!" said Berg.

"What?" said Stein.

"Do you see what street we're on?"

Stein glanced at the street sign as they crossed Reichenberger Strasse. "Yeah? So?"

Berg said, "Manteuffelstrasse! The Devil in Disguise Street! *This* is where the Devil got caught pretending to be a little girl!"

"What?!" said Stein and Max at the same time.

"Yah! The Devil was trying to trick some poor woman, and so he disguised himself as a little girl! But an angel—I think it was Raguel—spotted him. And he made the Devil grow back into his true form—but still with the little girl's dress on! Then Raguel made the Devil curtsy to the woman and apologize for bothering her! Oh, it was the talk of the town for decades!"

Stein was laughing right along with him, "When was this?"

"Oh, 1520 or thereabouts. Whew, good old days, eh?"

"Yeah," Stein agreed. "Like one hundred percent fewer Nazis back then."

Max emerged from Manteuffelstrasse and saw the sunken, tree-lined canal that ran through the Kreuzberg neighborhood. Either side of the canal were grassy banks, with benches and weeping willows. Nannies played with children in the grass. An old man fished in the green canal waters.

Max took a left and walked a block. "There," he said.

Facing the canal was a tall church made entirely of bricks. Max had always loved this church as a boy. Most churches were made of large gray stone, but this one was a bright brick red.

At the corner of the church there was a thick hedge that circled the small grassy churchyard. Between the hedge and the wall of the church was a very small gap.

Max scanned the area around him, saw that no one appeared to be watching, and swiftly ducked through the gap.

"What is he doing!?" Berg demanded.

"If you'd been paying attention during training," said Stein, "instead of trying to sabotage him at every turn, you would know."

"So you tell me!"

"Well, unfortunately, I wasn't paying attention either."

Max walked stealthily beside the brick church—the grassy churchyard, scattered with gravestones, was on his right. He came to the back of the church, and found himself in a small flagstone area with a drain in the middle. Max followed the back wall of the church, counting the bricks under his breath, "One, two, three, four . . ."

When he got to the fourteenth brick, he stopped. He angled his body so his back was facing the churchyard.

"He's peeing, isn't he?" said Berg. "Why did he have to leave Pastor Andreas's apartment just to pee behind a church?"

"He isn't peeing," said Stein.

At Max's waist was a brick, the fourteenth one across and the eighth one up from the ground, that had no mortar around it. If you weren't looking for it, you would never have noticed it.

Max put his thin fingers into the space where the mortar should have been, glanced once over his shoulder to make sure that no one had come into the churchyard, and slid the brick out from the wall. Then he reached into the hole, grabbed something, slid it into his pocket without looking at it, and replaced the brick.

He pretended to button up his pants, and he walked back to the churchyard, and then out onto the street.

"Oh," said Berg.

Max walked a couple of blocks and found a bench overlooking the narrow park that the Kreuzberg canal ran through. He glanced around: A mother smiling at her playing children under a willow down by the bank. An old man feeding some sparrows on a nearby bench. Another man sitting on a hillock in the little park, eating a sandwich from a paper wrapper. Max watched the sandwich eater to make sure that he wasn't paying attention to Max. He didn't seem to be. He kept dropping pieces of meat into his lap, and then cursing and trying to wipe mustard off his trousers.

As Max removed the slip of paper from his pocket, he explained to Stein and Berg, "The red sign is the signal that there's a message for me in the dead letter box. The loose brick behind the church is the dead letter box. This is the letter. Instructions from London. Already."

He opened up the slip of paper. His fingers were trembling. In German, it read:

Go?

Max took a pen from his jacket pocket and wrote:

Go.

Then he put the paper back in the dead letter box and replaced the brick.

It had begun.

CHAPTER Seven

That evening after dinner, Pastor Andreas turned on the wireless set in the living room and settled into his wingback armchair. Max sat down on the floor, his back against the sofa. Just as he used to in his apartment. Except his parents were usually right behind him. Supporting him.

The wireless was one of the original models of the mass-produced plastic People's Receivers that had supposedly been designed by Joseph Goebbels himself. They were cheap enough that just about every German could afford to buy one. Which was the point.

Goebbels had realized early on that radio was the most powerful way to spread his master's voice across Germany. After Hitler rose to power, he put Dr. Joseph Goebbels in charge of all radio broadcasting, as well as movies and newspapers, through his Ministry of Propaganda and Popular Enlightenment.

Which ran its most important operations out of the Haus des Rundfunks. The Funkhaus, for short.

Which Max was supposed to infiltrate.

The plan was this: In the far southwest of Berlin, among the leafy boulevards of a wealthy neighborhood called Steglitz, there was a certain radio shop. This radio shop was known to be frequented by "the most trusted voice in Germany," the lead news broadcaster on German radio and head of the news division for the Ministry of Propaganda—Hans Fritzsche.

Max would go to this radio shop and wait for Hans Fritzsche to stop by. Then Max would somehow have to impress Hans Fritzsche. This would be tricky, to say the least. His best chance, Uncle Ewen had theorized, was for Max to befriend Fritzsche's son, Freddie.

Freddie was a chubby, soft, lonely boy. A perfect target for a plan like this.

Max would become friends with Freddie and then use his brilliance with radios to get close to Hans Fritzsche. This process would take months—if Max was lucky.

Ultimately, if all went well, within the year Max would ask Hans Fritzsche for a job at the Funkhaus. It could be any job; in the mail room, perhaps, or as a messenger boy. As long as he was inside.

Once installed in the Funkhaus, Max's mission would be to memorize every name, every office, every technical detail he heard.

And then await instructions for his Grand Finale.

Max had no idea what the Grand Finale would be. An

explosion? An assassination? Something that would destroy the Nazi propaganda machine from the inside?

Hopefully.

"This is Hans Fritzsche." The sound of "the most trusted voice in Germany" emerged from the tinny coils of Pastor Andreas's People's Receiver. Instantly Max fell totally still.

"Good news from the Ministry of Propaganda and Popular Enlightenment," Hans Fritzsche said. "The ProMi tells us that a completely scientific study, performed with state-of-the-art techniques developed here in the German Reich, has found that more than *ninety-three percent* of Germans approve of how the Nazi party is running the government. No government in the history of opinion polling has ever scored so high.

"But that is not all the opinion poll found! On a scale of cold to warm, nearly *one hundred percent* of the German people have warm feelings toward our Supreme Leader, Adolf Hitler. This is unprecedented."

Max stole a glance at Pastor Andreas. The pastor's eyes were focused on the rug, and his brow was a series of lines.

"Now, I have promised always to be truthful with you," Hans Fritzsche went on. "And there is something troubling that must be acknowledged." Both Max and Pastor Andreas looked at the wireless set, as if Hans Fritzsche was speaking directly to them. "According to these poll results, it seems the Supreme Leader *may* have made an error."

Max caught his breath. Accusing Hitler of making a mistake could get you imprisoned—or worse.

But Hans Fritzsche continued to purr into the microphone, smooth and assured as ever. "In light of these poll results, when our Supreme Leader promised that his Reich would last a thousand years, he may have *underestimated*." Max could hear the smug laughter in Hans Fritzsche's voice.

As the newsman went on to describe how their Supreme Leader had just convinced Hungary to join their righteous cause against the Western colonialist oppressors, Max switched off the radio.

He turned to Pastor Andreas and said, "Is that true?"

Andreas's brow was still a stack of furrows. "Is what true? That Hungary is joining the Axis?"

"No," said Max. "Is it true that *everyone* likes Hitler?"

"Well, I assume they aren't polling the *Jews*," Stein said.

"Or the disabled, the Romany, gay people, immigrants . . ." Berg replied.

But Pastor Andreas shrugged. "Are you surprised?"

"Yes!" said Max. He was thinking of the two cops who'd stopped him on Friedrichstrasse. The mean one, with the teeth rotted by schnapps, certainly loved Hitler.

But did the other? Do they *all*? *Really?*

"I'm not surprised," said Pastor Andreas heavily. "Even the pastors I work with at my church are pretty much all proud Nazis." Pastor Andreas looked like he'd bitten into a rotten fruit. "Which feels so deeply *stupid* to me. If you pay any attention to what Hitler says, it is very clear that he is *anti*-Christian. He *certainly* does not believe that the meek shall inherit the earth, as our Lord Jesus Christ said. He believes the strong must *conquer* the earth. He takes the disabled, and he puts them to *death*. That is *not* Christian."

"How could a Christian pastor possibly be in favor of killing disabled people?" Max asked.

Pastor Andreas was chewing on the side of his long finger. "I doubt many of them support *that*. But they still support Hitler." Max noticed that the ends of Andreas's fingers were all red. Like he spent a lot of time gnawing his fingers. "You're too young to remember this, Max, but before the World War—the first one, I guess we should say now—before the first World War, we were a great nation. The strongest in Europe. The war starts, and we're winning. We take the eastern part of France. Then things shift and we're stalled there in the fields of France, so maybe it's a stalemate." Pastor Andreas weighed his long hands like scales, even. "That goes on for a while . . . and then, *suddenly*, they're saying we've *lost*! How did we lose? No French or British troops got anywhere *near* Germany! Our men were still in the trenches in *France*! It was the shock of it, Max. It's hard to understand if you weren't there."

"I must admit," said Berg, "I was confused, too."

"Then came the peace treaty." Pastor Andreas shook his head. "You can't understand how that ruined the country. Before the war, I had a hundred-thousand marks in the bank. I wasn't rich, but I could have retired on that. Gotten a little cottage by the Wannsee and read my books." Max looked at the small bookshelf crammed with black and brown and red spines. "A few months later, our money has lost all value, and I can't buy that cottage—I can't buy a *candy bar* with a hundred-thousand marks. Do you understand that, Max? Can you imagine feeling like you're a well-off man in the strongest country in the world, and then, suddenly, you're a starving man in a conquered nation? Without a *single troop* setting foot on our soil? Just the *shock* of it could shake your faith, Max. It did, in fact. It shook my faith, and the faith of many, many others."

"It sounds like a bad dream," said Max.

"Yes! That's right!" Pastor Andreas clapped his long hands once. "Very perceptive of you. And then a *different* dream started. We couldn't tell if this dream was a good one or a bad one. *I* couldn't tell. My fellow pastors and I debated it, all the time. The Nazis seemed like bullies and gangsters. But they were saying 'Band together! Hold your head up! *You* didn't do this—*they* did—and we can fix it together!' And suddenly men are marching through the streets and people are getting excited! The *young people* are getting excited! This is the future!

"These men take power—through villainy and lies, yes. The

Reichstag catches fire, Max, and they pretend we're under attack . . . but they got the army up and running again! The economy comes roaring back! Maybe I *can* buy that cottage after all!" Pastor Andreas is getting worked up. Max had never seen him preach in church, but this was clearly what it would be like.

"These men are telling us Germany is great again! Yes, they also tell us some stupid, awful, evil stuff. But who cares? And yes, they can be bullies. But they are *our* bullies! Bullies for Germany! It feels nice to have bullies on *your* side!"

"I said that to you one time," said Berg.

Max remembered. It was in the courtyard of St. West's. Max had been gazing at Circuitt and Bonner, wondering why the other boys liked them. And Berg had said: *Because everyone is scared. All you humans. All the time. You are scared of being beat up, or of being alone, or of your own thoughts. At least if you've got a bully on your side, you've got one less thing to be scared of.*

Pastor Andreas was still preaching, but very quietly now. "Some days, Max, some days . . . it is hard to feel my faith in God. Especially in those awful days when Germany had been defeated. Our buzzer rang ten or fifteen times a day, Max, beggar after beggar—people who had owned shops on this very street!—pleading for a few slices of bread, or a mouthful of cheese. And then Germany becomes strong again. The pews in my church are empty, but the streets are full of singing children, children carrying torches and bellowing Nazi hymns to the fire-lit sky. Those days, too, my faith wavers, and I wonder if it wouldn't be easier to believe in Hitler."

Pastor Andreas's voice dropped so low he seemed to be speaking only to himself. "Better to believe lies and live proudly than believe the truth and have to eat tree roots for dinner." He looked up at Max. "That's what we've decided in Germany. Can you blame us?"

CHAPTER Eight

The next morning, once Max had finished his hard-boiled egg and rinsed his plate, he set out on a walk.

Mission One. Day One.

Max had been tempted to start Mission Two first. But, as brilliant as Max was, he couldn't think of *how* to start Mission Two without walking straight up to the Gestapo and asking what they'd done with Jacob and Miriam Bretzfeld. Which was a great way to get himself killed.

So Mission One it was.

For now.

The fastest way to get to the little radio shop in Steglitz would have been to catch an overground commuter train, the S-Bahn, from the grand Anhalter train station. But Max wanted to feel Berlin's sidewalks again. They weren't like London's sidewalks. There was a little more sky here. The smells were different. Also, the *zeitgeist*—the general *feeling*—was different.

Berliners bustled past Max, greeting acquaintances, smiling at strangers, exhausted from overwork and *thrilled* about it.

The war was going well for Germany. Britain would surrender soon; all the news reports said so. Germany's disastrous, messy experiment with democracy was over, and a strong leader was in charge at last. Germany was again a world power. The beginning of the Thousand-Year Reich was proceeding just as the Supreme Leader had promised it would.

Two hours later, Max stood in front of a small store on a tree-lined boulevard. Through the shop's large glass windows, on which were stenciled the words PFEIFFER'S RADIOS, Max could see half a dozen wireless sets, polished and beautiful. But Max wasn't looking at the radios. He was looking at a little bell, hanging just inside the glass door to the shop.

And suddenly he was remembering walking into Herr Hoffman's butcher shop with his mother, many years ago . . .

Herr Hoffman's was around the corner from their apartment. Some of their Jewish friends would trek halfway across the neighborhood to buy their meat from the kosher butcher, but Max's family wasn't all that observant. They didn't buy pork, but otherwise they were happy to patronize Herr Hoffman's. Not only was it just around the corner—Herr Hoffman was also always kind to them.

He was equally kind on this day. Except that when Max's mother pushed open the door and the bell jingled, Herr Hoffman raised his right hand and said, "Heil Hitler!"

Max's mother froze.

Formerly, "Heil Hitler" had been how Nazis greeted one another. But now that Hitler had gotten himself named Supreme Leader, "Heil Hitler" was becoming a common greeting in Germany. Instead of good morning or good evening. "Heil Hitler."

Max's father had decried it as insane. "What kind of nation says 'hello' to each other by bellowing out their allegiance to some political leader? Can you imagine the English saying, 'God save the King!' every time they meant 'Cheerio'? Or the Americans saying, 'Hail to the Chief!' instead of 'Howdy'? Is Germany a nation of bootlickers? Or lunatics?"

But now Herr Hoffman was saying it. And if someone said it to you, you were supposed to say it back.

Max's mother replied with a flip of her hand and something that sounded kind of like "Heil Hitler." Max, even at age six, couldn't believe it. She bought her plucked whole chicken and hustled out of the store.

"Did you say 'Heil Hitler,' Mama?" Max asked as they hurried down the street.

"What? Of course not!" she whispered fiercely. "Don't be ridiculous! I said 'Ein Liter.'" Which was slang for heavy drinker.

Max stared up at his mom. She stared back down at him.

And then they started to laugh.

Max had to admit that Ein Liter, *if you just mouthed it, looked a whole lot like* Heil Hitler.

So that's what Max and his mother had taken to saying whenever someone greeted them with "Heil Hitler." "Ein Liter." No one ever seemed to notice. And Max and his mother would smile secretly to each other.

But they started schlepping across the neighborhood to the kosher butcher anyway.

Max pushed open the door of Pfeiffer's Radios. The bell jingled.

"Heil Hitler!" said the mustached man behind the counter.

"Heil Hitler!" Max responded.

He wasn't going to risk it. Not now.

Max looked around at the walls, breathing in the smell of plastic and soldered metal. On the wall to the right were shelves of radios. People's Receivers from 1938 and 1936, and one of the original 1933 models, which was probably just there for show. There were also AEGs and Siemens. All approved by Goebbels's men at the Funkhaus, with no shortwave capabilities, which made it much harder to receive broadcasts from outside of Germany.

On the opposite wall of the narrow shop were posters. The largest was the radio schedule for the day. Around it were flyers for various radio clubs and advertisements for new models of wireless sets. There were also big empty yellow patches on the wall where schedules of foreign broadcasts used to be posted . . . and weren't anymore.

Max glanced at the shopkeeper. Herr Pfeiffer was in his fifties, with a thick mustache like a push broom. He looked just like the picture Uncle Ewen and Lieutenant Chumley had shown Max.

"Can I help you?" Herr Pfeiffer asked.

"I'm just looking around, if that's okay," said Max.

"Enjoy yourself," said the shopkeeper, and he went back to reading a magazine. Beside him, a Siemens 22GW radio played a Liszt lieder softly.

The bell jingled as the door opened again.

A man entered, cradling a 1933 People's Receiver.

He dropped it onto the counter.

"Broken," he said.

"Of course it's broken," said Herr Pfeiffer. "With you banging it around like that."

"It was broken before I brought it here," the man retorted. He was wearing a brown felt hat that he pushed back from his sweating forehead. "Can't get it to play anything."

"Let's take a look," said Herr Pfeiffer. He took a screwdriver from the wall behind him and opened the case of the PR33. Max slowly moved toward the counter.

The shopkeeper peered at the magnetic coil and wires inside, frowning so his mustache bristled. He straightened up, took the electrical cord, and plugged it into an outlet on the back wall. The radio crackled to life. It sounded like it was throwing up.

"Turn the dial," said Herr Pfeiffer.

The man in the felt hat turned the dial.

The radio continued to vomit.

Herr Pfeiffer unplugged the radio. "It's your coil. Gone bad.

These Goebbels's Snouts are cheap. Especially the 1933. I'm surprised it's lasted this long."

"I'm not buying a new radio, if that's what you're implying," said the man in the felt hat.

"Suit yourself. But I can't fix this."

"You can't give me a new . . . whatever you said?"

"Coil? No. They stopped making the 1933 coils years ago. You can't get them."

"My radio looks just like that one," said the man, pointing at the PR33 on the shelf near the counter.

The shopkeeper's mustache bristled more. His upper lip looked like the back of a porcupine. "You want me to disassemble that radio to give you a part? Why would I do that? Then I have a broken set and you have a working one."

"I'll pay you! Isn't this a radio store?"

"You can buy this one, full price. But I'm not breaking my forty-mark radio to sell you a part for five marks. That would be stupid. Buy a new radio."

"This is preposterous!" The man in the felt hat was becoming very agitated. "You have the part I need *right there*!"

"What don't you understand? I'm not ruining a forty-mark radio for a five-mark part!"

Both men were now yelling.

"I'm going to report you to the Consumer Protection Agency! We'll see how this ends!"

"You're going to *report* me?! Because *you're* cheap?!"

Which was when Max said, "Excuse me, do you have a paper clip?"

"WHAT?!" the shopkeeper shouted, turning on Max.

"Do you have a paper clip? I might be able to fix his coil."

"With a paper clip? I very much doubt it," said Herr Pfeiffer.

But the man in the hat said, "What if he can?"

"If you don't mind," said Max to the radio's owner, "I could give it a try."

The man looked at Herr Pfeiffer. Herr Pfeiffer looked at Max. Max looked at them both.

The shopkeeper said, "If he breaks the radio, I take no responsibility."

"The radio's already broken," said the man with the hat.

So the shopkeeper rummaged in a drawer behind the desk and then handed Max a paper clip.

Max turned the radio around. Herr Pfeiffer leaned his soft belly all the way over the counter to watch.

There appeared to be nothing wrong with the copper wire that was coiled around the magnet. But Max had seen tiny breaks in this model before. He straightened out the paper clip and laid it over the coiled copper. Then he asked the shopkeeper to plug the radio back in. Herr Pfeiffer did, without objection this time. The radio emitted the horrible sound again.

Max moved the paper clip back and forth over the coil, until—

"Guten Abend, ladies and gentlemen—"

Max removed the paper clip. The garbled sound returned. He laid the paper clip back on the coil. *"We have breaking news from the negotiations with Romania. It appears . . ."*

"It works! He did it!" cried the man in the felt hat.

Max asked the shopkeeper to solder the paper clip to the copper wire, while he held it in place. The shopkeeper did, happy to have satisfied the man in the felt hat. Then he screwed the plastic cover back on. The radio played the news report flawlessly. The three of them listened in appreciation for a minute. Romania, it seemed, would be joining the Axis. More good news for the Reich, the German people, and Adolf Hitler.

"That's Hans Fritzsche," said the shopkeeper, and then he added proudly, "Did you know that he's a customer of mine?"

The man in the felt hat was surprised and impressed.

Max pretended to have the same reaction.

"Did you hear him last night?" the man with the felt hat was asking the shopkeeper.

"Of course," Herr Pfeiffer replied. "Never miss him."

"He was funny, wasn't he? The way he called Churchill 'You old crook!' Oh, that made me laugh." The shopkeeper laughed, too, and they kept repeating it: *"Du alte Gauner! Du alte Gauner!"*

Max said to Stein and Berg, "Why is that funny?"

Berg shook his head and shrugged his tiny shoulders. "The Germans aren't funny anymore. Back in the days of the Chatti and the Cherusci tribes, they were funny! Hermann the German had a great sense of humor!"

Stein raised an eyebrow. "Debatable."

The man with the felt hat shook Max's hand. Then he turned to Herr Pfeiffer. "How much do I owe you?"

"For what? I didn't fix it! Pay the boy!"

The man with the hat was confused. "He doesn't work here?"

"No!"

"Well, he should!"

Both men laughed. The man with the hat asked if he could pay Max, but Max refused. So the man left with a bemused smile and a working PR33.

Once the door jangled shut, Herr Pfeiffer looked at Max. "How did you learn to do that?"

Max shrugged. "I like radios."

The shopkeeper patted the counter. "I always say you young ones understand technology better than we old men ever will. Listen, I can't hire you because I'm barely squeaking by as it is—these damn Goebbels's Snouts leave no room for profit. But you're welcome here anytime. I'll let you look at the sets—even open them up, if you're careful." He gestured at the radios on the shelf. "Like that Victrola over there. Modified for the German market, of course. But she's a beaut."

Max hung around looking at the radios—and waiting for

another customer to come in. One in particular, actually. No one did, though.

As Herr Pfeiffer was closing up, he said, "Come back, Max. Any time at all."

And Max said, "How about tomorrow?"

Herr Pfeiffer smiled and said sure.

Max returned the smile. First cog, in place.

If Jean were here, Max was certain that she would have said, "Well done, soldier."

CHAPTER Nine

Max took the S-Bahn back to Kreuzberg. He arrived at his apartment building, began to climb thc stairs, and knew immediately that something was wrong. The door of the Persickes' apartment was so wide open it blocked the landing, and loud voices were ricocheting into the stairwell.

"Who's in there?" Max asked Stein and Berg.

"How should we know?" Stein retorted.

Max put his hand on the banister, unsure whether to climb or turn and leave.

Which is when Liesel Persicke stuck her head out the door. "Here he is," she said.

Too late.

To Max, she added, "Come on."

And her squinting glare followed Max as he climbed the stairs toward her. "You're so slow," she said.

Max didn't say anything.

He followed her inside the apartment.

His apartment.

It was completely the same, and completely different.

He turned from the doorway into the living room, where a young boy was playing on the rug with tin soldiers. It was a different rug, slightly larger than the one Max's family had had. The Persickes had a different sofa, too—but it was in the same place as theirs had been. There was an extra chair in the living room, which felt *so* wrong, for no reason that Max could justify. There was also a 1940 People's Receiver against the wall. If only the Persickes could have heard the set that used to sit there.

From the kitchen a woman's voice called, "It's our new neighbor! Welcome, young man!"

Frau Persicke stepped into the living room, wiping her hands on an apron. She was a thin woman with horselike teeth and a very intense look in her eyes. "Heil Hitler!" she said. "Very nice to meet you."

Max hesitated for just an instant, and for some reason he imagined Liesel, who was standing beside him, counting the milliseconds it took Max to return a strangled "Heil Hitler."

Pastor Andreas was sitting on the sofa in the living room. He smiled at Max apologetically and said, "The Persickes have been kind enough to invite us to dinner." He added, laughing, "I didn't dare refuse."

The pastor made it sound like a joke, but he held Max's gaze for just a little longer than natural.

"Maxy, they're informants," said Stein. "Careful what you say."

"Yeah, we got it, thank you," Berg replied.

From the extra chair in the living room, Baldur Persicke, the True German watchmaker, stood up and extended his hand. Max shook it.

"Adolf, shake your new neighbor's hand!" Frau Persicke barked from the kitchen, where she'd returned to preparing the meal. It smelled like soup.

The little boy on the rug looked up at Max, wiped his runny nose with his hand, and then extended the same hand to shake. He seemed to not be aware of what he'd done.

Max said, "How about the other one?"

So the boy extended the other hand, and they executed the rare left-handed shake. The boy thought it was funny.

"Sit! Relax!" said Baldur Persicke. "Make yourself at home."

And Max screamed, "THIS *IS* MY HOME!"

But just to Berg and Stein.

He sat down on the couch with Pastor Andreas.

"Liesel," said Baldur Persicke, "come, sit." He gestured to the small space next to Max on the couch.

"Ew. No," said Liesel, and she went into the kitchen to help her mother.

"Nice place," said Max.

Baldur Persicke nodded. "Not bad. Gift of the German state. The previous occupants were . . . well . . ."

Max and Pastor Andreas fell very still.

"Filthy Jews!" Frau Persicke called from the kitchen. Max

felt Pastor Andreas exhale heavily beside him. “Good riddance, right?” she shouted.

Suddenly, little Adolf stood up and stuck a tin soldier in his mouth. He grabbed a pillow and shoved it clumsily under his shirt. “Who ah I?” he asked.

“What?” said Max.

Baldur Persicke said, “He wants you to guess who he is.”

Max looked at the boy striding around the room, his stomach sticking out, puffing on the tin soldier like a cigar. “Cheerio!” said the little boy. “Cheerio!”

“Uh . . .” said Max.

“Winston Churchill!” the boy announced, and then he started pretending to shoot a machine gun, and then he fell down dead. “Oh! Cheerio! I’m dying! Cheerio!”

Max didn’t know whether to laugh, or scream in horror.

“That’s the most disturbing thing I’ve seen all day,” said Stein. “Which, in Nazi Germany, is saying something.”

The little boy named Adolf got up from the floor, came up to Max, and said, “Excuse me.” Max didn’t know what the little boy wanted now. Adolf pointed at the pillow behind Max’s back. Max leaned forward, and Adolf grabbed the pillow. He shoved that in his shirt also, so he was now bulging grotesquely. He hunched over, rubbed his hands together and hobbled around the living room with a horrible leer on his face. “Who am I now?” he asked.

Max had no idea.

"A Jew!" the boy laughed.

"Okay, now *that's* the most disturbing thing I've seen all day," said Stein.

Berg replied, "I'm sticking with Churchill being shot to death by a machine gun."

Little Adolf was taking the pillows out of his shirt now, loving the attention Max and Pastor Andreas were giving him. He climbed up on the couch next to Max. "Who am I?" he asked. And then he started shouting nonsense words, spitting all over the place, gesticulating ridiculously with his hands.

Max stared. There was only one person that this little boy reminded him of now, but he didn't dare say it.

Liesel and Frau Persicke had come into the living room to watch the performance.

"Blah blah blah Germany!" the little boy shouted, waving his arms wildly. "Blah blah blah England!"

His family was laughing and shaking their heads, trying to figure out who the boy was meant to be. "Roosevelt?" his father guessed.

"Roosevelt's a cripple, Dad," said Liesel. "So obviously not."

Little Adolf kept shouting. "Blah blah blah the Jews! Blah blah blah living room for Germans! Blah blah— OW!"

With two swift steps, Frau Persicke had stepped forward and smacked her son hard across the side of his face. Little Adolf tumbled down from the sofa and crumpled into a ball on the rug. "Don't you *dare* mock the Supreme Leader like that!" She smacked him once more, on the back of the head.

Then she said, "Now everyone sit down for dinner."

Never in his whole life did Max expect to see someone strike a child in *this* apartment. Little Adolf was curled up and crying on the rug.

Max slipped his hands under the small boy's arms and lifted him to his feet. *"Come on,"* Max whispered. *"You'll feel better when you've had some food."*

As everyone slurped the thick, bland potato soup Frau Persicke had made, she said: "You young ones simply don't know how *lucky* you are."

Max tried not to laugh. *Lucky* wasn't the word he would use to describe his situation.

Frau Persicke went on. "You can't possibly understand what it felt like *before* Hitler."

This made Max glance at Pastor Andreas, who raised his long his gray eyebrows back at him.

Liesel saw the pastor's meaningful look. "What was *that*?" she snapped.

Pastor Andreas smiled benignly at the suspicious girl. "I was just saying the same thing to Max yesterday. Please, Frau Persicke, continue."

Frau Persicke said, "Germany was a tragic place. We had

lost the war. This nation, our Fatherland, was wounded. You children have only known Germany now that we are great again. But we were like a . . . like a wounded lion. Beautiful, proud, but on the verge of death."

Her husband nodded sagely.

"It was so sad," Frau Persicke went on. "And we were so angry. Did I ever tell you kids about the time my family took me to the Rhineland?"

"About a million times," Liesel said, rolling her eyes.

"But *they* haven't heard it," Frau Persicke said, pointing her needle nose at Max and Pastor Andreas. "I was on a family vacation to Western Germany, the Rhineland, in 1924. Do you know that the Rhineland was occupied by France then? Can you imagine? A part of your nation, with foreign soldiers patrolling the streets? You can't imagine that, how could you? Well, it happened. We were on a train, and French soldiers walked into our train car. My mother *screamed.*" Frau Persicke looked around the table meaningfully. "Do you know *why* she screamed?"

"Because she hated the French?" Pastor Andreas guessed.

"Because they were *African*," said Frau Persicke, horror dripping from the word.

Max felt like he must be missing something. "What did they do?"

"Do? Nothing! They said 'Sorry to disturb' in horrible German. Oh, I will never forget it!"

Everyone was silent while Frau Persicke collected herself.

"You children cannot imagine living in a country where *Africans* have guns and can order you about. Where *Jews* sit in the Reichstag, telling us white Christians what to do." She shuddered. "*That's* why I won't let my son make fun of our Supreme Leader. Because Hitler has solved all that. He has tended to the lion's wounds, and fed it milk with his two hands, and now it is strong again, and on the prowl at last. As a proud, blond beast should be."

There was a moment of slurping soup. Pastor Andreas awkwardly offered a "Well said, Frau Persicke."

"I am so jealous of my sister, Marie," Frau Persicke went on. "She has three sons. Three! All soldiers marching across Europe to defend their precious Fatherland! One is in the Netherlands, another in France, another in Poland." She looked at Liesel. "And here I am, stuck with a *girl* who will *never* fire a rifle for the Supreme Leader. Life just isn't fair."

Liesel was scowling into her soup, like she'd heard *this* a million times, too.

Max said, "It really isn't."

CHAPTER
Ten

Max couldn't sleep. It felt like he was covered in fleabites. Or like the air was so stagnant and stuffy that there was no oxygen to inhale.

Or maybe it was that a horrible family of Nazis was living in his family's apartment, and he had no idea where his parents were.

"How am I supposed to find them?" he moaned.

"You're *not*," Stein reminded him. Stein's head was on the pillow next to Max's, and his legs were crossed and propped up on Max's left shoulder. "Ewen told you—if you get caught looking for them, you're *all* dead!"

"Besides," said Berg, reclining just the way Stein was, "why would we help you anymore? We helped you in England, and you brought us back here!"

"You helped me with the Green Cops."

"Yah, because that was funny."

Max shrugged, which made the kobold's and the dybbuk's feet rise and fall. "You didn't *have* to come to Germany with me. You could have just gotten off my shoulders. You still could. Be my guest."

"Yah, well, I would!" said Berg. "Except . . ." He glanced over at Stein.

"Are you feeling it, too?" Stein demanded. "Like his shoulders are . . . *sticky* or something?"

"Yah! When I got off to go to the alley, it was like some magnetic force was pulling me *back* to him! Why?! What does it mean?!"

Stein shook his head as he stared at the ceiling in Pastor Andreas's living room. "Maybe it means we're on his shoulders for a reason."

"To heckle and annoy him more?"

"Or maybe we're supposed to be helping him."

"No. I don't believe it. I refuse," said Berg.

They lay there in silence, the three of them, for a long while.

Finally, Max clocked Stein out of the corner of his eye. "You could *try*, you know. Just *try* to help me find them. See if it feels . . . *right.*"

Stein sighed.

Berg said, "Don't do it!"

Stein said, "Why would his shoulder be sticky, unless we're supposed to help?"

"I don't know! God is really confusing!" Berg retorted.

More silence. Then Stein said, "There's a place on Leipziger

Strasse. The Berlin Jewish Housing Authority. Keeps track of all the Jews in the city."

"THANK YOU!" Max shouted.

Berg muttered, "Traitor."

CHAPTER Eleven

The next morning, Max walked to Leipziger Strasse, a huge road that ran through the center of Berlin. People bustled past here, just as they did in Kreuzberg. But they didn't wear the half grin of working themselves to exhaustion for the same great cause.

They looked haunted, paranoid, and weary, nearly to the point of death. They hurried down the streets, to the munitions factories where they were forced to work for barely any pay. Or they cradled their tiny ration of food from the grocer, their bony hands and wrists gripping their paper bags tightly.

Max walked past a narrow cobblestoned alley filled with small shops—all closed. Their windows were replaced by plywood boards, spray-painted with Stars of David, or the word *Jude*, dripping down the boards in red paint like blood.

This was the remnants of Berlin's Jewish community.

By the first week of November 1940, more than half of Berlin's Jews were gone. They had fled Germany, or been arrested, or had been forcibly moved to work camps where they would make guns and bombs for their Nazi masters.

Or they had died. The leading cause of death among Berlin's remaining Jews was drowning. Themselves.

Those who were still in Berlin lived like this. And many of them lived here, at the shabby end of Leipziger Strasse. Just a few years ago, it hadn't been shabby at all. There had been department stores, and busy little shops, and singing and life and triumphant military parades full of proud German Jews, and Simchas Torah celebrations in the street.

Not anymore.

Max followed Stein's directions across Leipziger Strasse to a narrow five-story building nestled between two much larger ones. Inside, on the wall at the base of the stairs, was a board with moveable letters. Max scanned the uninterpretable bureaucratic names, until he came to the fifth floor. Reich Association of Jews in Germany—Berlin Jewish Housing Authority, Floor 5.

"Like I said," Stein announced.

"Like an idiot," Berg snapped back.

Max moved toward the dark and dirty stairwell. The steps were stone, but small dips had been worn into them by the hundreds of feet climbing and descending them every day. Max started up.

The Jewish Housing Authority was a small, messy office, with a single desk in front of two closed doors. An old woman with little glasses and her hair tied up in a tight bun was moving files from one stack to another, and then from a third stack to the second, and then from the second stack back to the first.

"Hello," Max said.

She looked up, blinking through her tiny spectacles. "Hello, dear," she said. "Can I help you?"

"I'm looking for . . ."

"*Careful*, Max," said Stein.

". . . for two people."

"Yes?" said the woman. "Are they Jewish?"

The way she said "Jewish" made it very clear to Max that she, too, was Jewish.

"Yes," Max said. He walked up to her desk, and the stacks of files looked like a city of skyscrapers. "Their names are Jacob and Miriam Bretzfeld."

"Bretzfeld," she said. "Bretzfeld. Hold on." She started searching through the stacks. "The B files are around here somewhere."

Max, sympathetically, said, "Shouldn't they get you some file cabinets?"

And then a man's voice boomed across the small office. "Are you questioning how the Supreme Leader keeps track of his *Jews?*"

And the way *this* voice said "Jews" made it very clear that he was *not* one.

Max looked up. One of the doors behind the desk had opened and standing in it was a man with a crooked boxer's nose, pale blond hair plastered to his head, and wide gray eyes.

He wore a long black leather coat that nearly reached his ankles and, beneath it, a dark gray officer's uniform.

Which made Max's blood run cold.

Dark gray meant *SS*.

"Max," said Berg. "Run."

When Hitler had taken power, he'd deemed the German army not loyal enough. Not young enough. Not *enthusiastic* enough.

And so he had created the SS, a parallel army of fanatics, radicals, and murderers. Young men who loved Hitler even more than they loved Germany, and who would do anything—absolutely *anything*—he told them to.

The long black leather coat meant the man wasn't just any SS officer, either. He was some sort of commander—in other words, one of the most effective and important fanatic murderers in Hitler's personal army.

Stein said, "I'm sorry, Max. I just peed on your shoulder."

Max glanced at the old woman with the spectacles. She appeared terrified. From behind the leather trench coat peeked another man with a short beard and heavy rings under his eyes. He seemed just as terrified as the woman.

Berg said, "Get out of here, Max. Leave. Exit. Depart. *Now*."

But Max knew very well that if he tried to flee, this man, whoever he was, would follow.

And Max got the distinct impression that, if this man was following you, you would not get very far.

"I asked you a question, son," he said slowly. He had a deep southern accent, like Hitler's, but his was somehow lazier and yet more clipped and precise. "Do you think you know better than our Supreme Leader?"

Max inhaled and tried to think of Kathy Kangaroo. But he could feel his pulse pounding in his neck. Not from fear. Or maybe partly from fear. But mostly from rage. There was something particularly odious about this man. Max couldn't quite put his finger on what it was. Maybe it was that Max was so close to finding out if his parents' whereabouts were in these files, and this SS jerk was standing there *smirking* at him, trying to bait him.

As calmly as he could, Max said, "You'd just think that they'd want the place that keeps track of Berlin's Jews a little more *organized.*"

The SS commander's wide-set eyes rested on Max. "You think you're clever, don't you?"

"No sir."

"You think you're cleverer than me?"

"Of course not, sir. Definitely not."

The SS commander eyed Max for another moment, appraising him. "You're lying. But that's all right. I happen to agree that this place is a dump." Then he said to the old lady: "Go ahead. Find them."

The woman began to riffle through the files with shaking fingers. "Bretzfeld," she muttered. "Bretzfeld. Hold on." She looked over the top of her spectacles and then through them and then over them again. "The Bs are around here somewhere!" A handful of files slid to the floor, spraying their papers across the dirty tiles. She cursed and bent down to gather them back up.

Max's impulse was to help her—but he caught himself. No self-respecting German would help a Jew. At least, not in front of an SS officer.

As the lady cleaned up the files from the floor, the officer said to Max, "And why, may I ask, are you looking for *Jacob* and *Miriam Bretzfeld*?"

For a moment, Max's mind was perfectly and totally empty.

"I hope you have an answer for this!" Stein barked.

Max remembered Kathy pulling on his rucksack as he panicked . . . until he had realized what she'd wanted. And had given it to her.

Max spat, "They owe my boss money. Stinking Jews."

The old lady and the bearded man both looked shocked. But the mouth of the officer in the trench coat curled into a smile. "Well, I wouldn't expect to get that money back. You know how Jews are with money."

Max forced himself to roll his eyes. "Don't I ever. Cheats, every one of them." And he thought of the receipts his father kept, files and files, and every one reckoned to the penny to be sure his customers were never cheated.

The SS commander said, "What is your name, young man?"

Max swallowed. "Max Maas."

The SS commander removed a small notebook and an even smaller pen from an inside pocket of his uniform jacket. He wrote the name down.

"Where do you live?"

Max lied fluently. "Falkensee." This was a suburb of Berlin. It was where his imaginary father lived. He'd worked it all out with Chumley and Uncle Ewen.

"You don't go to school? You work?"

Max nodded.

"Where?"

Max hesitated. Then he gave the address of Herr Pfeiffer's radio shop.

The officer put away his little pad and pen and gazed at Max. He said to the secretary, "Well? Have you found the thieving Jews?"

The old lady shook her head. "They're not in official Jewish housing," she said, almost relieved.

"They haven't been consolidated yet?" said the SS commander. "Sounds as if we'd *both* like to know where they are."

He took out a business card and handed it to Max.

It read:

Doctor Gustav Adolf Scheel. Commander, Sicherheitsdienst.

He wasn't *just* SS.

He was *SD*.

Max tried not to curse out loud.

When Hitler had taken over, he also deemed the German army's spy service, called the Abwehr, not loyal enough, not young enough, not enthusiastic enough. And so he had created the *Sicherheitsdienst*, the SD. A personal spy service within his personal army, tasked with catching and executing disloyal Germans and enemy spies.

Doctor Commander Gustav Adolf Scheel was a spy hunter.

"If you find them, come see me," said Commander Scheel, indicating the address below his name: Prinz-Albrecht-Strasse 8. The headquarters of the Reich Security Main Office. "Prove how clever you really are."

Max swallowed and said nothing.

Commander Scheel added casually, "And if you don't come see me, maybe I'll come see you." Then he left. They heard his black leather boots tramping down the stone steps.

Max turned and tried to smile apologetically at the old lady and the bearded man, but they were staring at him with undisguised hatred. So Max slipped the business card into his pocket and followed the SD commander down the stairs.

Max emerged onto Leipziger Strasse just in time to see Commander Scheel closing the back door of a large, shiny black Mercedes. As it pulled away, Max saw Scheel consulting his little notebook.

"I'm sorry," said Berg. "I peed on your shoulder, too."

CHAPTER Twelve

That afternoon, Max returned to the radio shop, shaky but desperately trying to hide it. He had made a terrible blunder going to the Jewish Housing Authority office. Now a commander in the SD knew about Herr Pfeiffer's shop. Why hadn't he lied? Invented some fake job, with a fake address?

"I didn't actually expect you to show up!" said Herr Pfeiffer as Max pushed open the shop door, announced by the tinkling bell. "Shouldn't you be in school?"

Max froze.

Why wasn't he in school? He had a cover story, but he was so thrown by the encounter with Commander Scheel that for a moment he couldn't remember it.

"Uh, you're going to need an answer, Max," said Stein.

Max was aware. "I'm not going to school," he said.

Herr Pfeiffer's face reddened. "Not going to school! Why?"

Max tried to sound as pathetic as he could: "Because I just moved to Berlin. To live with my uncle. And I'm not enrolled in a school here. Yet."

Herr Pfeiffer's gaze was stern and disapproving.

Until Max saw a little smile dawn under his push broom mustache. "Well, we ought to do some learning, since you're supposed to be in school. So how about *you* teach *me* how you fixed that customer's PR33."

They spent the morning looking at the coil of the PR33 on the shelf, and then at the insides of other radios in the shop. Herr Pfeiffer was all right, it turned out. He nodded along with the news reports of German victories in the war, but when Dr. Goebbels's voice blared out of the speaker, he turned the volume down.

Not off. That could have been considered anti-Nazi. A crime.

But just a little lower.

Herr Pfeiffer looked sheepishly at Max. "His voice is so harsh."

Max wanted to believe there was another reason Herr Pfeiffer had turned the volume down. But he didn't dare ask.

Max went to the radio shop each day that week. Herr Pfeiffer let him open up the sets, like he'd promised, and tighten their tubes or check the wiring. He repaired radios, studied sets whose technical plans he hadn't memorized already, and waited for the next phase of Mission One to begin.

It would have been the perfect job, except that every time the door opened and the little bell jingled, he expected Doctor Commander Gustav Adolf Scheel to walk through the door, his long black trench coat billowing behind him. And then, even though it never was Scheel, the customer *still* shouted "Heil Hitler!"

Finally, on Saturday at around eleven in the morning, the door opened, the bell jingled, and a boy walked in. He was just about Max's age. Pudgy. Light freckles. White-blond hair flopped over one half of his forehead.

Freddie Fritzsche.

And behind him, his father. Slicked-back hair. Wide mouth. An air of supreme assurance. Hans Fritzsche. The most trusted voice in Germany.

The next phase of Max's mission was underway.

"Heil Hitler!" shouted Freddie.

"Heil Hitler!" Herr Pfeiffer shouted back enthusiastically.

"Heil Hitler!" Max said loudly. But he kept his eyes on the PR38 he was repairing.

"Good morning, Herr Pfeiffer!" Freddie said cheerfully.

Herr Pfeiffer smiled and his mustache porcupined. "Freddie! Good to see you! And Herr Fritzsche! What a pleasure!"

Freddie Fritzsche came right up to the counter where Max was working. The PR38 had no cover on it, so the speaker, coil, wires, and tubes were all exposed between them.

"Are you here to pick up your radio parts pack, Freddie?" Herr Pfeiffer asked.

"Yes sir!"

And then Hans Fritzsche spoke for the first time. "Our little radio engineer is very excited."

Max's stomach dropped about a foot. Hans Fritzsche's speaking voice sounded *just* like it did on the radio.

While Herr Pfeiffer went into the back, where special orders were kept, Freddie leaned over the open PR38, trying to see what Max was doing.

"Excuse me," said Max.

"Yes?" said Freddie.

"You're in my light."

"Oh." Freddie backed up.

Stein said, "Uh, Max, isn't this *the target of your mission*? You might want to be a little nicer to him."

Hans Fritzsche was examining a new AEG-Super model that was on display near the front window. His back was to them. Max was trying to focus on the trimming job he was doing, which would clear up the reception at the top of the radio's range. It should have been simple. Except, at the moment, Max could barely remember which wire was the current and which was the ground.

"Whatchya doing?" Freddie asked.

Max looked up. Apparently annoyed. "Trimming this PR38."

"Oh," said Freddie. Grinning.

Hans Fritzsche looked over his shoulder. "Don't bother the boy, Freddie. He's working."

Just then, Herr Pfeiffer emerged from the back. "Oh, I'm sure Freddie isn't bothering anyone. This is Max. He just showed up this week. He's been helping me around the shop. Say hello, Max."

Max said hello. With absolutely no enthusiasm whatsoever.

"What's Max's problem?" Stein asked Berg. "Is he *trying* to blow the mission?"

Berg shrugged. "Hopefully. Then maybe we could get out of the land of Nazis and back to the land of well-behaved imperialists."

Hans Fritzsche came to the counter and paid for the do-it-yourself radio set.

"I'm going to be building my own radio model this weekend," Freddie said to Max.

"Huh," said Max, not looking up from his work.

"Have you built a radio before?"

"Sure."

The adults were silent, watching this exchange.

"If I need help, do you think I could come back here this afternoon?"

Without looking up, Max said, "The shop closes at four on Saturdays."

"So, maybe if I came at three? If I need help? Will you be here?"

Max hesitated. He looked at Herr Pfeiffer. "Will I have time to help him?"

Herr Pfeiffer was staring at Max in disbelief. His voice was loud and sharply clipped when he said, "If *Herr Fritzsche's son* needs help with a radio, *yes, you will have time to help him.*"

Max looked at Freddie in the face for the first time. He shrugged. "Sure."

Freddie smiled uncertainly. Nodded. And then he backed out of the store, clutching the radio parts in his arms. Hans Fritzsche waved distractedly as they disappeared.

As soon as the door jangled closed, Herr Pfeiffer rounded on Max. "What on *earth* was that? You will show some respect to our customers! Especially to the *voice of Germany's* son! For *God's sake*!"

"Sorry," said Max. "I guess I get nervous around famous people. I've never met one before."

Herr Pfeiffer softened a little. "Nervous? You didn't look nervous. You looked like you couldn't care less."

"Sorry," said Max, looking at his shoes.

Stein said, "Wait a minute. Maxy . . . were you just playing it cool?"

Max smiled inwardly.

Berg chuckled in disbelief. "I think he was! Okay, call me reluctantly impressed."

Herr Pfeiffer was looking at the door anxiously. "I hope he comes back."

"Are you kidding?" Stein said. "Did you see the way that boy was looking at Max? He's coming back."

CHAPTER Thirteen

Freddie didn't come back.

"Well, you blew it," said Stein as Herr Pfeiffer was locking up the shop. "Played it a little *too* cool, didn't you?"

Berg was laughing. "Thank you, Max! Mission over! Can we go back to England now?"

Max was kicking the sidewalk, feeling like the world's biggest idiot.

He had sized Freddie up as a kid who wanted the approval of cooler kids. Well, *every* kid wants the approval of cooler kids. But Freddie looked particularly desperate for it. And if Max had acted like *he'd* wanted to be friends with *Freddie* . . . well, then he'd just be another kid who was impressed with Freddie's famous dad.

At least, that's how Max had sized him up.

It seemed like he'd sized him up wrong, though.

Herr Pfeiffer shut the front door and locked it. Then he turned to Max. "You better hope that the Fritzsches come back soon. Otherwise, you can tell your uncle to enroll you in school, because I'm done with you."

Max continued kicking the pavement. If Freddie didn't come back, the British secret service would be done with him, too. Maybe he *should* go back to England.

And then Herr Pfeiffer said, "You lucky devil."

Max said, "What?"

"Look."

Max turned. Freddie was hustling up the sidewalk, carrying the do-it-yourself radio set. He was beaming.

"Sorry! It took me longer than I thought! But I did it!" he called.

"Wonderful!" cried Herr Pfeiffer. Then the shopkeeper grabbed Max by the sleeve and pulled him close. He whispered, *"What are you doing this afternoon?"*

"Uh . . . I don't know," Max said, trying to yank his arm free. But Herr Pfeiffer was not letting go.

"You're admiring Freddie Fritzsche's radio. That's what you're doing. Do you understand? Or you can forget coming back to this shop. Hans Fritzsche's business is worth ten little snot-nosed radio geniuses. Understand?"

Herr Pfeiffer straightened up. "Freddie! Let's see what you've done!"

Freddie held out the radio.

"Does it work?" Max asked sullenly. Herr Pfeiffer kicked him in the ankle.

"Yes!" said Freddie. And then his face fell. "But I can't show you, because it doesn't have a battery. I have to plug it in."

"You can plug it in inside the shop!" said Herr Pfeiffer, turning to unlock the door.

"No!" said Max.

Herr Pfeiffer froze. Max could feel him slowly turn, like he was going to strike him.

Max said, "Herr Pfeiffer, aren't you visiting your mother this afternoon?"

"Don't worry, she'll be fi—"

To Freddie, Max said, "We could go back to your place."

Freddie Fritzsche whispered, "You want to come over to *my* house?"

Max shrugged and half rolled his eyes. "Yeah. Sure."

Freddie's smile dawned slowly, and it made Max's heart hurt just a little.

Freddie was a kind kid.

And Max was acting like a complete jerk.

But he wasn't about to stop.

"Come on!" Freddie said, leading the way.

Max stole a glance at Herr Pfeiffer. The shopkeeper gave a stern nod of approval. Max huffed, slumped his shoulders, and followed Freddie.

"I take it all back," Stein said to Berg. "Our Maxy is a genius."

Berg put his head in his hands. "Yah, a genius with a death wish."

CHAPTER
Fourteen

The Fritzsche home was on a shady street in the Steglitz neighborhood, not too far from Herr Pfeiffer's radio shop.

Max walked in silence, which was easy because Freddie, lugging his homemade radio set, wouldn't stop talking.

"This isn't my first custom set, you know. It's my *third*. Well, the first I totally ruined by plugging it into the wrong current, which completely fried it, which was actually pretty funny once I got over it, but at first I was *so* upset, and my dad said . . ."

Max just let Freddie ramble on, as if he didn't care what he said. As if he was just going to his house because his boss was making him. As if his whole mission didn't depend on the next hour.

As they crossed a small street, Freddie yelled, "Watch out!"

Max jumped back. A car sped by.

"Thanks," said Max, his heart pounding.

"Look left, *then* right," Stein reminded him. "You're not in England anymore."

"I know," Max replied.

"You better hope your little Nazi friend didn't notice," said Berg.

"I *know*," Max answered testily, angry with himself.

Luckily, Freddie had gone back to his monologue about his custom radio set, and what his dad had said, and on and on.

Max was surprised by the Fritzsches' house. Unlike the neighboring traditional suburban German homes, the Fritzsches' was one sleek story of dark brick, with long rectangular windows. When Freddie brought Max inside—still yammering away—Max was even more surprised.

Whenever he had seen newsreels showing the homes of high-ranking Nazis, they were always decorated the same way—tall white columns and crimson fabrics and gold leaf everywhere. It was Hitler's preferred style. But Hans Fritzsche hadn't designed his home according to the tastes of the Supreme Leader. His house was sleek and ultramodern. There was no ornamentation on the furniture, no lintels above the portals. Everything was curved and smooth, with beautiful fabrics of different types—deep green velvets, thick beige rugs, cherrywood desks that were simply, beautifully practical. Hitler, who considered himself an art critic and a design expert because he'd nearly gotten into art school, called this modern style "degenerate" and, worse, "Jewish."

Max wondered if there were more ways "the most trusted

voice in Germany" differed from the Supreme Leader. He filed that question away for later and focused on Freddie.

They went downstairs into an unfinished basement. Freddie placed his radio set on a tall plywood table. Behind the table, a rack of tools had been screwed into the wall.

"Nice setup," said Max, gesturing at the worktable and the tools. He meant it.

"Yeah, my dad got it for me for my last birthday. I'm thirteen. What about you?"

"I'm twel—" Max began, and stopped. Horror swept over him.

His birthday had been yesterday.

He had completely forgotten.

Suddenly, all of his birthdays began to rush through his brain. When he turned five, and his father had come into his room and Max had sat on his lap and they'd talked about what it meant to be five. When he turned eight, and for his party he and his classmates had waged a massive battle using fallen leaves in the park by the canal. When he turned twelve, and he'd sat around the dining room table at 28 Kensington Court, trying to avoid the invasive sympathy of the Montagu family by staring at his plate of white birthday cake as he swallowed mucusy tears.

He had intended to spend his thirteenth birthday with his parents.

"I'm thirteen," Max finally managed to say.

But Freddie had already moved on. "So, what's your favorite radio program?" he asked. "Mine's *The Comedy Hour*. Did you hear it this morning? It was *so* funny. What's yours?"

Max nearly said, *This Is Hans Fritzsche*, but then he realized that would sound like he was trying to flatter Freddie. So instead he said, "*Jazz Cracks*."

Freddie said, "What?"

Oh no.

"What do you mean, *Jazz Cracks*?" Freddie said, squinting under the lank lock of blond hair that hung over his eyes. "That's on *Die Deutschen Europasender*. They don't play that here. That's on the radio in England."

Max stared at Freddie.

"Max," Stein said. "What have you done?"

Max's mind was racing. Half of it was trying to concoct a plausible explanation for why his favorite show was something only heard in England. But the other half was still wondering how he had forgotten his own birthday, and whether Uncle Ewen and Uncle Ivor and the Montagus remembered it. And whether his parents remembered, wherever they were.

Come on, Max! he chastised himself. *Focus! He's going to tell his father! Focus!*

Freddie's eyes got really wide. "Wait . . ." Freddie said. So Max waited, his throat constricting as the moments passed, his brain constricting as if he'd forgotten to breathe. Maybe he had.

Freddie, in a hushed voice, asked, "Did you . . . *rig your radio* so you can listen to *Europasender?*"

"Uh . . ." Max said.

"Is that even *possible*?" Freddie asked.

"Uh . . ." Max said again.

"SAY YES!" Stein shouted.

"Yes!" said Max.

"Show me!" said Freddie. "Show me how to get *Europasender!*"

"Um . . . sure . . ." said Max.

Max had no idea if it was possible to get the *Europasender* on the new German sets. They were specifically designed so they couldn't pick up shortwave radio broadcasts.

But if he couldn't, then how could he explain how he'd heard *Jazz Cracks*?

Freddie was staring at him expectantly, awaiting the impossible.

And Max could hear the soft footfalls of Hans Fritzsche, moving around upstairs.

"First," said Max, trying to buy time, "let's see how your set works."

Freddie plugged it in. Light instrumental music came out of the tinny cone that served as a speaker. So it worked, but the reception was poor. As he took off the plastic casing to reveal the wires and tubes and coil inside, Max desperately scanned the radio's innards for a workaround to the shortwave inhibition.

"Let me show you how to get better reception," said Max. Freddie leaned in and watched Max's deft fingers at work. Max could feel the warmth of Freddie's cheek next to his own, and he suddenly wondered if Freddie had ever been this close to a Jew before.

He decided not to ask him.

As Max trimmed the oscillator, the crackle in the reception cleared up. Max could feel a grin spreading across Freddie's face.

"Now show me how you get the *Europasender.*"

Max gazed at the innards of the radio like they were going to kill him.

Which they very likely were.

As Max unplugged Freddie's set and then took it apart, Freddie began yammering again.

"A lot of people want to know what it's like having a famous radio broadcaster for a father," Freddie said. "It's no big deal. I mean, it's normal to *me.* I've met Dr. Goebbels. Once I even went to a banquet where Hitler spoke, but I didn't get to meet him. I will one day, though. Probably pretty soon."

Max tried not to roll his eyes. If Freddie bragged like this all the time, it was no wonder he desperately needed a friend.

"But having a famous dad also means," Freddie continued, "that I don't really *see* him all that much. I mean, he's got to prepare for his broadcasts, which are three times a day. And he tells everyone else what to broadcast, too. So he's got to gather the information from all the reporters around Germany and really the whole world. And then . . ."

Max tried to block out what Freddie was saying and imagine some way to get this longwave radio receiver to behave like a shortwave radio receiver. All the simple ways were blocked. There was no room to wrap a long wire around the workings—there were tiny barriers between the coil and the speaker. Max cursed silently.

"My mom took my little sister back to Bavaria, where my grandparents live. She said Berlin is no place for a little girl. But *I* get to stay."

Because Max thought he should probably say *something* while he fumbled with the wires and transformer, trying desperately to make them violate the laws of physics, he asked, "Why is Berlin no place for a little girl?"

"The British bombing, of course," Freddie replied, as if this were obvious.

"The British planes can barely reach Berlin," Max retorted as his frustration with the receiver mounted. "Besides, they wouldn't bomb civilians. That's what the Luftw—"

Max stopped himself.

He'd nearly said, *That's what the Luftwaffe does*. But he hadn't. Thankfully. What was wrong with him? Why was he so rattled? Was it because of his birthday? Or this damn radio set? Or being in the home of Hans Fr—

A voice rose from the far, dark side of the basement. "You

think the German air force is bombing civilians? And that the British *wouldn't*? Is that what you were going to say?"

Max and Freddie both straightened up and spun around.

Hans Fritzsche emerged from the shadows.

"Where on *earth* would you have learned lies like that?"

Hans Fritzsche was smiling, and his voice was as soft as a lurking tiger's rippling haunches.

CHAPTER Fifteen

Max and Freddie both dropped their hands to their sides like they'd been doing something illegal. Which, technically, they had been.

Hans Fritzsche's eyes moved smoothly back and forth between the two boys. "Who," he said to his son, "is this young man in my basement?"

"This is Max," said Freddie, swallowing. "The boy from the radio shop."

"So, *Max from the radio shop*, have you gotten my son's radio to work?"

Max was paralyzed. It felt like a dream, hearing the most famous voice in Germany say his name.

Or, maybe, a nightmare.

Freddie piped up, "I got the radio to work, Papa, before Max came over!"

Hans Fritzsche dismissed his son. "But it sounded like you were popping corn down here. Terrible quality."

"I fixed that," said Max quietly. And then he stole a glance at Freddie's face.

The boy looked stricken. He wanted his father's admiration so badly, and Max had just stolen it.

"I don't doubt it," said Hans Fritzsche casually. "And what are you doing now?"

Freddie saw his opportunity for revenge.

Would he take it?

"Max said that his favorite radio program is *Jazz Cracks*."

Yes, he would.

A shadow passed over Hans Fritzsche's face. "*Jazz Cracks*? Really?"

"But I said that's on *Europasender*, and it wasn't possible to hear in Berlin."

"Indeed . . ." said Hans Fritzsche. His voice seemed to be purring again. His large, dark eyes roved from Freddie to Max and back.

"But he said he knew how to change a radio to get it."

"That would be a neat trick," purred Hans Fritzsche. "It would also be *illegal*."

Max's lungs collapsed.

"Still," Hans Fritzsche went on, "I'd like to see it."

"It's over. He's dead," said Stein.

Max felt like he was swallowing screws, but he managed to say, "Really? Even though it's illegal?"

Hans Fritzsche said, "We're all friends here."

"Would it be unnecessary to point out that you are *not* all friends?" Berg volunteered.

Max turned back to Freddie's radio set. He had shoved a pin into the wire coils, loosened some screws, tightened some others, run new wire between them all over the plastic barriers, and reversed the tiny powerhouse. He gazed at his mad improvisation.

"I don't know if this set can pick it up," Max said. Sweat was beading on his lip. "Probably not . . ."

But Freddie had already dived under the table to plug it in.

It crackled to life. Static. Freddie stood up. There was a combination of pity and pleasure on his face that only the Germans have a word for: *schadenfreude*.

His revenge was complete. Max was no better at the radio than he was.

Max reached out and hopelessly turned the dial.

More popping and crackling.

"I hope you have another explanation for how you listen to *Jazz Cracks*," said Stein. "Because you're probably going to have to give it to the Gestapo."

Herr Fritzsche's chin jutted out; his upper lip began to curl.

And then, as Max aimlessly spun the dial, they heard comically upper-crust English: "Hallo, friends! This is your patriotic correspondent Lord Haw-Haw! Haw haw haw! It's time for . . . *Germany Calling*!"

Max slowly turned to Hans and Freddie Fritzsche. He was just as surprised as they were. "Uh . . . there . . ." he stammered. "It works."

Lord Haw-Haw's show was a staple of the Nazi programming broadcast to England.

"See, Papa?" said Freddie, changing allegiances in an instant. "He's a *Funkmeister*! A radio wiz!"

Hans Fritzsche's face had relaxed. "Indeed." He addressed Max. "If you are listening to foreign radio broadcasts, especially non-German stations, that would explain your . . . *misconception* about the Luftwaffe. It's a bad habit, in addition to being illegal."

"Yes sir," Max said quickly. "I won't do it anymore."

Hans Fritzsche loomed above Max, considering him. After a moment, he said, "It seems my son has not only made a friend, he's made a *talented* friend." And he sounded so surprised that Max was sure that Freddie would droop again.

But he didn't. Freddie was beaming.

"The housekeeper has put dinner on the table," Hans Fritzsche said. "Time for Max to go home."

"Can he come again sometime?" Freddie asked.

Max tried to hide his desperation as he waited for the famous broadcaster's answer.

Hans Fritzsche lifted a trimmed eyebrow. "Does Max *want* to come again?"

Max said, "If it'd be all right with you?" And he smiled warmly. Not at Freddie. At Hans Fritzsche.

Hans Fritzsche nodded and turned to go upstairs. "Anytime you like, Max."

Freddie turned to Max. "Tomorrow? Could you come tomorrow?"

From the staircase, Hans Fritzsche called out, "Freddie! At least *try* not to appear so desperate."

Freddie froze. Max could see that he had Freddie's confidence, his happiness, practically Freddie's whole *life* in his hands.

Max said, "Shop's closed tomorrow. I can come."

And Freddie was floating like he was filled with helium.

As he left the Fritzsche house and stepped into the dark street, Max felt elated. That had gone *unimaginably* well. A week in Germany and he was already friends with Freddie Fritzsche, already approved of by Hans Fritzsche, already a trusted visitor in their home. This was quicker progress than Uncle Ewen had even been willing to contemplate when he'd laid out the scheme on the eighth floor of the hotel on the Thames.

But there was another feeling inside of Max's body. Maybe down around his stomach. Or lower even, in his bowels. It wasn't fear—though Max felt plenty of that. It wasn't worry for his parents—though he felt that more than anything. It was a different emotion.

Berg said, "So you are going to *use* that boy Freddie? You are going to twist him around your finger and then betray him?"

"So what?" said Stein. "Max is doing the same thing the

Nazis do: using someone to achieve a goal. What do the philosophers say? The *ends* justify the *means*?"

But Berg said, "Some say that, and I reject it! To defeat a monster, Max, do you have to *become* one?"

Max answered quickly. "I'm *not* becoming a monster." Now he could name that feeling in his gut—guilt.

He pushed it down. Shoved it under the stairs with his terror, his doubts, his memories of Major Jameson. He couldn't afford to feel any of that. Not if he was going to succeed in his mission.

"*They're* the monsters," he added forcefully.

To which Berg replied, "Is Freddie?"

CHAPTER Sixteen

It was early Sunday morning when the buzzer rang in Pastor Andreas's apartment.

Max had been eating a slice of toast with butter on it, preparing for his day at the Fritzsches'.

The toast fell, face down, on the table.

Pastor Andreas froze with his coffee an inch from his lips.

Max hurried to the window and looked outside while Pastor Andreas advanced on the intercom with dread.

"Hello?" he said, holding the black button.

"Good morning," a voice crackled in reply.

Max was peering down into the street, looking for Commander Scheel's long black Mercedes, or maybe an SS van with soldiers pouring out of its double doors. But there was only a small black car that had pulled halfway up onto the curb.

The voice from the intercom continued: "I'm sorry to bother you so early on a Sunday. I was hoping to catch Max before he went out."

Pastor Andreas shot Max an anxious look as he said into the grille, "I'm sorry, who is this?"

The voice through the intercom said: "My name is Lieutenant Colonel Alexis von Roenne. I'm with the Abwehr. May I come up?"

Pastor Andreas's eyes rolled back in his head like he was about to faint.

The Abwehr was the army's spy agency. Not the SD. The *original* one. Their spies were a little older. And perhaps slightly less fanatical. But they were also probably better trained and certainly more experienced. And if they caught Max, he would go to the same rooms in the basement of Prinz-Albrecht-Strasse 8 for "interrogation."

"Don't let him in!" Stein shouted.

"Climb out the back window!" Berg cried.

"There's nothing out the back window," said Stein. "He'd fall three flights into an alley."

"That sounds better than whatever this guy is going to do to him!"

But Pastor Andreas was already pressing the button that unlocked the door downstairs.

Max stood by the window, unable to move. Pastor Andreas hurriedly cleaned up Max's toast and the cups. On the stairs, they heard the Persickes' apartment door open, and Liesel's voice shout, "Heil Hitler!"

The response was too quiet to be heard.

There was a gentle rap on the door.

Pastor Andreas opened it. "Please," he said, "come in."

Into the apartment stepped a small man. He had a very smooth face, a high, shining forehead, and he wore perfectly round glasses that reflected the morning light from the windows. His uniform, the muted green of the German army, had an impressive row of decorations over his heart.

"I'm sorry to bother you," he said again. "I'm sure you're getting ready for work, Pastor." Pastor Andreas went to church on Sundays, of course. "If you would like to continue with your day, please, don't let me disturb you. I only need to speak with Max here."

"Oh Lord, he knows everything," Stein whimpered.

"Forget the back windows," said Berg. "Just jump out of this one."

Pastor Andreas replied, "If it's all right with you, Lieutenant Colonel, I'll stay with the boy while you talk to him." His voice was trembling, but his eyes were resolute.

The German intelligence officer smiled. "If you wish." He gestured at the small couch in the living room. "May we?"

So Max and Pastor Andreas sat on the couch, and Lieutenant Colonel Alexis von Roenne sat down opposite them in the wingback armchair. He took off his glasses, then untucked his tie from his green jacket and used it to polish the lenses. He looked apologetic. For what, Max could not guess.

Or maybe he could.

"If you don't mind, I'd like to tell you a story," said Lieutenant Colonel von Roenne. "It may sound fantastical. But I *suspect* . . ." He lingered on the word *suspect* far too long for Max's comfort. ". . . that you will believe it. As a member of the Abwehr, my job is to read intelligence reports, delivered to us from all over the world, and to tell the Supreme Leader what they mean." He sat inhumanly still. "I have developed a technique for this work. Which I will share with you because I have the feeling that you, Max, are a very clever young man, and might appreciate it."

"HOW DOES HE KNOW EVERYTHING ABOUT YOU?" Berg wailed.

"I believe," von Roenne said, "that from a few shreds of fact, one can reconstruct an entire truth. Show me the tracks of a British truck in the mud and I will tell you where the British are getting their war materiel from, when that materiel was delivered, and which port it was likely delivered to."

"Like Sherlock Holmes," Max said.

"Good God, Max, keep your mouth shut!" Stein cried.

"The window is right there, Max. Go for it," Berg said.

Von Roenne's face had lit up. "Yes, Max! Exactly like Sherlock Holmes. Do you see? I had also surmised that you were well-read, from tiny scraps I have picked up over the last week, and, *voila!*, so you are."

Max looked at his lap. "Why have you been picking up scraps about me?" he mumbled.

"I TOLD YOU TO SHUT YOUR TRAP!" Stein bellowed.

Pastor Andreas's leg was bouncing with nervous energy.

"Well," Lieutenant Colonel von Roenne replied, "this is where the fantastical story comes in. May I tell you?"

Max was absolutely certain that he had no choice, so he said nothing.

Von Roenne took Max's silence as assent. Or submission. In a quiet and precise manner, he began his story.

"When reading the intelligence notices from across Europe last Monday morning, I discovered a very concerning report. About a dead British paratrooper, lying in a field."

"It's over," Stein said quietly.

"What was particularly concerning about this report was that this dead paratrooper was wearing a *double harness*. Max, do you see the significance of that detail?"

Max looked through von Roenne's full-moon spectacles, straight into his eyes. "A double harness . . . Does that mean there should have been somebody else?"

"Indeed, Max. Indeed, there should have been. Now, the ground was hard that morning, and no footprints could be found. But there were broken branches in the hedge that separated the field from the road. And that road led to Berlin."

Max said, "All roads go two ways."

The small lieutenant colonel paused. And then he threw his head back and laughed. "Very good, Max. Yes, they do. And this road led both to Berlin, and to the small town of Marwitz. But there were no reports of any strangers arriving in Marwitz.

Or in any of the towns farther along the road." Von Roenne was smiling at Max now, like a teacher smiles at a promising student.

"So, I turned my attention to Berlin, of course," the intelligence officer went on. "I began by scouring the police reports. And indeed, two Grüne Polizei on patrol had encountered a *boy*. At *three* in the morning. Walking *alone*. They had written down that he was going to his uncle's house. But they had *failed* to write down the address of this uncle's house, or this uncle's name. They have been reprimanded severely for this oversight."

Inside, Max was beginning to crumble. Berg and Stein were now trembling and gripping Max's neck with their tiny fingers. Pastor Andreas was gazing out the window. Max suspected that he was silently praying.

"So, what information did I have?" von Roenne went on. "Just that some boy was walking the streets of Berlin. There were a dozen other reports from that night that seemed more likely candidates for our missing parachutist. So, I filed that one away in the back of my mind and moved on to more promising leads. But then—"

Lieutenant Colonel von Roenne stopped. Suddenly, very forcefully, he stomped the floor. Which produced a muffled "Ow!"

"You have a very . . . *interested* neighbor," von Roenne said. "Young, but very committed to the Nazi Party."

Pastor Andreas nodded.

"I am sure you will not be surprised to learn that she submits regular reports to your block warden, who dutifully passes on those reports to the local Gestapo office."

Pastor Andreas's jaw was flexing when he said, "Not surprised in the least."

Von Roenne took off his glasses, examined them, apparently determined that they did not need polishing, and put them back on. "I began reading Gestapo reports concerning the night our mysterious parachutist went missing, to see if there was a fragment of information that I could pair with the police reports. And I found one, reported by your nosy neighbor down there, about a boy who arrived at this apartment between four and five in the morning."

Max, at that moment, could have strangled Liesel. He really could have.

"A quick glance at a map of Berlin confirmed that it would take approximately two hours to walk from the location of the mystery boy's encounter with the Grüne Polizei to this building. So"—von Roenne opened his hands—"I have found the boy. Is it not so?"

Silence.

And then Max said, "It is so."

"NOOOOOOOO," Berg wailed.

"DON'T GIVE YOURSELF UP!" Stein cried. "RUN! FIGHT! MURDER THIS BESPECTACLED CREEP!"

"I did walk across Berlin that night, to get here, to my uncle's house, as I told the Green Cops," Max went on, focusing all his energy on maintaining the bluff he had begun with the Green Cops. Just like he would have at the poker table with Ewen and Chumley and Jean and Lord Rothschild. "But I have never even seen a parachute. I was leaving my father's house. He was drinking. He gets . . . violent. I'm sick of it."

"Yes, of course," said von Roenne. "Tell me, then, what is your father's name and address?"

Another brief moment of silence.

Then Max said, "Leo Maas. Coburger Strasse 25, Falkensee. The garden apartment in the back."

It was the address Chumley had told Max to give. Max had no idea who lived there, or if it even existed.

When Lieutenant Colonel von Roenne heard it, he smiled at Max in a disconcerting way. Like he had *expected* Max to say that.

"Good. Very good." The intelligence officer stood up and stretched out his hand. Max stood, too, and shook it. Lieutenant Colonel Alexis von Roenne's hands were soft. "It's been a pleasure to meet you, young man. A very interesting mind you have. I can tell. I'll see you again."

It wasn't a threat.

It was a fact.

Once von Roenne was gone, Pastor Andreas grabbed Max and hugged him tight. *"What are we going to do?"* he whispered.

"Nothing," Max whispered back.

"Are you *joking*?" Berg cried.

"Nothing?! Do NOTHING?! That's what your plan is?" Stein shrieked.

There was only one thing Max could do—report this encounter to Uncle Ewen, using the dead letter box behind the church. But if he did that, Ewen would certainly end the mission and bring him back to England.

But Max wasn't going back to England. At least, not without his parents.

CHAPTER Seventeen

Freddie was sitting on the low brick steps outside his front door, like a dog waiting for his master to come home.

As soon as Max saw him, that uncomfortable feeling bubbled up in his gut again. He pushed it down almost before he could remember what it was called. Shoved it back under the stairs, where Major Jameson's body was now stowed awkwardly, barely hidden at all, thanks to Lieutenant Colonel Alexis von Roenne.

Freddie stood up and waved. "Come around back! I want to show you something."

"Aw," said Berg. "Your sweet little sucker is so excited to see you."

It was a warm day for November, and birds were dancing around the branches of the low-slung apple trees in Freddie's backyard. There was a short brick wall that ran around the perimeter of the yard, separating it from the neighbors. There was also a small outdoor dining set—a circular table and chairs, made of thick iron, painted white.

On the table was a rifle.

Max stopped as soon as he saw it. "What do you have that for?" he asked.

Freddie picked it up. "Isn't it cool? I got it from my Hitler Youth group. I've been practicing all week!"

"Practicing? In your backyard?" Max was incredulous.

"Yeah! Check it out!"

Freddie hoisted the wooden rifle to his shoulder and pointed it at the far wall of the garden. There were half a dozen empty bottles lined up. Freddie threw the rifle's hammer and pulled the trigger.

The *BANG* Max expected never came. Instead, there was a soft pop.

"Oh! It's a pellet gun!" said Max.

Freddie stared at him. Then he started to laugh. "Did you think they were handing out real rifles to thirteen-year-olds to take home with them?"

Max shrugged. "They give you daggers . . ." Long daggers with decorative handles were standard equipment for every boy in the Hitler Youth and the Young Folk, which was the division for boys under fourteen.

Freddie was speechless. Then he said, "You're not a member of the Hitler Youth?"

Max had made another mistake. When you turned ten, you were required to register for the Young Folk, unless you were

Jewish, disabled, or had committed some "dishonorable acts" and were forbidden to join. But before Max could cover his error with a lie, he noticed Freddie's expression.

Freddie was *thrilled.*

"You should join my group! It's amazing! We go hiking and sing songs and shoot things! Wanna see my dagger? It's upstairs!"

"Maybe later," said Max. "I like radios better than weapons."

This was true.

"Oh," said Freddie. He put down the rifle, momentarily embarrassed. Then he rallied. "Still, you should come on our trip next weekend! It's going to be incredible! We're going camping! Come with us!"

Max didn't reply. Nothing sounded worse than spending an entire weekend with a group of adolescent Nazis.

"Max," Stein hissed. "Say something."

Max said quickly, "I can't. Gotta work at the shop on Saturdays until four."

"Come *on*," said Freddie. *"Please?"*

And suddenly it was as clear as the sun in the cool blue sky why Freddie wanted Max to join his group. He was terrified to be alone in the woods with Hitler Youth bullies.

As was Max.

Freddie just said, "Think about it, will you?"

At the sound of a door opening both boys spun around.

Hans Fritzsche was standing on the back porch. He was wearing a smoking jacket and holding a pipe. He was smiling with one corner of his mouth. Just like Uncle Ewen.

"Look who it is. The *Funkmeister.*"

"Hello, Herr Fritzsche," said Max.

"Heil Hitler, Max," Herr Fritzsche replied.

The tin can of Max's heart crumpled a little more. "Heil Hitler," he replied as Hans Fritzsche watched him carefully.

Then the broadcaster sauntered down into thc backyard.

"I thought you had to work this morning," said Freddie plaintively to his father. As if he were saying, *I don't want to share my new friend with you. Can you leave us alone, please?*

But if Hans Fritzsche understood, he didn't show it. He pulled a painted iron chair away from the outdoor table and sat down, folding one leg over the other and lighting his pipe. It had a beautiful rosewood bowl and an ebony stem. "Nice day, isn't it?"

"Yes, Herr Fritzsche," Max said, wondering what the most famous radio personality in Germany wanted from him.

Maybe he didn't want anything. Maybe he merely wanted to enjoy his own backyard. He was watching some sparrows fighting in a tree.

But then he said, "I was impressed with your skills on the wireless set yesterday. What you did to Freddie's radio was highly . . . *unconventional.*"

Max was instantly flooded by two contradictory feelings: elation and terror.

Max swallowed as he said, "Um, thank you, Herr Fritzsche."

"I was thinking about something you said, though," Hans Fritzsche mused. He puffed thoughtfully on his pipe.

Max tried to play it cool. Which was harder than usual, because Hans Fritzsche's voice had always sounded to him like the Voice of God. "Yes, Herr Fritzsche?"

"You said—or almost said—that you didn't think the English would bomb the civilians of Berlin. I find that curious."

Max said nothing at all.

"The English, it seems to me, are the most warlike people in the history of the world," Hans Fritzsche went on.

"Uh, have you looked in the mirror?" Stein retorted. "I think Germany just declared war on everyone!"

But Hans Fritzsche said, "Think about it. From the very day that the English realized they had ships to sail the seven seas, they have been taking their guns and their flags and subjugating every nation of the globe! They sailed to Africa, enslaved the people there, and exploited their land for every precious stone they could find, did they not?"

Max supposed they did.

"They sailed to the New World and killed most of the people there and locked the rest away on 'reservations,' to make room for British farms and industry. And now the Brits have the gall to criticize what Hitler is doing in Poland. He got the idea from them!"

Max asked Stein and Berg, "Is that true?"

Stein said, "I don't know where Hitler got the idea. But it does seem kinda similar. . . ."

"The British landed on the subcontinent of India, and planted a flag, and said 'We own all of this!' Hundreds of millions of Indians, and some small island off the coast of France owns it?" Hans Fritzsche laughed. "That's moxie, I tell you!"

Max was trying to figure out if Hans Fritzsche suspected that he'd been living in England . . . or if he was just trying to convince Max of English villainy. If it was the latter . . . well, it was kind of working.

"Then they went to China, and they couldn't conquer that country, so they sold them opium! Drugs! Got half the country addicted, so they couldn't resist the English merchants selling their woolen socks!" Herr Fritzsche exclaimed as he knocked his pipe out on the arm of his chair, making a clanging sound like a cracked bell. "This is all fact, all written down even in English history books."

Max didn't dare doubt him.

"And then, of course," said Hans Fritzsche, "their greatest crime of all. They occupied Germany, after the first World War. And they made Germany a colony, too. This is what England does. They conquer every corner of the globe, and then they squeeze it for everything it's worth."

Which was just what Uncle Ivor had said.

"Are we expected to become the next tragedy in the history of Western colonialism? If a hunter came into a lion's den with a rifle, and the mother lion killed that hunter, would we blame the mother lion? Are we not allowed to strike out, in order to survive? And if we strike back, to protect ourselves, our wives, our *children*, from the rapacious greed of the colonialists and bankers in London and New York, who could blame us?"

"No one!" Freddie cried.

"Wrong," said Hans Fritzsche. "The British propagandists could, and do. The American Jewish interests, in Hollywood and New York, blame us. They blame us for standing up on our own feet. They have starved and imprisoned our people for the last twenty years, and now that we *dare* to strike them, to get their boot off our necks, they call *us* monsters?

"Well," concluded Hans Fritzsche, "if defending ourselves is monstrous, let us be monsters."

Freddie beamed at his father. He looked to be on the verge of breaking out in applause.

Silence settled over the yard. The only sound was the twittering of birds and the clamoring questions in Max's brain.

Finally, Freddie said, "Papa, don't you think Max should come on my Hitler Youth trip next weekend?"

That seemed to rouse Hans Fritzsche from some deep thoughts of his own. "I'm sure he's got his own group."

"No! He doesn't!"

Fritzsche turned his deep eyes on Max, and Max felt utterly naked. "You don't belong to the Young Folk?" Hans Fritzsche asked him. "However did *that* happen?"

Max was now ready for this. "I had a group," said Max. "When I was living with my father. But since I came to live with my uncle in Berlin, I haven't joined one."

"Well then, we should rectify that!" Hans Fritzsche exclaimed, standing up. "I'll put in a call to the Hitler Youth leadership office."

"Um . . ." said Max.

"Just tell me your full name, your old address, and where you're living now, and I'll make a call."

"A call to the Hitler Youth, or the Gestapo?" asked Berg.

"Because you've already got that little sadist with the glasses from the Abwehr on your tail. Why not get all the German security services in on the fun?" Stein added.

Max slowly recited both his imaginary father's address in Falkensee and Pastor Maas's address in Kreuzberg, as well as his false last name.

Hans Fritzsche smiled. "Very good," he said. He turned and walked briskly into the house.

"Isn't this exciting!" Freddie said to Max.

It was so exciting Max thought he might faint.

They took turns shooting with the pellet gun while they waited for Hans Fritzsche to come back. Freddie was abysmal. He couldn't hit a thing. Max was equally terrible. But he was fairly certain that was because his hands were shaking so hard.

Ten minutes later, Hans Fritzsche reemerged from the house and smiled.

"It's all set. Next weekend, you'll join Freddie on the retreat."

Max managed a barely audible "Thank you, Herr Fritzsche."

Hans Fritzsche's deep, dark eyes never left Max's sweaty face.

As Max walked away from the Fritzsche home that evening, he said to Berg and Stein, "I have to admit, I'm feeling a little confused."

"So am I," Berg agreed. "I am confused as to why a Jewish child insists on running around, playing at being a spy, in *Nazi Germany*."

Max ignored him. "Is it true that Britain just wants to colonize Germany, like they have everyone else in the world?"

Stein *tsk*ed Max. "Who started this war?"

"Well, Germany . . ." said Max.

"Right," Stein went on. "Despite Prime Minister Neville Chamberlain groveling at Hitler's boots, asking him not to."

"But hasn't England really done all those things?" Max pressed. "Haven't they conquered and exploited half the world?"

"Well, we don't know a lot about what happens outside of Germany. But from what we've heard . . . Yeah, seems accurate."

"So why should the British fight Germany, when Germany's only trying to conquer a few of its neighbors?" Max asked. And then he immediately said, "Oh. That sounded way stupider when I said it out loud."

Stein chuckled. "Yeah. Just because Tommy likes to punch people in the head doesn't mean that Gerry can kick people between the legs. They should *both* stop."

"But is Germany really any more evil than England?" Max asked.

Berg sighed heavily. "Max, let's review: The Nazis have created a state of terror. Every book that contradicts their views has been burned. The people are afraid of telling the truth, for fear that they will be taken away to a concentration camp. Newspaper buildings have been set aflame and newspapermen bullied until they either jumped out their office windows or only report what the Nazis want people to hear. Disabled people are being put to death. Germany has become a nation of lies and of terror. And this terror is spreading across Europe at lightning speed, behind bullets and bombers and tanks and men with skulls painted on their helmets."

Stein cut in: "The Brits have done a lot of evil things over the last many centuries. Most of the terrible things the Germans are doing to their own people, the British have done to others. So how do you compare evil? What do you do? Count the dead? The wounded? The starving? The Boss didn't explain how to compare two evils at the beginning of time. But Germany didn't used to be like this, Maxy. These Nazi psychopaths have created a whole nation *committed* to evil. Doesn't that feel *different*?"

And then, quietly, Berg added, "Also, where are your parents?"

To which Max, after a sigh, replied, "Right."

CHAPTER Eighteen

Max spent the next week working in the radio shop during the day, and sleeping fitfully on the couch in Pastor Andreas's study at night.

Once, he had a terrifying dream where he was tuning his family's radio set for his father, after a long day of work. Hans Fritzsche's voice came on, and Max turned to his father to ask if he wanted to hear *This Is Hans Fritzsche*—but it was Hans Fritzsche, not his father, on the sofa. And he was saying the words that they were hearing on the radio. Max had no idea what that dream meant, but he woke up with sweaty sheets twisted around him so tight that when he tried to wrestle out of them, he fell to the floor with a bang.

Which made Liesel pound on her ceiling and yell at him to keep it down.

The one bright spot was that, ever since his success with the Fritzsches, Herr Pfeiffer practically treated Max like a son. Like a German son, of course, with a stern German father. But still, Max could see the twinkle in Herr Pfeiffer's eye whenever Max fixed a customer's wireless set that had seemed utterly beyond repair. And more than once someone had come in and said, "Is the Funkmeister here?" And every time, Herr Pfeiffer would nod toward Max and beam.

On Friday, Max was working on a Siemens 95W and Herr Pfeiffer was humming through his mustache while listening to a low, sultry voice on the Victrola.

Stein was squinting at the shopkeeper. "You know what—I think I've seen Herr Pfeiffer before."

Berg was lost in the music. "Yah?" he said absently.

"But where?" Stein murmured.

Berg's eyes were closed and his head was swaying. "Did you ever hear Josephine Baker sing this song live, back in '26?"

"That's it!" Stein shouted. Startled, Berg gripped his chest and emitted a strangled "Ack!"

"*That's* where I saw him!"

Berg scowled at the dybbuk. "What? Who?"

"That's where I saw Herr Pfeiffer! At the Josephine Baker concert!"

"Impossible."

Max was finishing up his work on the Siemens. "What are you two talking about?"

"In 1926, at the Metropol. September, I think," said Stein.

"October," Berg corrected him.

"October, that's right. Josephine Baker," Stein murmured, remembering.

Max said, "Who?"

"What do you mean, *who*? You've never heard of Josephine Baker?" Berg snapped.

Max said, "No . . ."

Stein said, "Of course not. Her music is illegal now."

"Who is Josephine Baker?" Max asked again.

"The greatest entertainer who ever lived, that's who," said Stein. "When she came to Germany, every immortal being dragged their *tuchuses* down to the Metropol theater! We packed it to the rafters. More metaphysical energy in one spot that night than at any time since Eden, probably."

"Okay . . . I still don't know who she is," said Max.

Berg said, "Singer. Dancer. Comedian. Some people thought she was a spy. An American Black woman, though she lived in Paris. Knew karate, incidentally."

"I saw her kick the stuffing out of some toughs in an alley one time," Stein added. "Spinning roundhouse to the head, *and* she could hit the high notes."

Max looked skeptical. "And Herr Pfeiffer went to her concert? At the Metropol?" It was hard to picture the stout, stolid shopkeeper at a nightclub.

"Go ahead," said Stein. "Ask him about it."

Max closed up the Siemens's smooth, dark wood and walked up to the counter where Herr Pfeiffer was totaling his sums and humming.

The shopkeeper looked up over his reading glasses. "Well, Max? I thought I asked you to work on the 95W."

"Yes sir. I finished."

"Already? Really? Okay. So, you need something else to do?"

"I actually wanted to ask you a question, Herr Pfeiffer. If you don't mind."

Pfeiffer took off the reading glasses and placed them on top of the receipt book. He pursed his lips and his mustache bristled.

"This song on the radio."

Herr Pfeiffer's eyes narrowed. "Yes?"

"Didn't Josephine Baker sing it?"

Herr Pfeiffer's face began to redden.

Max suddenly suspected he'd said something wrong.

"You know Josephine Baker?" Herr Pfeiffer's pocked cheeks were ruddy, like he was very angry. The silence in the shop felt dangerous.

"Okay, maybe I made a mistake," Stein said.

"Retreat!" Berg cried. "Retreat!"

But Max's curiosity was piqued. He looked over his shoulder to be sure no one was coming into the shop. And then he plunged ahead. "I know how to listen to foreign radio stations. I've heard her name a few times." Max thought this was probably true. "They always talk about her with such *awe*."

Herr Pfeiffer's face was getting redder and his eyes were getting wider.

"I'm sorry!" Max added quickly, in a hushed voice. "I know I'm not supposed to listen to those stations! I'll stop! Please don't tell!"

Herr Pfeiffer's voice was a low growl when he said:

"I saw Josephine Baker once."

Max held perfectly still.

"It was at the Metropol. She was on tour from Paris."

"Ha!" Stein cried triumphantly.

Herr Pfeiffer had stopped talking.

Max waited.

That was it.

So, very cautiously, Max asked, "How was she?"

Herr Pfeiffer's face was the color of a brick now.

Max quickly added, "Awful, right? Decadent, degenerate, dis—"

"She was a genius, Max."

Slowly, Max said, "She was?"

"The greatest performance I ever saw."

Max said, "Can you tell me?"

Herr Pfeiffer wiped his nose, which had begun to drip. He looked fiercely at Max. "Even *talking* about this could get me in trouble."

"But please, Herr Pfeiffer," said Max. "Please. I want to know."

"You will tell no one?"

"Who would I tell?"

"Hans Fritzsche. Or his boy."

"Never. I swear on my life, Herr Pfeiffer. And you could tell the Gestapo that I listen to illegal radio stations. So, we're even."

Herr Pfeiffer turned away.

Max deflated.

Herr Pfeiffer said, "Close the shop. It's lunchtime."

Max hurried to the door and flipped the sign so it read CLOSED from the outside.

Then he hurried to the small back room, where Herr Pfieffer had moved to.

"We won't be even," said Herr Pfeiffer.

"Huh?" Max asked.

Herr Pfeiffer didn't explain. Instead, he said, "Josephine Baker could sing. She could dance. And she had the funniest patter you've ever heard. In English, French, German . . . switching back and forth at lightning speed. You couldn't believe what you were hearing. Half the time, Max, I was roaring with laughter. And then she'd sing, and I'd be weeping by the end of the song, Max. *I* was. And look at me. Do I look like a weeper?"

Max glanced up at the shopkeeper. He did not.

Herr Pfeiffer said, "This was back when I was at university. Well, sort of." He chuckled. "I was skipping every class and getting together with my friends, and we were making radios. Oh, what a time for radio, Max! There were no regulations, not like now. If you could fix it right, you could pick up broadcasts from Paris, from Moscow, from New York, from . . . Australia."

Max looked sharply at Herr Pfeiffer. On the word *Australia* his voice had cracked. It was cool that he could hear radio from Australia, but Max had no idea what would make Herr Pfeiffer so emotional about Australian radio.

Herr Pfeiffer was gazing far away. "We loved the broadcasts from New York," he went on. "Direct from Harlem. That music was the best. Still is. Nothing has ever been made that's better, and it never will be, Max."

"Yes, Herr Pfeiffer."

"We started to go to the clubs so we could hear the music live. Be *right there*. The drums changing the rhythm of your heartbeat. The bass changing the timbre of your soul."

Max had never heard Herr Pfeiffer talk like this. It was *very* strange. The stern shopkeeper was a model of sensible Germany.

"We all went together, but my classmate Philip and I . . . we went to every show we could. There was a year, the Josephine Baker year, 1926, when we went to a show every single night, Max. Three hundred and sixty-five nights of live music. You could do that then. Philip and I got an apartment together, because we never went to bed before sunrise. Oh, what a year that was."

Max said, "That sounds amazing."

"It was. It was."

Max said to Herr Pfeiffer, "And then?"

Herr Pfeiffer looked at Max and said, "And then 1933 came, and Hitler became Chancellor. And they closed the clubs. Most of them. And they banned Black people from performing. Which pretty much killed the music scene. There were a few good Jewish jazz clarinetists. But, of course, they couldn't perform either."

"Right," said Max, trying to keep his voice level.

"And then came the Night of the Long Knives. Do you remember that?"

"No," said Max.

"Of course not. You must have been a small child. Do you know who Ernst Röhm was?"

"No," said Max again.

Pfeiffer chuckled ruefully. "Amazing that his name has been wiped from history already. Röhm was the second most powerful man in the Nazi party, after Hitler. He led the Brownshirts, who were the soldiers of the party back then. Röhm commanded four million Brownshirts. The Germany military only had a hundred thousand men at that time! Also, Röhm was gay."

"Really?" Max asked. The Nazis said terrible things about gay people. How could the second most powerful man in the Nazi party have been gay?

"Röhm was fairly open about it," said Herr Pfeiffer. "Phil and I often saw him at the jazz clubs with a boyfriend. But then Hitler began to fear Ernst Röhm's power. Millions of

Brownshirts could have easily overthrown Hitler, if Röhm told them to. So Hitler struck first."

"What did he do?" Max asked.

"The Night of the Long Knives. Ernst Röhm was grabbed out of his bed and put to death. As were many of his top lieutenants. The reason given to the public? They were gay."

"But that wasn't why?"

"That had never been a problem before," said Herr Pfeiffer. "Really, it was because Hitler was afraid of Röhm. I'm sure of it. But after that, everything changed for gay people in Germany. Pretty soon, Phil's name showed up on a list."

Max didn't make a sound.

"I don't know how. *My* name didn't get on that list. Just Philip's."

There was a long, long silence.

"Did he disappear?"

Herr Pfeiffer wiped his nose again. "No. Many others on that list did. Friends of ours. They were all arrested and sent I don't know where. All I know is that they never came back. Phil got lucky, thank God. He found a visa for Australia."

Oh.

Australia.

"He got on a steamship and I never saw him again."

Herr Pfeiffer's mustache had tears in it.

"We used to write, every week. Now, with the war, I haven't heard from him in almost a year."

Herr Pfeiffer hid his eyes behind one plump hand. Then he wiped his face.

"So," he said, sniffling hard. "You can see, Max, why you and I are *not* even."

Max spoke quietly and urgently: "I swear, on the *lives of my parents*, that I will never tell a soul."

Herr Pfeiffer shrugged and sniffed once, hard. "The Gestapo knows already. I'm sure of it. They read all the mail. When they want to get rid of me, they will." He sighed. "Still, it's better never spoken of again."

Max said, "I promise." He turned to give Herr Pfeiffer some privacy—and then he stopped. "Can I ask you one more question?"

The shopkeeper threw up his hands and laughed through his tears. "What do I have to hide now?"

"How can you support the Nazis after that? How can you admire Hans Fritzsche so?"

Herr Pfeiffer's head tilted to one side. "Support?" he said. "Admire?"

He took out a handkerchief, blew his nose, and put the handkerchief back in his pocket. "Max," he said, "I am *terrified* of the Nazis. Every day when I walk home, I am waiting for a van to pull up beside me. For the Gestapo to drag me in and take me to a camp. Every morning when I arrive at the shop, I am sure it will be closed, with boards over the windows and the word *pervert* in dripping red paint. I do not *admire* Herr

Fritzsche. I am *scared to death* of Herr Fritzsche. I am scared to death of them all, Max."

Suddenly, a sharp rapping came from the front door. All the blood drained from Herr Pfeiffer's face.

"I'll see who it is," Max said. "Take your time."

Herr Pfeiffer nodded and began to scrub tears out of his mustache with his snotty handkerchief.

Max looked over the counter and through the glass door. It was the man with the felt hat, with his PR33 radio under his arm.

"Don't worry," said Max. "It's okay. It's just a customer. I'll let him in. Everything is okay, Herr Pfeiffer."

From the backroom, Max heard a muffled "Is it, Max? I don't think so. I don't think it is."

CHAPTER Nineteen

Saturday morning. The day Max had been dreading.

It was dark when Max started through the streets of Kreuzberg for Freddie's house. He hadn't slept at all the night before. He had tossed and turned on the short sofa, throwing pillows on the floor, picking them up, then throwing them on the floor again.

The idea of spending two days—and one night, one awful, terrifying night—in the wilderness with a bunch of Hitler Youth . . . Max was almost hoping that Lieutenant Colonel von Roenne or Commander Scheel would show up to take him away first.

"Are you *sure* you have to do this?" Stein asked as Max trudged, shivering, through the streets. "I mean, those Hitler Youth kids are *monsters*. They're breeding a *generation* of monsters."

"Don't remind me," Max said. But yes, he had to do this. Nothing else would advance his mission like this could. Hans Fritzsche seemed to *like* him. It was unbelievable, really. *The* Hans Fritzsche, the most trusted voice in Germany, liked *Max*.

The Funkhaus was just one step away.

Hans Fritzsche's beautiful BMW 327, painted in two tones—mauve and tan—was parked in front of the Fritzsche house when Max arrived. Hans Fritzsche stood beside the open trunk. He smiled and waved at Max. Max waved back and managed the best approximation of a smile he could muster.

"Good to see you, Max," said Hans Fritzsche as Max climbed into the back seat. The front door of the house banged open and then shut, and a moment later Freddie ran and threw himself into the BMW, landing on Max and laughing.

"Hey Max! Good morning! Are you excited?"

Max nodded and stared out the window and wished he was *anywhere else.*

On the drive, Hans Fritzsche turned on the radio. The Berlin station bloomed to life from the speaker on the dashboard. For the first few minutes, they listened to old Bavarian folk songs with oompah-oompah horns and a marching rhythm.

Then a voice came on the radio to announce a replay of Dr. Joseph Goebbels's speech from the previous evening.

"Did you hear this?" Hans Fritzsche asked, looking over his shoulder at Max.

Max told the truth. "No sir."

"It was good. Listen."

Hans Fritzsche turned up the radio.

"My dear German friends!"

Berg groaned. "Of all the reasons I got on that ferry," said Berg, "this man's speeches was number one."

Dr. Joseph Goebbels, architect and master of German media, director of the Ministry of Propaganda and Popular Enlightenment, and close advisor to Adolf Hitler, began to bray into the microphone: "What a great day to be German! It is a day of thunderous laughter! Ha ha ha!"

Max caught himself as he began to roll his eyes. The laughter was so fake, so forced. It was embarrassing.

"Ha ha ha!" Goebbels laughed. "Just this week, we have heard the most laughable lies coming from the shores of Britain! The English plutocrats, the rich Jews and inbred lords, look foolish today! Ha ha ha!"

Max glanced quickly at Freddie, and then at Hans Fritzsche. They were both enjoying this.

Goebbels's smug voice continued:

"They have told their people that Germany, great Germany, tried to invade Britain, and failed! What? We did? Did I *fail* to notice? Ha ha ha! Of course not. When we invade, with the full might of the German navy, the air force, and the army united as one clenched fist, we will smash the teeth from their grinning mouths!

"So why did they *say* we invaded, when we did not? Because the British do not fight their wars with guns alone. No! They fight their wars with *lies*. Yes. They always have. They tell the people of India, 'We are just here for tea, and we'll pay you for it!' and then they starve them to death by the millions! They tell the German people, 'Just give up your guns, and all of Europe will live in peace,' and then they reduce this great nation to a mass of starving, mewling prisoners!"

Hans Fritzsche hit the steering wheel to show his approval.

"Well, we have something far stronger than their lies!" Goebbels thundered, which made the speaker crack with static. "We have our National Community! We are not divided, like the British, between rich and poor! We are all children of the Fatherland! We are not weakened, like the Americans, who invite every brown, black, and yellow man into their country—and then hypocritically keep them separate by law and custom, all so they can more easily *exploit* them! No! We are *one* people, a *German* people, strong and united!"

Hans Fritzsche said to the boys, "We worked on that part together, Dr. Goebbels and I."

The radio blared away: "And while we have a variety of viewpoints in our great nation, a great diversity of opinions, a total freedom to think whatever our conscience calls for . . ."

"We do?" Berg asked.

"Yeah, if we want to end up in a concentration camp," Stein replied.

". . . there is one opinion that *unites* us: We love our

Supreme Leader! We *all* love the wise, the caring, the thoughtful Adolf Hitler!" The crowd *roared.*

Max thought of Herr Pfeiffer, crying into his bristly mustache. He thought of Pastor Andreas, terrified that the child downstairs would inform on him to the Gestapo. He thought of his mother, tears streaming down her face as she put Max on the train, knowing she might never see him again—all to escape the wise, the caring, the thoughtful Adolf Hitler.

"Yes, we are united by our love for our Supreme Leader, Adolf Hitler, into one great National Community! No *lie* can break that bond! So what do we say to the British and their lying radiomen? We say: Ha ha ha!"

The strains of violins from Wagner's "Ride of the Valkyries" began, and Hans Fritzsche snapped off the radio and sighed contentedly.

In the ensuing silence, Max thought about what Goebbels had said: *No* lie *can break that bond!*

That implied . . . that *something could.*

Max wondered what that something might be. He filed this question away for later.

Aloud, Max said, "He sounds like an amazing man."

Hans Fritzsche nodded thoughtfully. "He is a genius, in his way."

"One day . . ." Max said, almost to himself, "one day, I'm going to shake his hand."

Hans Fritzsche glanced over his shoulder at Max. "Would you like that?"

"More than *anything*."

Hans Fritzsche returned his gaze to the road.

Stein was appraising Max. "Well, aren't you a crafty boy?"

Max smiled inwardly.

CHAPTER Twenty

The muster point for the camping trip was a dirt parking lot at the edge of the Grunewald—the forest that lay just to the west of Berlin.

There was already a group of about a dozen boys standing around in the cold morning air, all wearing the standard-issue winter coats and hats of the Hitler Youth. Most had good hiking boots on, too.

Not Max. He was wearing the same thing he wore every day.

"Not to worry," said Hans Fritzsche. "We'll get you a uniform."

Once they'd parked, the famous broadcaster sauntered up to the troop leader, a young man with a sharp hooked nose and very short cropped hair. When he saw Hans Fritzsche approaching him, he clicked his heels and shouted, "Heil Hitler!"

Hans Fritzsche lazily saluted back and then began talking and gesturing across the lot at Max.

"Papa will get you everything you need," Freddie assured him. "Come on, let's choose our packs."

There was a stack of enormous backpacks piled at one end

of the parking lot. They were each made of red canvas and about as big as Max. A dozen boys were there, trying on different packs, adjusting the straps, and laughing with each other.

A tightness gripped Max's insides.

It wasn't *only* that he was about to spend the weekend with a bunch of Hitler Youth. He would have felt this way about *any* camping trip. Even if all the boys were Jewish.

Thirteen-year-olds can be . . . well, awful.

"Hiya, Rolph!" Freddie called to one of the taller boys who was tightening a strap around his waist. Rolph looked up, rolled his eyes, and went back to working at the strap. Max noticed that Rolph's black hair was long and combed across his forehead in exactly the style of Adolf Hitler.

A small boy with two front teeth like a rabbit's stood beside Rolph. Freddie called to him, "Hey there, Peter!"

Instead of replying to Freddie, Peter looked across the parking lot at Hans Fritzsche walking toward them, holding a Hitler Youth coat, shirt, and hat.

"Hi, Freddie!" Peter said loudly. Loud enough for Hans Fritzsche to hear.

Max immediately knew two things about Rolph and Peter:

They were the cool kids.

Max hated them already.

Peter and Rolph and all the other boys stared as Hans Fritzsche gave Max the uniform. "They didn't have any boots for you, Max," Fritzsche said apologetically. "You'll just have to prove you've got tougher feet than the rest of these limp noodles."

All the boys laughed loudly.

Even though it wasn't remotely funny.

"Nice to see you, Herr Fritzsche!" Rolph and Peter both called as the famous radio man waved and walked back to his two-tone BMW. Then, much more quietly, but still loud enough for Max and Freddie to hear, Peter said, "How on earth could Hans Fritzsche have a son like Freddie?"

Rolph looked right at Freddie as he said, "I have no idea."

Freddie deflated like a punctured tire.

"Well," Berg observed, "this seems like the beginning of a *lovely* weekend."

CHAPTER
Twenty-One

Max was in pain from the first moment of the hike.

The troop leader, Rudi, set a blistering pace. Max's shoes had thin leather soles and were not made for hiking. Also, he couldn't get the straps of his pack right. Whenever he tightened the strap on the left shoulder, the whole pack would tilt to the right side. So he'd tighten the strap on the right side, and the pack would tilt the other way. Then both straps would be digging so hard into his shoulders that he'd loosen them both. And the pack would tilt back to the left.

"You look like an old smokestack," Stein informed him helpfully.

"You're wheezing like an old smokestack, too!" Berg added.

Freddie was just ahead of Max, and he wasn't doing much better. His chubby cheeks were as red as the canvas sack, his blond hair was matted against his head with sweat, and he kept stopping to catch his breath, causing Max to crash into him.

"I hate this I hate this I hate this," Max muttered to Berg and Stein. He stubbed his toe on a rock. "Ow!"

"You okay?" Freddie called back.

"Fine," grumbled Max. And then he continued mumbling, "I hate this I hate this I hate this."

Soon, to help the boys keep pace, Rudi the troop leader started a song:

Ohhhh, Jews are sinners . . .

"Here we go," muttered Stein.

They kill German kids, don't you know!

"We *don't* know—because they don't!" Stein shouted.

They cut the little kids' little throats!

Berg hid his face in his hands.

The filthy, scheming Jewish filth!

"What exquisite poetry," Stein said. "I love the pointless repetition! How avant-garde!"

All of the boys knew the song, and they sang it loudly and cheerfully, in time to the marching of their boots.

Max was in the very back, because he was so slow. Which meant, luckily, that no one noticed him not singing. Instead, he spoke to Berg and Stein. "I don't get it. I still don't. Why do they hate us so much? What did we actually *do*?"

"Do?" Stein replied. "To make them hate you? Nothing!"

"Then *why*?"

Berg shrugged. "Germany has been Christian for a thousand years. Which makes Jews *different*. And it's easy to blame whoever is different. The bishops and kings of Germany have *always* blamed the Jews for *whatever* goes wrong, so the people won't blame *them* for their problems. But the Jewish people didn't do anything to deserve it. We would know. We've been here all along."

They stopped for lunch by the Teufelssee—the Devil's Lake—a beautiful lake, ringed by icy rocks.

Max immediately took off his scuffed shoes and rubbed his aching feet. Which proved a mistake, because his socks got wet from the damp ground. He began to shiver.

"Great," he said to Berg and Stein. "Now I'm going to die of hypothermia out here with a bunch of Nazis."

"Of all the ways I see this weekend going," Stein replied, "that's one of the more optimistic scenarios."

"I want to go home," Max moaned silently.

"Where, exactly, is that?" Berg asked.

To which Max had no answer.

CHAPTER
Twenty-Two

Rudi, the troop leader, passed around dried sausages and hunks of cheese. Rolph held out a sausage to Freddie, but when Freddie went to take it, Rolph flipped it to Peter, who caught it and passed it along to someone else.

Rolph held out another sausage, and again Freddie went to grab it—and again Rolph flipped it to Peter.

Every time this happened, the boys in the group laughed harder. Including Freddie. But Freddie was laughing in that desperate way, Max could tell, which was dangerously close to crying.

While this was going on, a canteen of hot water, mixed with a dash of schnapps, was passed around. Max took a sip. The schnapps burned his throat, but the drink made warmth radiate out from his chest.

"Oh great, now they're giving kids alcohol," Stein complained.

Just then, Max realized he had to pee.

It came on fast. Must have been the schnapps. Plus the sound of the Teufelssee, its water lapping against the rocks.

Max bent over to put his shoes back on. He hurried to tie them up.

Suddenly he had to pee so badly that his fingers were fumbling with the laces. Finally he just jammed on the untied shoes and sprinted for a nearby tree.

"You're too close!" Stein said. "If they see . . . you know what . . . you're dead."

"Quite literally," Berg added.

Max stopped.

Of course.

Max was circumcised. Like nearly all Jewish boys. Like none of these boys.

He hustled a little deeper into the woods, and now he was beginning to lose control of his bladder altogether.

But was he still too close?

So he waddled just a little farther, trying to unbutton his pants at the same time.

At last, with blessed relief, he peed on a tree.

When he finished, he buttoned up again . . . and saw that he had urine all over his trousers.

Max walked back toward the edge of the lake. The day was cold, but Max burned. His neck burned, his face burned. He was *so* embarrassed. He broke a thin sheet of ice that lay atop the lake and splashed water on his hands, and then on his pants, glancing over his shoulder to see if the boys were watching him. They weren't.

"I'm sorry, Max," Stein said quietly. "As if this day weren't bad enough."

"Raise your hand if you want to go back to England!" Berg said.

Four small hands went up.

Max, face bright red, returned to the group, hunching over to hide what had happened.

"Max! Why are you all wet?" Rudi asked.

"Did you pee yourself?" Peter barked.

"He peed himself!" Rolph laughed.

"He peed himself! He peed himself!" the boys all chanted, and despite being the leader, and older, Rudi didn't do anything to stop them.

Max sat down, bent over, and tied his shoes properly. It helped him focus on not murdering Peter and Rolph.

"I don't understand why you went so far away in the first place," Peter said. "There are plenty of trees right here."

"Maybe," said Rolph, "he's got a tiny pecker and he didn't want us to see."

All the boys *really* laughed at that.

"Come on," said Rudi. "Let's go."

But as they hefted their packs onto their backs, Peter said, "Or maybe it's because he's a Jew."

Max froze.

Skinny, bucktoothed Peter was squinting at Max, appraising the effect of his words.

Stein cursed. “How can boys be so *stupid* . . . and so *smart* . . . at the same time?”

The other boys were laughing, saying things like “Freddie’s friend is a Jew!”

Freddie said, “He’s not!”

“I think he is,” Peter taunted.

“He isn’t!”

Max put a hand on Freddie’s shoulder. He tried as hard as he could to make it stop trembling. He said, “They know I’m not. They’re just teasing. Ignore them and they’ll stop.”

But they didn’t stop.

Kids know, somehow, when they’ve hit a nerve.

“Jew boy Jew boy Jew boy,” Peter taunted. He slowed his pace, allowing Max and Freddie to go ahead of him so he could sing it in Max’s ear. “Jew boy Jew boy Jew boy.”

The words stabbed at Max, like a small knife in the kidney, over and over and over again.

“Shut up!” Freddie cried. “Stop it!”

But that just made Peter say it more.

“You know,” Rolph called back, “I think he *might* be a Jew, *for real.* And I bet Freddie knows it.”

Max’s feet were wet and totally blistered. His back and his

shoulders were bruised and aching from the ill-fitting pack. His pants were soaked and frigid. And Peter *would not shut up.*

Max bent down to retie his shoes. All the other boys kept walking, except Peter, who waited, quietly taunting him: *"You're a Jew boy. We're going to kill you. We'll kill your parents."*

Finally, Max looked up. "You know what, Peter? I have a secret to tell you."

Peter stopped his singsong chant.

Max glanced up the path. The others were out of sight.

"Do you want to know the truth?" Max said.

Peter grinned. "That you're a Jew?"

Berg and Stein both screamed at Max to shut his mouth.

Max glanced over his shoulder again. "I don't want anyone else to know this, but . . ."

Peter's eyes widened in eager anticipation. "Yes?"

Max gestured for him to come a little closer, checking again to be sure they were alone.

Peter bent down.

Which is when Max swung the rock that he'd been gripping in his hand and connected with Peter's head.

Peter screamed and fell to the ground.

"OH NO!" Stein cried.

Max jumped on top of Peter and tossed the stone aside. He began pummeling Peter's rabbitlike face with his fists.

Stein was shrieking, "You're going to kill him!"

"Good for you!" Berg shouted.

Max hit Peter again and again. He hit him to the rhythm of the song they'd sung about filthy Jews. He hit him to the rhythm of Peter's singsong taunts. He hit him for every time Max had been forced to say "Heil Hitler!" to a customer in the radio shop. He hit him and hit him and—

Suddenly, Max was lifted into the air.

Rudi had grabbed Max under the arms and was swinging him away from Peter. Rudi tossed Max in a heap at the base of a tree.

Rudi and Rolph were bent over Peter.

Peter wasn't moving.

CHAPTER
Twenty-Three

They had returned to the banks of the Teufelssee.

Peter was not dead.

Rudi had packed ice from the lake into a handkerchief and Peter, who could now sit up, was pressing it to his face. On the left side, then the right, then on his forehead, then on the left side again. And each time he moved it, he moaned.

They'd set up the tents. They weren't going any farther.

Berg and Stein were looking at Max with a touch of fear. And more than a touch of horror.

Rudi hadn't screamed at Max. Or threatened him. Or said he was reporting him to the police.

Not yet.

He had merely directed the other boys to make a bonfire, which was high and raging now. The thin winter light was already beginning to fade.

"Gather round, lads," said Rudi. "We need to talk."

They all found seats around the campfire. The heat was intense.

It reminded Max of the fires he'd seen when he was little, at the book burnings they used to have in Berlin, back when there were still offending books left to burn.

He wondered whether this fire was meant for him.

In the fading light, Rudi spoke at last. "What does it mean, to be a community?"

The boys were silent. The only sound was the cracking of the branches in the bonfire.

"I'll tell you what it means," Rudi went on. "It means no divisions. No strife. No fighting."

All the boys hung their heads.

"It means our enemies are *outside*. It means our rage should go *out*. Not at each other."

He reached into a pocket of his jacket and removed a piece of paper.

"Do you know what Hitler said?" Rudi began to read: " 'In my great work of educating this nation, I am beginning with the young. We old ones are used up. We are rotten to the bone. We bear the burden of a humiliating past. But my magnificent youngsters! Are there finer ones anywhere in the world? Youth must be indifferent to pain. There must be no weakness! No tenderness! Like beasts of prey. I shall eradicate the thousands of years of human domestication. Then I shall have the pure and noble natural material. With *that* I can create the new order!' "

Rudi looked up. The fire danced in his eyes.

"Our Supreme Leader does not want divisions between us. This is why the Jews must be expelled from Germany, or gotten rid of some other way. So Germany has no divisions. Our Supreme Leader also does not want weakness among us Germans. He wants strong boys, boys who can stand up to a threat. Who are not afraid of pain. Who are not afraid to *unleash* pain on others, if necessary."

Rudi gazed around at his troop.

Here it comes, thought Max. *Here comes the pain.*

"The Supreme Leader wants natural boys. Wild boys. Strong boys. Boys," said Rudi, "like Max."

"Huh?" said Stein.

"Huh?" said Berg.

"Huh?" said Max silently.

"Did you see?" Rudi continued. "Peter was testing him, and Rolph was testing him, and we were all testing him, weren't we? And did Max back down from a challenge? Was he afraid? Was he tamed? No, he was not. No matter what the Bible says, the meek will not inherit the earth. The strong will inherit the earth. No, that's wrong, too! The strong will *take* the earth. We should all aspire to be strong. Strong like Max."

The boys looked at Max. He was speechless.

"Hooray for Max!" Freddie cried.

And the boys echoed him, except for Rolph and Peter.

"Hooray for Max!" they cheered. "Hooray for Max! Hooray for Max!"

Max stood up, and the fire lit his face from below. Max thrust a hand in the air and cried, "Heil Hitler!"

And all the boys stood and cried, "Heil Hitler! Heil Hitler! Heil Hitler!"

That night, in the tent, as Freddie snored loudly, Max stared into the darkness.

"This is a land of monsters," Max said.

"It has become one," Stein replied.

"And you," Berg said to Max, "are learning to fit right in."

"I'm just pretending," Max told them. And then he repeated that to himself—*just pretending, just pretending*—as he fell into an uneasy sleep.

CHAPTER Twenty-Four

The next morning, they hiked out. Peter had recovered enough to carry his own pack, but he walked slowly, and quietly, and stayed far away from Max. Big, broad-shouldered Rolph now gave Max begrudging respect, and also a wide berth. Rudi winked proudly in Max's direction more than once. It was as if they had all discovered a future leader among their ranks, and each instinctively changed his own status accordingly.

In the parking lot, the parents waited in the weak sunlight of late autumn. Hans Fritzsche was signing an autograph for one of the mothers when the boys emerged from the trees.

Freddie ran up to his father. "Papa! Papa! You won't believe what happened! Peter was taunting Max, and Max hit him with a rock! And then jumped on him and pummeled him!"

The mother, who'd taken her little diary back from Hans Fritzsche, let out a gasp. It was Peter's mother. She rushed to find her boy.

"Oops," said Freddie. "Sorry."

"Sometimes," Hans Fritzsche told his son, "I think you were born without a brain."

Freddie instantly deflated. It was a sight Max was growing accustomed to.

Hans Fritzsche told Max and Freddie to wait in the car while he spoke to Rudi and made sure that Peter was all right.

Max sat in nervous silence.

Freddie said, “Thank you for going on the retreat.” Then he added, “I know you didn’t want to.”

Max turned toward Freddie. “Yes I did.”

Freddie smiled. “No you didn’t.” He glanced out the window, saw his father still engaged with Rudi, and turned back to Max. “I don’t blame you. They’re awful.”

Max caught his breath. “Who are?”

Freddie’s voice was quiet when he said, “All of them.”

Max gazed into Freddie’s freckled, pudgy face. He whispered, *“They really are.”*

Freddie leaned back against the headrest. “They really are,” he repeated. And he chuckled.

Max chuckled, too. And then they were both laughing. From disbelief that they’d survived the weekend and relief that they both felt the same way.

Stein said, “I can’t believe they’re laughing right now.”

Berg replied, “Humans are so weird.”

Then the door of the BMW opened and Freddie and Max both sat up and shut their mouths.

Hans Fritzsche slid behind the steering wheel, wearing a quiet smile.

They drove without speaking. The radio played vapid popular songs at a level barely loud enough to hear over the sound of the wheels on the road. Freddie stole glances at Max from time to time, his joy returning. He looked like he couldn't believe his good luck—that he'd managed to befriend, and introduce to his troop, the new bully.

Max couldn't believe it either. He'd never been the bully in his life. It felt . . . weirdly good.

"I was thinking about what you told us, Max," Hans Fritzsche said as he accelerated into a sharp bend in the road, the engine growling. "About how much it would mean to you to shake Dr. Goebbels's hand."

Max tried to keep his voice level when he said, "Of course, Herr Fritzsche. It would be a dream come true."

"He's coming to the Funkhaus tomorrow," Hans Fritzsche said in an offhand manner. "For the weekly meeting."

Max didn't say a word.

"Do you want to come with me?"

"Me too, Papa?" asked Freddie excitedly.

Hans Fritzsche squinted through the windshield. "Uh . . . I don't think so, Freddie. One child in the Funkhaus is enough. Besides, you've met Dr. Goebbels before."

"But I've never gone to work with you!" Freddie protested.

"Don't whine, for God's sake!" Hans Fritzsche snapped.

Freddie sulked while his father glared at the road ahead.

Finally, Max said, "I would be honored, sir."

"Good. It's settled. You know where the Funkhaus is?"

"Yes sir."

"Meet me there. Eight thirty sharp, outside the main entrance. If you're not there by eight thirty-two, I won't wait for you."

"Of course, Herr Fritzsche. I won't be late."

Hans Fritzsche said, "No, I don't think you will be."

CHAPTER
Twenty-Five

The Haus des Rundfunks, called the Funkhaus for short, was a massive, modern building on the western edge of Berlin. Hundreds of small windows peered down from a brick facade that stretched for an entire city block and rose five stories from the street.

Max waited on the sidewalk outside the front door. It was Monday morning, just before 8:30. People were rushing in and out of the building carrying attaché cases and folders, consulting their watches, and then quickening their steps.

"I've dreamed about this building my whole life," Max said to Berg and Stein. "But I've never seen it in person."

"How exciting for you," said Berg. "And even better, you get to shake hands with Joseph Goebbels, one of the most evil humans in history! So *that* should be fun."

Max wasn't listening. He was considering the pieces of the watch, spread out on black velvet. His mission was proceeding much faster than anyone had anticipated. Get a job at Herr Pfeiffer's? Check. Befriend Freddie? Check. Gain Hans Fritzsche's confidence? Check. Get invited to the Funkhaus? Check.

But now Max was at the most difficult stage yet. It was one thing to get into the Funkhaus. It was another entirely to *stay*.

"You know," Berg said to Stein, "I'm considering hopping off this kid's shoulder right now. I have a bad feeling about all of this."

Stein said, "Have you tried to get off lately? Even for a moment? I did. Couldn't do it! His shoulders feel stickier than ever."

Berg tried, just as an experiment, to leap down onto the pavement. "Hey!" he cried. "You're right! It's like there's molasses on my feet! What is the meaning of this?"

"I have no idea," Stein replied.

At 8:30 sharp, Hans Fritzsche strolled up the sidewalk and waved to Max, a bundle of rolled newspapers under his arm. Max nervously raised a hand in greeting.

Without a word, without a change in his expression, Herr Fritzsche motioned for Max to follow him through the glass front doors of the Funkhaus.

Just inside stood two uniformed SS guards. They glared down at Max as he hurried after Hans Fritzsche. He felt like a tiny fish swimming in the wake of a shark, as deadly barracudas eyed him hungrily.

Hans Fritzsche led Max into a bright, bustling, echoing lobby. As employees of the Funkhaus hurried past, every one of them deferentially ducked their head or murmured, "Good morning, Herr Fritzsche." Hans Fritzsche mostly ignored them as he led Max to an elevator.

There was no button to push. Nor were there doors waiting to open. The elevator shaft was exposed, and they just waited for the car to slide into view on its way up. When it appeared, Hans Fritzsche stepped on without hesitating, and Max leaped in after him. They glided to the fifth floor, where Fritzsche stepped off with ease, and Max tumbled out, nearly falling headfirst onto the patterned linoleum.

If Max was going to infiltrate the Funkhaus, he was going to have to get used to the elevator.

The fifth floor was a hive of desks. Clerks and secretaries scurried back and forth, reading newspapers and holding stacks of carbon copies. Hans Fritzsche led Max through the honeycomb of workers and pushed open a heavy door to reveal a large office with an imposing mahogany desk and windows that peered down onto the street.

Two men were standing in front of the desk, smoking.

"Good morning, Herr Berndt, Herr Diewerge," said Hans Fritzsche.

Max caught his breath.

Alfred-Ingemar Berndt. Wolfgang "Wolfie" Diewerge.

Max had studied their photographs, and files, for hours, back in England. And now here they were.

"Good morning!" Herr Berndt said, waving around a

cigarette in salutation. He was tall, with dark, greased hair and a long, large torso that was wrapped in an SS officer's uniform.

"Sorry to have occupied your office," said Wolfgang Diewerge. He was short and square—square head, square shoulders—and he had the face of a gangster's henchman. "They're doing some construction in both of ours. Putting in the new air-raid warning system."

"Also"—Herr Berndt grinned—"we couldn't find any ashtrays. So we decided to use yours." He smashed his cigarette in a large crystal ashtray on Hans Fritzsche's desk and then took a silver case from his pocket and lit another. "And who's this?"

"Herr Berndt, Herr Diewerge, this is Max Maas. A *Funkmeister*, and a very promising young man." Max shook hands with Berndt and Diewerge as Hans Fritzsche announced, "I've got to get my notes ready for Dr. Goebbels, if you'll excuse me." He sat down at his desk and spread the newspapers he'd been carrying out in front of him.

"Already done mine," Berndt gloated.

"No you haven't," Diewerge said. "You never prepare notes. You just steal other people's ideas and pretend you had them first."

Berndt grinned guiltily at Diewerge and then winked at Max. "First time at the Funkhaus?"

"Yes sir," said Max. "It's a great honor."

Wolfie Diewerge waved plumes of cigarette smoke away from his face. "Fritzsche, you can stop preparing for the meeting.

No point. I've got something that will knock everything else out of Dr. Goebbels's head. It's *that* good."

Hans Fritzsche stopped reading the papers for a moment. "Oh?"

"The Kaufman Pamphlet." Diewerge's curled smile revealed little dimples—also squares—on his cubic cheeks.

"Never heard of it," said Hans Fritzsche, and went back to the papers.

"Not yet. But soon all of Germany will know it by heart."

"Oh, do tell," said Herr Berndt.

Yes, please do, thought Max. If he wasn't able to make it back into the Funkhaus after today, he might as well gather as much information as possible right now.

"There is a certain pamphlet," Diewerge said, perching himself on the edge of the grand desk, "published by a Theodore Kaufman, of New Jersey, USA. A Jew. This pamphlet very explicitly calls for the *annihilation* of the German race. It is evidence, in black and white, that the Jews of America are planning to exterminate us all."

Max became very, very still.

The Nazis talked constantly about the global Jewish conspiracy. Max had grown up around Jews, had lived with Jews his whole life, and the only time he'd ever heard a Jew mention this conspiracy was while rolling their eyes.

"That isn't real, right? The global Jewish conspiracy?" Max asked Stein and Berg.

Stein said, "Jews are involved in exactly as many conspiracies as anyone else. None of them are global. And none of them are about exterminating Germans. Not any that I've heard of, anyway."

But it sounded like there *was* one, based in the United States of America.

Hans Fritzsche had put down his pen to listen to Wolfie Diewerge.

"The pamphlet is *real*?" asked Berndt.

"Absolutely real," said Diewerge.

"Do you know who is involved?" Hans Fritzsche wanted to know, getting excited. "The Rothschilds? President Roosevelt?"

"Well, at the moment it's just Theodore Kaufman, and his dad. And our Abwehr agent in Newark," said Diewerge, grinning wickedly. "Theodore is . . . well, he's a bit of a *loner*. Not too many *political contacts*, you might say."

"He's a crackpot, isn't he?" Berndt chuckled.

"Lives in his father's basement," admitted Diewerge.

Hans Fritzsche rolled his eyes and went back to his notes.

"But he really did print a few hundred copies!" Diewerge said. "Which is phenomenal for us! All we have to do is run off another few *million*, and make sure everyone in Germany sees them!"

Max worked up enough courage to say, "Why would you do that?"

Diewerge seemed surprised that their young visitor had

spoken. "Why?! The Supreme Leader needs the German people to fight harder! To work longer! There's a war on! If everyday Germans believe that the stakes of the war are their *total annihilation*, don't you think that'll goose 'em a little bit? Motivate them a little more?"

Max blinked through the smoke at Diewerge. "But that would be a lie."

All mirth and cheer dropped from Diewerge's face. "Young man," he said, his voice suddenly very flat and very serious. "This is *not* a lie. This is an *exaggeration*."

"Yes sir," said Max, cursing himself for not keeping his mouth shut.

Diewerge reached out and put a hand on Herr Berndt's shoulder. "What *Berndt* does is lie." And suddenly, he was laughing. "This guy is the biggest liar in the ProMi! You've heard of *The Protocols of the Elders of Zion*?"

Of course Max had. Everyone in Germany had heard of it. It was supposed to be the founding document of the global Jewish conspiracy. The Jewish plans to rule the world.

"The *Protocols* are a lie," said Diewerge. "A total forgery! But Herr Berndt here has made his career pushing that lie in every newspaper in the Reich!"

Berndt grinned guiltily. "Hey, I just give the people what they want. Play the hits, right?"

Max said, "But . . . I had to learn about them in school. I wrote *essays* about the *Protocols*." He had never believed anything he wrote about them, of course. Still, it was surreal to have these two men standing here and saying to his face that his school curriculum was utter hogwash.

Berndt leaned down and spoke to Max in a stage whisper. "Word to the wise, kid. Don't write the essays. Just shout *Heil Hitler* louder than the next guy. And if your teacher tries to flunk you, denounce him to the Gestapo."

Hans Fritzsche snapped his notebook closed. "That's *quite* enough mentorship from you two, I think." He rose from his chair. "I think it's time to greet Dr. Goebbels." He smiled at Max. "Ready for your big moment?"

"Try not to be so awed you puke on his shoes." Berndt grinned, grabbing Max's shoulder.

Max absolutely did want to throw up, but it wasn't from awe.

CHAPTER
Twenty-Six

They were back in the main lobby of the Funkhaus. Hans Fritzsche, Alfred Berndt, and Wolfie Diewerge were standing, shoulder to shoulder, facing the front doors. Max stood behind them. He peered through the sliver of space between their sleeves.

When the large clock over the security area read 9:02, the front door swung open and the two SS guards clicked their heels and shouted "Heil Hitler!" Anyone who had been passing through the busy lobby stopped instantly and turned.

Dr. Joseph Goebbels walked through the doorway.

Everyone in the lobby saluted and shouted "Heil Hitler!" Their voices ricocheted across the brick and tile lobby. It was deafening.

Dr. Goebbels saluted lazily and hobbled forward. Max had never seen Joseph Goebbels in person before. Why was he limping like that?

He asked Stein and Berg.

"He's got a club foot," said Stein.

"Really?" asked Max in disbelief.

"What, you're surprised that the chief Nazi propagandist—who advocates for the elimination of disabled people in order to strengthen the National Community—is himself disabled?" Berg said. "Also, Berndt over there has eleven toes."

Max glanced quickly at Herr Berndt's shoes. He couldn't see anything out of the ordinary.

"Not that there's anything wrong with having eleven toes, or a club foot!" Stein added. "Except that if they abided by their own policies, they'd have executed themselves by now."

Berg said, "Hypocrites, liars, and murderers, as far as the eye can see . . . Here he comes. Smile!"

Dr. Goebbels had made it across the lobby, and the employees of the Funkhaus had resumed scurrying in every direction.

Greetings were exchanged among the men of the ProMi, and then, with great ceremony, Hans Fritzsche said, "Dr. Goebbels, I would like to introduce you to a very promising young radio engineer. Max, meet Dr. Goebbels."

Dr. Joseph Goebbels was small, barely taller than Max. His nose was long and ratlike, and his eyes were deep set and shadowed, as if one of the most powerful men in Germany had spent his formative years being afraid.

"Heil Hitler!" Max shouted, and he gave the most energetic Nazi salute of his life.

"Max's dream was to meet you and shake your hand," Hans Fritzsche informed his boss.

Goebbels seemed to hesitate for a moment, before he

relaxed and his face broke into a wide, satisfied smile. "Well, well. Good to meet you." He stuck out his hand, and Max reached out and shook it. Goebbels turned to Fritzsche. "And will this young radio engineer be joining our meeting?"

"Ah, no, Dr. Goebbels. Now that he's met you, he can be on his way."

Suddenly, Max decided to improvise. "Please, Herr Fritzsche! May I stay?"

"What?" Herr Fritzsche sputtered. "That was *not* the plan, Max. We have *work* to do."

Berndt was looking down, embarrassed. Wolfie Diewerge was smirking. Dr. Goebbels's reaction to this small scene was just beyond the edge of Max's peripheral vision.

Max hung his head. "I'm sorry."

Then he remembered what Rudi had told the Hitler Youth group. About the New Germany.

He raised his head. "I am sorry to be so bold," he went on. "But it *was* my dream to meet Dr. Goebbels. *Now* it is my dream to learn as much from him as I can. I just want to ask him a few questions, if he has time. I may never see the great man again. I want to seize my chance."

He was speaking about Dr. Goebbels in the third person, but he had turned to stare straight into his dark eyes.

No one spoke for a moment.

Then Joseph Goebbels's mouth curled into a smile.

"Why not?" he said. He seemed to be quite pleased. "Have

someone give him a tour! He can see what a cutting-edge radio operation looks like! Then, if there is time after our meeting, maybe he and I can chat for a moment longer."

"You . . . want to *chat* . . . with Max?" Hans Fritzsche asked, bewildered.

Goebbels winked at Max. "Yes. I think I do."

"Oh *no*," said Berg. "I think he . . . *likes* you."

Stein shuddered. *"Gross."*

CHAPTER Twenty-Seven

Joseph Goebbels and his propaganda men went downstairs to a small recording hall, where they would listen to Dr. Goebbels set the agenda for the week, and where Wolfgang Diewerge would present the next great Nazi lie.

Meanwhile, Max waited by the security desk—glancing uneasily at the uniformed SS soldiers. Hans Fritzsche had telephoned up to his office and asked one of his young employees to come down and give Max a tour. He watched the elevator, waiting for his guide.

The car slid into view and Max stopped breathing.

A young woman smoothly stepped off and began to stride across the linoleum floor. And for one mad moment, Max thought it was Jean Leslie walking toward him.

The young woman walked right up to him and stuck out her hand, and just like Jean's, her elbow bent more than 180 degrees. "Hi," she said. "I'm Melita Maschmann. You must be Max."

Max nodded. Now that she was right in front of him, she

was definitely not Jean. Her teeth were too straight. Her chin was a little less sharp. But the resemblance was distracting.

"Follow me," she said, and he did.

Max tried to remember everything he saw and heard, in case this was his only visit to the Funkhaus. He simultaneously tried to invent a plan to ensure that it was *not*. And simultaneously simultaneously he repeated Melita's name over and over under his breath so he wouldn't accidentally call her Jean.

"It's ironic that *I'm* giving you a tour," Melita said as she walked with him across the busy, echoey lobby. "I've only worked here for three weeks." They passed through a wide passageway, and the linoleum floor gave way to thick orange carpet. Melita pulled open a heavy door, revealing a large concert hall. Max stared up at the ceiling, far above him, where strangely shaped panels hung. To soften the sound, Max knew, for recordings.

"What were you doing up until three weeks ago?" Max asked her.

Melita replied proudly, "I was in Poland, helping prepare farms for German settlement."

"So . . . you're a farmer?"

Melita laughed dismissively. "No. We were moving the Poles out of their houses, and making sure they didn't steal or destroy anything before German settlers could move in. I was helping create the *Lebensraum* the Supreme Leader has always promised us."

Lebensraum ("living space") was probably Hitler's favorite word. The great German people needed more room to live, he said. They needed to be like the Americans and stretch across a continent. And just like the Americans, they pretended that the continent was vast and empty, only populated with people who weren't really people at all.

Max asked, "Did you like the work?"

"Oh, it was *glorious* out there." Melita sighed dramatically. "In Germany I never felt like I was *useful.* Even the laborers and servants who worked for my family hated me, I could tell. They thought I was a spoiled rich girl. And they were right. But out there, I was *doing something* with my life. Something our nation *needed.*"

It struck Max that Jean Leslie had joined the secret service in Britain for similar reasons.

"Also," Melita added confidentially as she led Max backstage, where harps and kettle drums and xylophones waited for the next performance, "my parents are uptight prigs. *So* conservative. When I joined the Nazi party, at fifteen, it drove them *crazy*!" She laughed.

"Where did the Poles go?" Max wondered aloud.

"What Poles?"

"The ones you moved out of their homes."

"Oh." Melita shrugged. "I don't really know. Some became laborers here in Germany, working in the factories. Others . . . I'm not really sure." Then she smirked. "Well, I know where the Jews went."

Max's insides chilled. "Where?"

"Ghettos first, and then off to the concentration camps," she said. "Thankfully."

Max must have given Melita some sort of look, because she saw his face and said, "To keep us safe. We can't have Germany's enemies living freely within our borders." Max nodded quickly and vigorously.

Melita took Max past dressing rooms, opening doors for him and showing him where famous singers and conductors had readied themselves for concerts that had been broadcast live over the radio. They descended some concrete stairs and came out in a long basement corridor. "More recording studios down here," she said, "and that's the small concert room where Dr. Goebbels is leading the meeting."

Max thought he should probably ask more about the meeting.

Or about how the Funkhaus functioned.

But he was disturbed and distracted by Melita's nonchalance about sending Polish families to who-knew-where, and Jews to concentration camps.

She took them into a recording studio that had guitars and violins and cellos hanging from the walls. As the soundproof door closed behind them, Max asked her: "Did it ever bother you?"

"*Max* . . ." Stein said, in a warning tone.

"Did what ever bother me?" Melita asked.

"Making people leave their homes."

The dybbuk covered his face. Berg was watching nervously.

Melita turned to face Max. She seemed . . . uncertain. "Well, it was *hard*. And dangerous. The Poles and Jews were very angry at us. We always had to watch our backs. Sometimes I used a whip—I'd crack it over their heads, to get them moving. And I had a very loyal dog, a German shepherd, who helped keep them obedient, but . . ." She trailed off. "That's not what you mean, is it?"

"No," said Max. "That's not what I mean."

Melita sat down on a tall stool. And she said:

"Maybe one time."

CHAPTER
Twenty-Eight

Max, very gently, said, "Can you tell me about it?"

Melita Maschmann turned her head sideways, and hair fell out from behind her ear and across her face.

"I was walking by myself," she said. "To a large country home that I was supposed to appropriate for our officers. I was on a dirt road, with blooming yellow flowers on either side. It was quite beautiful, and I was feeling rather proud that day of the role I was playing in Germany's future. Then, suddenly, a man jumped up out of the ditch that ran along the side of the road and started yelling at me. I ran from him. He ran after me, shouting and waving his arms. I don't speak Polish, so I don't know what he was saying, but I was pretty sure he was going to kill me."

"That sounds terrifying," said Max. It took all his strength to act sympathetic to Melita.

"It *was*," she agreed. "But then I saw a grand house in the distance, and I cut into the tall yellow flowers and ran across the field, all the way there. I banged on the door, screaming for help."

Melita reached out behind her, for no reason Max could tell, and plucked a string on a double bass that hung on the wall. The sound reverberated through the quiet, soundproof room.

"The door opened, and an old woman was standing there. She was dressed in clothes that seemed to have been expensive once, and she held her head up like she was nobility. I begged her to let me in, gesturing wildly behind me. I don't think the man had even followed me, but she did let me in. Even though she didn't seem to speak any German, and I didn't speak any Polish, she understood my cries and pleas well enough. I washed my face in the washroom and calmed myself down, and she gave me some milk to drink."

Melita sighed. "It was only then that she touched the pin on my lapel. This one." She let her finger graze a tiny porcelain swastika on her green blazer. "And that's when I realized that *this* was the home I was supposed to be scouting for appropriation."

"Appropriation means 'stealing,' right?"

"Max!" Berg hissed. *"You'll give yourself away!"*

Melita shook her head—but then she began to nod. "I suppose so. But it's war, Max. Anyway, this old noblewoman gestured for me to follow her. She was so proper—she reminded me of my *mother*. Ugh. Except she was silent as a ghost. She took me through the house. In each room, she would stop and let me look around the room, and then she would continue on. Kind of like the tour I'm giving you now." Melita laughed. But the laugh had a lump in it.

"She never said a word. But I followed her with an increasing sense of shame. It felt like she was saying, 'Look at this beautiful home, built by my family, where we have lived for generations. We have never done a thing to you. But you will expel us and drive us into misery.'

"Finally, she guided me outside again, to the field of yellow flowers, and then to the main road. The man was gone. I didn't even say goodbye. Tears were flooding my eyes, and I ran all the way back to the German base."

Melita sat in silence.

Max said, "So *that* bothered you."

"Yes," Melita said, and she used a sleeve to wipe her face.

"But that was the only time?"

Melita shrugged. "You know, it's strange. I never once thought of that woman while I was working on the farms, whipping the air above people's heads so they would hurry onto the cattle cars. I didn't think about it. I didn't think about her. If I had thought of her, how could I have done my work?"

"How could you have?" Max echoed softly. Though he meant something different than she did.

Melita shrugged. "I suppose there are thoughts that we all avoid. Feelings that we can't afford to have. Right?"

Max wondered if that was true of all Germans these days.

And then he thought of the space beneath the stairs of his own mind.

He wondered if it was true of *everyone*.

Melita stood up. "Come on. I don't want to think about this anymore. Let's go."

As they left the studio, Stein said, "You humans really *hate* being uncomfortable, don't you?"

"It's why they do pretty much everything," agreed Berg, "to avoid being uncomfortable."

Melita and Max walked out of the studio and back into the hallway. "Hey!" someone shouted.

They spun around.

A thick man was hustling down the hall toward them. "What were you doing in there?"

Melita raised her chin. "I was giving this boy a tour. Herr Fritzsche's orders."

"Oh," said the man, slowing down. "Dammit, what a day."

"Is there something wrong, Herr Hadamovsky?" Melita asked, perfectly composed. Max could easily imagine her watching dispassionately as every inhabitant of a Polish town was packed into a boxcar by soldiers, a German shepherd barking at her knee.

"Yes, there's something wrong! The transmitter is still acting up! I have no idea what's going on. Can you tell Herr Diewerge when he's out of the Goebbels meeting?"

"Of course, Herr Hadamovsky."

The man nodded and stalked away, muttering about finicky transmitters and winter weather and whether or not they would have a hot lunch in the cafeteria that day.

Melita showed Max into a long room, with an entire wall of gray machines. Dials fluctuated, meters whirred, and the whole room vibrated with an ambient electric hum.

Max froze in the doorway.

"You can come in," Melita assured him.

Max murmured: *"The transmitter."*

"Uh . . . yes, that's right."

"*The* transmitter. For the Berlin station, the *Deutschesender*, and the *Europasender*."

Melita chuckled. "I've never seen someone so excited about a large box of bolts and wires before."

"This isn't a box of bolts and wires! This is where the sound captured by the microphones in the studios gets converted to radio frequencies so the broadcast tower can beam the waves all around Europe! This is where lead gets turned into gold!"

Melita laughed out loud at Max. "I'm glad you like it so much," she said. "Their meeting is just down the hall. Do you want to wait here and admire your precious transmitter until they're ready for you?"

Max turned to her, and he did not have to fake his enthusiasm when he said: *"Could I?"*

Melita laughed again. "Sure. I'll let Herr Fritzsche know this is where he can find you when he's free."

"Thank you. And . . ." Max added, ". . . thank you for telling me what you told me."

Melita pushed a lock of hair behind her ear, just as Jean would have done. She shrugged, nodded at the floor, and left.

Max walked quietly to the door, counted to ten, and then closed it.

CHAPTER
Twenty-Nine

Max walked slowly from one end of the transmitter to the other. It ran thc whole length of the room. He was admiring it, certainly. He'd never seen a transmitter that was larger than a sewing machine. This one was larger than a car.

But he was also scouring the dials for information.

Once he got to the far end of the transmitter, he walked back, just as slowly. Then, where a number of meters waggled in a neat line, Max knelt. He took a small screwdriver out of his pocket.

"Why do you have that?" Stein exclaimed.

"It's from Herr Pfeiffer's shop," Max answered.

"I don't care where it's from. Why do you have it? Did you come here this morning *expecting* to be left alone with Germany's most powerful radio transmitter?"

"Of course not," Max said. "But I wasn't going to be unprepared, if the opportunity presented itself."

"Always four steps ahead," Stein murmured.

"Frankly, it's creepy," Berg replied.

Max removed the top screw from a gray panel and placed it in his pocket.

"Max," Berg said, "if they find you, you are dead. Literally dead."

Max removed a second screw.

"How long is that meeting supposed to last?" Stein asked.

Max removed a third screw.

Berg said, "Forget the meeting, don't engineers come in and out of this room all the time?"

Max removed the fourth screw and then gently laid the gray panel on the concrete floor.

Max considered the bundles of thick cords that ran into a black box. He exhaled. Then he unscrewed the cover to the box, revealing six large tubes. Copper wires connected the tubes to the thick cords.

Max smiled and chuckled to himself.

Crouching, balancing on his toes, Max carefully inserted the tip of the screwdriver between two copper wires. He put a little pressure on the screwdriver. Ever so gently, he waggled it back and forth, back and forth, until there was a space between them. He removed the screwdriver and—

"WHAT ARE YOU DOING?!"

Max toppled over.

The door to the hallway was open, and Herr Berndt was standing in it, his face red, his eyes blazing. He rushed into the room and grabbed Max by the wrist and hoisted him clear off the ground.

"Ow!" Max cried. His arm was being wrenched out of its socket.

More men hurried into the transmitter room. Hans Fritzsche, Wolfie Diewerge . . . and after them, Goebbels himself.

Dr. Joseph Goebbels was staring at Max, hanging like a caught fish.

Goebbels looked . . . hurt.

Then, finally, one last man walked in, whose mirrorlike eyeglasses Max remembered all too well.

Lieutenant Colonel Alexis von Roenne.

"What is *he* doing here?" Max exclaimed, but only to Stein and Berg.

"Catching an enemy spy red-handed?" Berg suggested.

Max felt the tendons in his shoulder being stretched dangerously close to snapping.

Hans Fritzsche put his face right up in front of Max's. "*What* is the explanation of this?" he demanded.

Max whimpered. Tears were leaking from the corners of his eyes.

Alexis von Roenne looked like he already knew which instruments he'd be using to torture Max.

"*What were you doing*?! *Answer* me!" Spittle was flying from Hans Fritzsche's mouth. Berndt's hand was so tight around Max's wrist it felt like their skin might fuse together.

"I . . . I . . ." Max tried to speak. "Can you put me down?" he pleaded.

Herr Berndt barked, "You're going to be hanging in an interrogation cell soon enough, so you might as well get used to it!"

"I was . . . I was fixing it!" Max pleaded.

"Fixing what?" Hans Fritzsche said.

"The transmitter!"

The men all fell silent.

"Put him down," Hans Fritzsche commanded.

Herr Berndt dropped Max, hard, on the concrete floor.

Now his knees hurt almost as much as his shoulder.

The men stared down at the boy crouched on the floor of the transmitter room in the Haus des Rundfunks.

Max took one long breath and then made himself stand up.

He looked around the room, from Hans Fritzsche to Alfred Berndt to Wolfie Diewerge to Joseph Goebbels himself. And finally, to Alexis von Roenne.

Slowly, Max spoke: "I heard Herr Hadamovsky say that the transmitter was 'acting up,' which I figured meant it was going in and out. He couldn't explain it. Whenever I have a transmitter that's acting finicky, it's usually the copper wires from the vacuum tubes. They're so delicate. They're easily bent. I figured they were touching one another."

The men all stared at Max. Their faces still registered a spectrum of emotions, ranging from enraged to scandalized.

But another possible emotion was emerging.

Max thought that, just maybe, it was curiosity.

"Find Herr Hadamovsky," Max said. "See if it's improved."

But they didn't need to find Herr Hadamovsky, because just then he barged into the room.

"What's happened?" he demanded, breathing hard.

Dr. Goebbels turned to him and said, "*You* tell *us*. How is the signal?"

"Cleared up!" Hadamovsky exclaimed. "Clear as a bell! How'd you do it?!" Then he noticed Max, and the open panel. "What's *he* doing in here?"

"He," said Dr. Joseph Goebbels, "is replacing you."

CHAPTER
Thirty

The four of them sat in a fancy, modern conference room.

Dr. Joseph Goebbels sat at the head of the long, brightly polished table.

On the left side of the table was Hans Fritzsche.

Next to him was Max.

Across from Max was Lieutenant Colonel Alexis von Roenne. He was polishing his glasses with the fat end of his tie.

Well, there were six of them in all, counting Berg and Stein. But nobody counted Berg and Stein.

Goebbels leaned back in his chair and smiled over tented fingers. "So, this remarkable young man's life ambition was to shake my hand. Now that he's achieved it, he wants to ask me a few questions. Whatever shall he do when he's achieved *that* goal?"

"I'm sure he'll come up with something," Hans Fritzsche replied. "He is a talented and driven boy. Although he is also bold, bordering on reckless."

"Good. We like that," Goebbels replied.

Max was smiling blandly and trying as hard as he could not to stare at Lieutenant Colonel von Roenne. What was he doing here? Why hadn't he spoken yet? Why was he just polishing his glasses and looking at his lap? It was the most important moment of Max's life—he had an audience with Joseph Goebbels himself—and all he could think about was the representative of the army's spy agency whose presence no one had explained and who still hadn't said a word.

"Well, Max?" Hans Fritzsche began. "You've got about ten minutes with the great Dr. Goebbels before he has to hurry off to other things. I suggest you make the most of it."

Max forced himself to focus on the task at hand. First things first: "Are you really giving me a job?"

Goebbels appraised Max for a moment. "Would you like to work here?"

"More than anything," Max replied quickly.

Goebbels cocked his head at Fritzsche. Fritzsche gave a small shrug.

"Was that a *yes*?" Stein asked.

"It looked like a *yes*," Berg marveled.

Goebbels said to Max, "You can assist Hadamovsky. He's been here for seven years and still doesn't seem to know how a radio functions. And to think, until two years ago, that sweaty pig *ran* the place. It's a miracle we weren't accidentally broadcasting the BBC the whole time!"

Hans Fritzsche laughed heartily. Alexis von Roenne gave a small, polite smile.

Max could have stood up and danced.

Fritzsche said, "Anything else, Max?"

Certainly. But what? What would British Intelligence want Max to ask if he had only ten minutes with the architect of Germany's propaganda machine?

Max cast his mind back. To sitting with Chumley and Jean and Ewen and Admiral Godfrey in the hotel on the Thames. Then further back, to discussing propaganda with Ewen in cottage number 3 at Tring Park. Then further back still. Finally, his thoughts landed on the Montagu family, walking past the broken teeth of bombed-out houses and puddles reflecting dying fires, as Uncle Ewen swore, *How in God's name does Hitler get them all to go along with it?*

Max took a deep breath. Might as well go big.

"Dr. Goebbels, what is the secret to the success of your propaganda?"

There was a moment of silence.

Then Hans Fritzsche and Joseph Goebbels both burst out laughing. Even von Roenne grinned.

"What?" asked Max, not getting the joke.

"You sound like a regular radio interviewer!" Hans Fritzsche chortled. "I should let you interview von Roenne, instead of me!" Max stole a glance at the small, bespectacled spy. He was here to be *interviewed*?

So he *wasn't* there for Max.

"You be careful, Fritzsche," Goebbels quipped. "Or he'll replace *you* once he's done replacing Hadamovsky!"

Max smiled at the grinning men and waited.

"The secret to the success of *my* propaganda, eh?" Goebbels repeated, obviously delighted with the question, emphasizing the word *my* and flashing a mouthful of large yellow teeth. He rose from the table and put his hands on the back of his chair.

"Fifty thousand years ago," Goebbels said, "our German riverbanks and valleys were inhabited by a different kind of man from us. We call him Neanderthal. He was tall, and strong. He was the apex predator of Europe. He could kill mammoths and saber-toothed tigers and anything else that crossed his path."

"But then," Goebbels went on, starting to limp around the large conference table, "a new type of man emerged. We call him *Homo sapiens*—'knowing man.' Or *humans*. And within a few short millennia, all the Neanderthals were *gone*."

Goebbels was now standing directly behind Max. He laid his hands on Max's shoulders. Max shuddered. But Goebbels kept a firm grip on him.

"Oh, scree and slag, his hand passed *through* me!" Stein screamed.

"I need a shower! I need a shower!" Berg wailed.

Goebbels continued. "So, what happened to the Neanderthal? One-time king of Europe?"

Goebbels leaned down so his face was beside Max's ear. His breath stank. Stein crawled down Max's arm to put some distance between himself and the Nazi propagandist.

"We murdered them," Goebbels whispered. *"Murdered them*

all." He straightened up. "But how? Neanderthals were larger than we, and tougher, too. Perhaps it was because we made tools and weapons, and Neanderthals did not? No! They made spears, just as we did. But perhaps it was our brains? Our cunning? Well, maybe. But Neanderthals had *larger brains than we do*!"

Goebbels lifted his hands from Max's shoulders and continued his slow limp around the room. Hans Fritzsche watched him with admiration. Alexis von Roenne's expression was . . . *different.* Max couldn't read it.

Max said to Stein and Berg, "Is this true? Did humans kill the Neanderthals?"

"I'm afraid so," Stein replied.

"Humans are the worst," Berg said.

"Mosquitoes are the worst," Stein corrected him.

"Nope. Humans one, mosquitoes two," said Berg.

Dr. Goebbels had returned to the head of the table, waiting for Max to ask the next question.

Max obliged. "So how did we do it, Herr Doctor?"

Joseph Goebbels raised his head as high as it could go—which was not very high—and spread his hands out before him like he was presenting a feast. "We did it with *stories.*"

This was *not* what Max had expected him to say.

"Yes, I can see you're surprised! Even our secretive friend here is surprised." Goebbels laughed, pointing at Alexis von Roenne. "But it's true!"

"*Is* it true?" Max asked Stein and Berg.

"I'm not sure," Stein replied. "Lemme hear him out."

Dr. Goebbels sat down. "What made humans unique is that we painted tales of great hunts on cave walls. We made gods out of wood and stone and clay. We could *imagine*. Which means we *could tell each other stories*."

Alexis von Roenne had started to polish his glasses again.

" 'So what?' This is what you're thinking," Goebbels said, laughing. "What's so powerful about stories? Well, the Neanderthals lived in clans of ten, maybe fifteen individuals. But we humans? We banded together in great numbers! A *hundred* of us could sweep into a valley. And as strong and tough, and even smart, as those ten Neanderthals were, they were no match for a *hundred* humans. So we invaded their valleys and we murdered them."

Max felt slightly sick to his stomach.

Goebbels suddenly banged his palms on the table. "How could *we* create groups of a hundred, Max, when they could not? Because of *stories*. Because we humans told stories of gods, commanding us to capture the valley from on high. We told stories of *us* against *them*! Stories that said *we* are good, *they* are bad! *We* are a tribe, and *they* are our enemies! *We* have to kill them before *they* kill us! And when a great leader arose in any human clan, it was because he was a master storyteller. And his stories inspired these early humans to band together into one great tribe, into one great *race* that could conquer the *world*."

Dr. Goebbels leaned back in his chair. He had sweat on his upper lip. "And we did. We used our stories to band together and murder every Neanderthal. And the world is now ours."

"And this? Is this true?" Max asked Stein and Berg.

"I don't remember it happening exactly that way," Berg replied.

"But you gotta admit it," Stein added, "it's a pretty good story—I mean, if you're into stories about mass murder."

Goebbels pushed his chair back, and he was standing again, one finger raised in the air—and now it sounded like he wasn't just speaking to them in this room, but that he was thundering through an echoing public address system to a hundred-thousand Nazis, bathing in their roaring adulation.

"And this is what the Aryan race will do again! A Great Man has risen, a he-man, a *demigod*, and we will follow him! We will follow our beloved Supreme Leader to conquer, capture, or exterminate every other race—before they band together and exterminate us!"

Suddenly, Goebbels became very quiet. "And *how* will we do this, Max?"

Right on cue, Max answered: "Through stories."

"That's right," Dr. Goebbels said, his voice now at normal decibels again. He sat down, as if they were resuming a routine meeting.

"We will conquer the world the same way our ancestors did. By telling stories. And *this* is my special responsibility.

Here at the Funkhaus, mouthpiece of the ProMi, we create grand narratives: about Germans versus the world, about survival, about the villains of other races—and especially about the Jews, who look just like us and are therefore the most dangerous of all our racial enemies. We tell these stories over and over and over again. In comedy programs, in news reports, in speeches. We tell them in newspapers, on posters, in classrooms, at Hitler Youth weekend retreats. Over and over and over again." Dr. Goebbels waved his hand in the air like a conductor. "Over and over and over. With these grand stories, we can bind our people together. We can make a National Community. We can unite—not a hundred humans—but a hundred *million*."

Dr. Goebbels sighed contentedly. "*That* is my secret. We have a grand story, and we tell it *ruthlessly*. Do you understand, young man?"

"I *think* so . . ." Max replied. "In order to convince Germans to murder other groups of humans, you tell them stories. You tell them these stories over and over and over again, until they believe them. Until they will *die* for them. Until they will *murder* for them. Another word for *stories* is *lies*. You tell the German people *lies* until they will throw other humans through plate glass windows, steal their homes, drop bombs on their cities, drive them into ghettos, whip them into cattle cars, and work them to death in concentration camps. You lie to them *over* and *over* and *over* again, until they have become a nation of fanatics and murderers. Have I got that right?"

The room was dead silent.

The room was dead silent because Max had not said one word of that out loud. He said it to Berg and Stein. He wasn't an idiot, after all.

"Yup, you got that right," Stein replied.

"I have one last question, Dr. Goebbels," said Max.

Goebbels was mopping his brow with a handkerchief. He looked out from under the white silk, and he seemed spent and annoyed. "Haven't I given you enough, young man?" But as he folded up his handkerchief, he said. "I will grant you *one* last question."

Max asked: "When can I get to work?"

CHAPTER
Thirty-One

Herr Hadamovsky stood over Max with his arms crossed and a very confused look on his facc.

Max had opened a panel on the transmitter to check the wires and the connections, and was lying on the floor, peering into the dark machine.

"You know, we never do this," Hadamovsky was saying. "I don't think it's necessary."

Max replied, "Maybe that's why your sound quality has been deteriorating."

"Deteriorating! That's preposterous! It has not!"

Max unscrewed more wires, checked to make sure their ends weren't fraying, and then screwed them back in.

"How long is this going to take?" Hadamovsky demanded.

Max peered down the length of the enormous transmitter. "Over an hour, certainly."

Hadamovsky huffed, explained he had to go talk to the engineers about the air-raid system installation, and told Max not to screw anything up as he left.

"Are you doing some spy stuff right now?" Berg whispered to

Max. He was sitting on Max's shoulder as usual, but since Max was lying on the floor it meant the kobold was completely sideways. "Installing listening devices or something?"

"Why would he install listening devices in the wiring of a *radio*?" retorted Stein, who was also completely sideways. "It broadcasts to the entire country. That's its job."

"I don't know!" said Berg. "I don't understand anything Max does!"

"I'm trimming the system," Max explained. "It's basic maintenance, and it seems like no one has done it in years. Probably not since Hadamovsky took over."

It was slow work, and it didn't take much thought. So as Max slid along the polished linoleum floor, he thought about how quickly he had succeeded in his goal of infiltrating the Funkhaus. Uncle Ewen had expected it to take months. Admiral Godfrey had thought he'd fail completely. Max allowed himself a moment of pride.

What was next for him? Now that he had a position here, he had to keep it. He also had to learn everything he could about how the place operated—Goebbels's villainous monologue this morning was a fantastic start, and so was the banter between Berndt and Diewerge. And, of course, above all, he had to be sure his real identity wasn't discovered.

And then, at some point, he would get further instructions from London. There would be a "Grand Finale," as Lieutenant Chumley had cryptically referred to it. Max hadn't a clue what that Grand Finale would be, but he hoped it was violent. Maybe they would give him one of Lord Rothschild's explosive devices and he could blow up Joseph Goebbels.

Probably not.

But a kid could hope.

As Max continued to work on the transmitter, he said to Berg and Stein, "So what's the deal with Goebbels? How does a guy like that get to be so important?"

Berg shrugged. "He was made for this. He was a scared little schoolboy who was bullied for his deformity. That made him mean, and self-righteous, and a braggart. Finally, he found Hitler, in the very early days, before Hitler was important—and suddenly Goebbels had a bully of his own. He took it upon himself to brag for Hitler—he published articles about him, spread lies for him. But when Goebbels wrote to his family about his new devotion, they stopped speaking to him. And Hitler was all that Goebbels had left."

Stein said, "How do you know all that?"

Berg shrugged. "I possessed a distant cousin of his once. Heard it at a family reunion."

He took it upon himself to brag for Hitler. Max thought of the "grand stories" Goebbels and his ProMi told "over and over and over again."

And he remembered a conversation he had with Uncle Ewen back in Tring Park. Ewen had said:

In fact, Adolf Hitler himself wrote that the most effective kind of lie is the Big Lie. *He said that people won't believe small lies, because they themselves tell small lies every day, and so they recognize them. But the average person can't imagine someone would have the gall to tell an* enormous *lie, a* huge *fiction, a* total *falsehood, because it's something they couldn't get away with in their own lives. And so* those *are the lies that they believe.*

The Funkhaus was a factory, Max realized, and its product was Big Lies.

Herr Hadamovsky was grumbling when he came back in the transmitter room: "Everyone keeps complimenting me on how crisp the broadcast sounds today." Max smiled to himself and said nothing.

Hadamovsky watched Max work for a while. Then he made himself busy with some of the dials on the panels above Max's head. Then he went back to watching Max. "I would ask you to explain what you're doing, but I'm sure I wouldn't under—" Hadamovsky suddenly stopped speaking.

"What is it?" Max demanded of Hadamovsky. But then his voice died in his throat.

Standing in the doorway of the transmitter room was Lieutenant Colonel von Roenne. In the glare of the bare overhead bulbs, his eyeglasses were flashing.

CHAPTER Thirty-Two

"You scared the schnitzel out of me," complained Herr Hadamovsky to von Roenne.

"It's nearing lunchtime," said the little spy in the army-green suit.

Hadamovsky checked his wristwatch. "Er, so it is."

"I was wondering," von Roenne continued, "if you'd like to join me for your midday meal."

"Well, that's kind of you," Hadamovsky began, "but I think I'll just head to the cafeteria. Turns out it's rösti day, which is my favorite, and—"

"I'm sorry," von Roenne interrupted, "I was talking to the boy."

Max pulled himself into a sitting position.

Alexis von Roenne's glasses were reflecting the lights above, making it impossible to see his eyes. He was smiling vaguely. Or maybe he was frowning vaguely. Either way, he looked like he was apologizing for whatever was about to happen.

"Don't do it," Berg said to Max.

"Say you like rösti, too," Stein suggested.

"Who doesn't like rösti?" Berg agreed.

"It's the best," said Stein.

Max glanced from von Roenne, to Hadamovsky, to the door, and back to von Roenne. Calculating.

"All right," said Max to Alexis von Roenne.

"What? No!" Berg hissed.

Quickly, Max added, "Unless, Herr Hadamovsky, you need me . . . ?"

"No," said Hadamovsky. "You can take the rest of the day off as far as I'm concerned. Take the rest of your life off, for all I care." And then he said to von Roenne, "Excuse me. If you don't get in line early, all that's left is the burnt bottom part." And then he pushed past the small, precise Abwehr officer and lumbered down the hall.

Stein said, "What are you doing, Maxy?!"

"I had no way out."

"We had a whole rösti thing planned out for you!" Berg exclaimed.

Von Roenne smiled sadly at Max and said, "Shall we?"

As Lieutenant Colonel von Roenne led Max through the basement of the Funkhaus, then into the elevator, and out through the lobby, Max looked around desperately for Hans Fritzsche, or even Berndt or Diewerge. Anyone who might catch his eye, say hello, divert their course. But Max saw no one who might save him.

Von Roenne's small Opel coupe was parked across the street from the Funkhaus.

"Are you hungry?" the intelligence officer asked.

"Not really," Max replied. He was more likely to puke than be able to eat.

"Good. Me neither."

Von Roenne opened the car door for Max, closed it behind him, and then walked around to get into the driver's seat.

"What are you doing, Max? Get out! Run! You've been caught!" Stein pleaded.

"Why are you letting him take you without a fight?" Berg demanded. "When he gets in, punch him in the throat! Or between the legs! Or anywhere those swastikas were on that dummy! Then run!"

But Max had already thought it out, four, five, six, seven steps ahead.

His chances of getting away from von Roenne, in broad daylight, in a country with millions of soldiers and even more informants, were very small indeed. And of course, if he ran, his missions were over. No Grand Finale.

And, more importantly, no parents.

Maybe ever again.

Von Roenne was steering into traffic now. "I'd like to take you to my office," he informed Max.

"Of course." Max put his hands on his thighs to stop his legs from trembling.

They drove in silence for a moment. Then von Roenne said, "I was wondering . . . what brought you to Berlin?"

Max, very slowly, said, "I moved from my father's house to my uncle's house because—"

"No, not your cover story," said von Roenne. "I meant, what brought you *back* to Berlin, after you managed to escape to London?"

CHAPTER Thirty-Three

Stein and Berg were both screaming. Max couldn't make out *what* they were screaming, because he was on the verge of passing out, and also they weren't screaming words so much as just screaming.

"If you don't want to tell me," said Lieutenant Colonel Alexis von Roenne, "I completely understand."

Max couldn't have told von Roenne anything, even if he'd wanted to.

"Would you like *me* to tell *you* something instead?" asked the neat little spy with the round glasses.

Max didn't even nod.

"Do you know why I'm Hitler's favorite intelligence officer?"

Max had a few guesses. He did not offer them.

They were driving very slowly down Unter den Linden, one of Berlin's main thoroughfares. Cars were honking loudly and swerving around them. Alexis von Roenne didn't seem to mind.

"It's not because I'm a Nazi," he said. "I'm not. I've never joined the Nazi Party, in fact."

Had Max been breathing, he might have caught his breath. But he had none to catch.

"It's not because I flatter Hitler, either," von Roenne continued. "Unlike most of the sycophants in his inner circle."

Max kept staring through the windshield, fighting an urge to leap out of the moving car and into traffic. At least there would be oxygen outside of the car. There seemed to be none inside.

"I am Hitler's favorite intelligence officer, as Herr Fritzsche's radio program will call me," Alexis von Roenne went on with a hint of embarrassment, "because I can take a single scrap of data, and extrapolate from that a whole world. I explained this to you before, I believe."

Max almost managed to nod.

"And I believe I told you about the missing parachutist with the double harness. And how there was a suspicious Grüne Polizei report. And a corroborating Gestapo informant, the girl in your building. And then there was *you*."

Von Roenne drove into an underground parking garage and slid into an open spot. He pulled up on the parking brake.

But he did not get out, or even move to open his door. Instead, he stared straight ahead, still speaking.

"The address you gave me, where you said your father lived, is in fact a building owned by the British government." Max cursed silently and wondered how Chumley could have been so careless. "They don't know that I know," von Roenne said, as if reading Max's thoughts. "But I wasn't surprised by the address. What *did* surprise me was the history of the building where I found you. *That* is where the story became really gripping." He glanced at Max. Max was trying not to tremble visibly.

Von Roenne watched him for a moment, and then he opened the car door. "This is Prinz-Albrecht-Strasse 8. Home of the Reich Security Main Office, the Gestapo, and the SS. Most of my Abwehr colleagues work over on Tirpitzufer, but Hitler spends much more time here, and he likes to keep me close at hand."

"Not surprising," said Stein. "He loves creeps like you."

"Come," von Roenne invited Max. "Wouldn't you like to look inside?"

He got out, and Max dragged himself out after him.

Max said to Berg and Stein: "You know the tingly feeling, when your leg has fallen asleep, and you can't put any weight on it?"

"Yeah. That happens to us, too," Stein answered.

"Well, that's how my whole body feels right now. None of my limbs are working."

"Don't worry about it," Berg reassured him. "This guy is about to break all your limbs anyway."

They walked up concrete stairs, into a grand office building. Men in military uniforms and clerks and secretaries hurried up and down the hallways. What Uncle Ewen and Admiral Godfrey wouldn't *give* to see inside this place.

What Max wouldn't give to get out alive.

Von Roenne took Max to the elevators—and then past them, to the stairwell.

"Why doesn't he want to go in the elevator?" Berg asked.

"The elevator probably doesn't go down to the torture chambers," Stein replied.

"No, I bet it does."

Once on the stairs, von Roenne went up, not down. Max followed, silently.

Max was trying his utmost to organize his mind, just as Ewen and Chumley had taught him to do. The most important secrets safely hidden in the darkest corner of that place beneath the stairs. Then other secrets, ones that Max could give up and still survive, in front of that one. If Max played his part well enough, perhaps von Roenne would discover those secondary secrets and think he'd found all there was to find.

But of course, in a battle of wits between a thirteen-year-old boy and "Hitler's favorite intelligence officer," Max knew he didn't stand a chance.

Lieutenant Colonel Alexis von Roenne's private office was immaculate. Dozens of wooden filing cabinets, but not a file in sight. A broad mahogany desk, but not a single piece of paper left out. Von Roenne closed the door behind him.

And locked it.

"Max."

Max turned around and tried his best to keep breathing. Alexis von Roenne was looking at him almost sympathetically. Which was *even more* terrifying than if he'd looked at him like he was going to kill him.

"Max. Why, why, *why* did they send you back to Berlin?"

Max did not respond.

"You made it out!" said Alexis von Roenne, shaking his head. "You made it out, when so many Jewish children did not! And you came *back*?!" He tsk-tsked. "There must have been a very important reason for them to send you to Berlin."

Alexis von Roenne took off his glasses and polished them on his tie and examined Max thoughtfully.

"I have no idea what the play is here, Max," said Stein.

"You could always jump out the window," suggested Berg.

"You always want him to jump out a window!"

"Guilty as charged!"

Max said nothing. Alexis von Roenne had found his secret hiding place under the stairs and pointed right at Max's *most dangerous* secret: he was a Jewish spy, sent from Britain.

Max was dead.

Von Roenne sighed in a disappointed way and walked over to one of the file cabinets. He unlocked it and started thumbing through the files. He found the one that he wanted and scanned the pages. Then he dropped the file on the otherwise bare table and locked the cabinet again.

"Max, are you going to tell me why you're in Germany? I really think you should."

"I grew up here," Max said weakly.

Von Roenne nodded as if he'd expected Max to say that. "I know you did. I'll be right back." He went to the door, unlocked it, slipped into the hall, and closed it again behind him.

Max heard the door lock from the outside.

"Well, *now* what are you going to do?" Stein said, holding his little head in his warty hands.

"What do you think Lieutenant Colonel von Psychopath is getting?" Berg asked. "A club, to break your hands with? A lighter, to burn the bottoms of your feet?"

"Berg! Please!" Stein cried.

Max had picked up the file on the desk.

"Max!" Stein moaned. "What's the good of spying now, when you've already been caught?!"

The file was marked KNOWN INTELLIGENCE AGENTS—K-P.

With growing dread, Max looked inside. He found a list of names.

Kaiserling, Anton. Kentridge, Alice. Krauss, Tomas. Each name was followed by a location, and a few scribbled notes.

Max looked at the tab of the folder again. K-P. He quickly flipped to M.

He scanned the page, looking for Maas, Max.

He wasn't there.

He breathed a sigh of relief.

And then, farther down the page, he saw: Montagu, Ewen.

Max's heart sank. It had Uncle Ewen's home address, age, rank, and a physical description.

And then he saw the name below Uncle Ewen's.

Montagu, Ivor.

Huh?

Uncle Ivor didn't work for British Intelligence, did he?

Max's eyes moved across the columns, to the notes.

Oh.

No.

Uncle Ivor did *not* work for British Intelligence.

In neat block letters were written the words SOVIET AGENT.

Uncle Ivor was a spy for Russia.

CHAPTER
Thirty-Four

Lieutenant Colonel von Roenne came back into his office and locked the door behind him.

In his hands were . . . brown paper lunch bags.

"Max, why don't you have a seat?" he said.

Max collapsed in a sturdy wooden chair, leaving the folder open on von Roenne's desk.

Uncle Ivor was a spy? For Russia? For Stalin?

Stalin had a pact with Hitler. They had carved up Poland between them. Stalin's Soviet Union didn't have concentration camps, but they had gulags in Siberia, which were pretty much the same thing.

How could he? But, of course, the Soviet Union was communist, and Ivor was a devout communist. That was how.

Max thought back to what Ivor had said to him, the last time they'd been together. About writing to him, and not telling Ewen about it. About keeping him up to date.

Maybe Max had known then and hadn't admitted it to himself.

How much, Max wondered, was he not admitting to himself?

"Here," von Roenne said, handing Max a bag. "I got you potato salad. I'll take the pork sausage."

Max took the bag listlessly.

Alexis von Roenne settled into the chair behind his desk, putting his sausage to the side. "I know who you are, Max. I know that you lived with the family of Stuart Montagu, in London. That his brother, Ewen Montagu, of British Naval Intelligence, recruited you. I know that you were parachuted into Berlin on the night of November second, and that the commando whose chest you were strapped to died upon landing."

Max stared at the bag in his hands.

"What I *need* to know is *why* you are here."

Max kept staring at the brown paper.

"Max!" von Roenne snapped. Max looked up. "I am going to make a promise to you. I don't have to—I could turn you over to our interrogators and you would tell us everything you have ever learned from the day you were born in a matter of hours. But I will not do that, Max . . . *if* you tell me why you are here. In fact, if you tell me why you are here, I am very likely to let you go."

Max knew that von Roenne was lying. He had to be.

Max looked back down into his lap.

Von Roenne let a minute pass. And another. And one more.

Finally, he said, "All right. This is my final offer. I am going to tell you a secret, Max. It's a good secret, I promise. I will tell you my secret, and if you agree with me, that it really is a good one, *then* you can tell me yours. If you don't think it's a good secret . . . well, then you can take your chances with the interrogators. How does that sound?"

Max raised one eyebrow. He was fairly certain this "secret" would be a lie, or something frivolous and insignificant. But why not hear it?

So Max said, "Okay."

"My name," said the small intelligence man with the moon glasses, "is Baron Alexis von Roenne."

Max knew that. Except for the "Baron" part.

"Yes," said von Roenne, "I'm a baron. Nobility. I am also a Christian." He took off his glasses, peered through them, and put them back on his face. "I was raised with many beliefs. Some of those beliefs you might call old-fashioned. One of those old-fashioned beliefs is that I think society was divided into social classes for a *reason*. The farmers are born to farm, the workers are born to work, and the nobility are born to rule. In my view, the common man hasn't the time, the energy, or the intellect to make the complex decisions that are required when running a nation. This is what royalty and nobility are for. I have no love for democracy, Max, because I don't believe the people should rule a nation."

"This guy's secret stinks," Berg said.

As Max had expected.

Von Roenne continued. "But I am also a Christian. A *real* Christian. I believe, Max, that life is sacred."

Max wondered how you could believe life was sacred while working for the Nazi war machine.

"I believe there is one Supreme Leader, and He is in Heaven. Not in the Chancellor's office on Voss Strasse."

Max raised his eyebrows at that. It almost sounded like von Roenne was putting down Hitler.

"I believe," said von Roenne, speaking very slowly and very quietly, "that you shall love your neighbor as yourself."

"Yeah, right," Stein scoffed.

But Max was listening very carefully now.

"Even," von Roenne whispered, *"your Jewish neighbors."*

"He's lying," Berg said immediately. And then he added, "I mean, he must be."

Von Roenne was staring at Max very intently through his spectacles. "Max, my secret is this: I *hate* the Nazis, and *I hate Hitler.*"

Max remained very still on the outside, but his insides were trembling. That was not a sentence you could say in Germany. It was, quite literally, a death sentence.

Von Roenne was still talking. "I do not want Germany to lose the war, because I am German and my family is German and the last time we lost a war to Britain and the United States, we were punished so severely it nearly destroyed us. But if the only way to rid Germany of Hitler is for us to lose yet again—then I will do *everything in my power* to make us lose."

Max stared through Baron Alexis von Roenne's glasses, into his sad gray eyes.

For a long time.

A really long time.

And then Max said, "I think . . . I think you're telling the *truth*."

"You are an astute young man, Max," von Roenne replied.

"He *can't* be telling the truth!" Berg cried. "Can he?"

"He kinda *looks* like he's telling the truth . . ." said Stein, though he didn't sound too sure.

Max said, "All right. I'll tell you why I'm in Berlin."

So Max told Lieutenant Colonel von Roenne the truth. That he had been tasked with infiltrating the Funkhaus to learn everything there was to know about its operations and methods. That he was awaiting instructions for some undetermined "Grand Finale." That he hoped it would be violent, and that it would target Goebbels himself.

When Max had finished, Alexis von Roenne looked like he'd drunk a cupful of sour milk. "Max," he said. He sounded disappointed.

"What?"

"Max, what I told you was the most sensitive secret I could *possibly* tell you. Also, it was *true*."

"What I told you was true, too!"

"No, it wasn't."

"Yes! It was! It is!" Max retorted. He didn't understand what game von Roenne was playing.

Von Roenne stood up from his chair and came around to Max's side of the desk. He leaned forward until he was very close to Max. He smelled faintly of paper and very expensive cologne. "Young man, I have been sparring with Ewen Montagu for more than a year now. I have composed a very accurate picture of him. He is charming. He is secretive. He is smart. Max, believe me when I tell you: *This is not your mission.*"

Max stared at the German intelligence officer.

"Ewen Montagu would never send a boy on a potentially fatal mission for *that.*"

"I . . . I don't know what to tell you," said Max. "He did."

Von Roenne shook his head. "And why did you agree to this? Why on *earth* would a Jewish boy agree to be sent back to Nazi Germany?"

"THAT'S WHAT I KEEP ASKING HIM!" Berg roared.

Von Roenne had uncovered all of Max's secrets. He had dragged them into the light and strewn them out across the floor.

All, that is, except for one. The secret that even Ewen didn't know.

"I came back to find my parents," said Max.

The small man with the very round glasses sat there, considering. Then he began, slowly, to nod. At last, he said:

"All right."

"All right what?"

"I'll help you."

"You'll *help* me?"

"This is *not* how I saw this meeting going," Berg mumbled.

"Yeah, you saw him plummeting to his death from a window," Stein replied.

Max considered "Hitler's favorite intelligence officer."

Could he trust von Roenne? No, right? And yet . . .

Von Roenne spoke again: "I will help you. In exchange, I need two things: First, when you get back to London, you must tell Ewen Montagu everything—except, I beg of you, Max, do not tell him my secret. I trust Ewen Montagu—but I do *not* trust everyone he knows and speaks with." Alexis von Roenne looked meaningfully at Max. And then at his desk. The file.

Ivor. Von Roenne feared Ivor telling Soviet intelligence, who could then expose von Roenne.

"Second, and this is of *utmost* importance, Max. To you as well as to me." Von Roenne leaned in again, and this time, he got as close to Max's ear as he could without their cheeks touching. *"Don't. Get. Caught."*

He sat back up. "If you do, I can't help you. In fact, if you get caught, I will probably be caught as well. And then, Max, I cannot help Germany lose the war."

CHAPTER Thirty-Five

Baron Alexis von Roenne walked Max back to the stairwell. They descended from the fifth floor down to the fourth, the third, the second . . . when they heard, "Max Maas! Wait!"

Von Roenne and Max both froze.

Slowly, they turned.

Doctor Gustav Adolf Scheel, Commander of the SD, was hurrying toward them, his leather boots clacking on the stairs, his leather trench coat over his arm. "I know this boy! Alexis, what is he doing here?"

Von Roenne stopped and Scheel came to a halt a little closer to him than seemed reasonable. The small man in green looked up at the tall man in gray. They were like two captains of different sports teams, meeting in the center of the pitch.

Von Roenne said, "He is here, *Herr Doctor Commander*," and it sounded like a reproach, "because I ran into him at the Funkhaus, where he was meeting with Dr. Goebbels. He has just been given a new post at the Funkhaus, as technical assistant to Eugen Hadamovsky. I thought it prudent to check that he was secure before he took a position at such a sensitive ministry." Commander Scheel could not hide his astonishment. He turned to Max, seeing him in an entirely different light. But instantly his expression changed when von Roenne said, "I just happened to be there for an interview, so I decided to take the security review upon myself."

Commander Scheel spun back to von Roenne, and his voice had turned bitter. "You were there for an *interview*, were you? *La-di-dah*, aren't you fancy? Are they going to call it 'Hitler's Favorite Intelligence Officer' or something revolting like that?"

"Actually, that's exactly what they're calling it," von Roenne replied.

"They are? They are!" Scheel rolled his eyes. "Well, anyway, what was your conclusion, *Alexis*, after interviewing Max here?"

"That he is secure."

"Of course he's secure!" Commander Scheel said scornfully. "Do you know he's working for me?"

Von Roenne looked down in surprise at Max. "No, I did not learn that."

Max looked equally surprised. What was Scheel talking about?

"Yes! He's helping me find Jews and other illegals who are in hiding! Looks like 'Hitler's favorite intelligence officer' can't break a kid! Ha!" Commander Scheel crowed. A new thought seemed to strike him. "What about lunch, Max? You can update me on your progress for our, um, our work together. Oh, and incidentally, I have some information you might find interesting as well." Gustav Scheel was showing all his teeth in what seemed to be a sort of smile.

"Uh . . ." said Max.

"Good, it's settled!" Scheel announced. Then he sneered at von Roenne, "Sorry, Alexis, my regular table at Horcher only seats two. Otherwise, I'd *definitely* have invited you."

And he guided Max away from Baron Alexis von Roenne.

Max glanced over his shoulder at the brilliant spy. Von Roenne was watching him with an expression that Max could not place at first. And then he placed it.

It was fear.

They were seated at a table by a window. Waiters in white coats and black pants, with white towels over their arms, seemed to skate by as if their shoes had invisible wheels on the soles. The walls were wood paneled, the rugs were Persian, the windows were covered in lace, and men—all men, many in officers' uniforms—sat talking in two and threes and fours, or sat alone reading the day's newspapers.

Doctor Commander Gustav Adolf Scheel studied the menu. Max pretended to study his, while actually studying Commander Scheel. His broad shoulders. His wide-set eyes. His platinum-blond hair. His broken nose.

What did Scheel want? Why was Max here?

Scheel put down his menu. "Lobster for both of us, what do you say?"

Max said, "That sounds expensive . . ."

Scheel laughed, gratified. A waiter glided past and Commander Scheel grabbed his arm, nearly causing the man to fall over. Scheel handed the waiter both menus and said, "Two lobsters. And two glasses of *Kölsch*."

The waiter glanced at Max. "Beer for him? Sir, he's a little young . . ." The expression on Commander Scheel's face began to change—and instantly, the waiter was saying, "Of course! I'm so sorry. Right away."

Scheel turned back to Max as the waiter hurried off, and he was grinning again. "You see that? That's what *power* looks like, Max. Best feeling in the world. So tell me." He leaned forward. "Was von Roenne trying to recruit you as an informant? I bet he was, the little sneak. Listen, you don't want to fall in with those Abwehr losers. Most of them are defeatists and monarchists anyway. That von Roenne isn't even a Nazi! Did you know that? I bet he didn't mention that!"

"No," said Max, doing his best to act shocked. "He didn't!"

"See?" Commander Scheel said. "There's no future in the Abwehr. Hitler will liquidate it as soon as the war is over, mark my words. Up against a wall and shot, every one of them." Scheel was quite clearly looking forward to that moment. "No, the SS is where the future is. And the SD, for the really clever ones, like me. Who knows, Max? Maybe for you, too, one day, if you choose the right allies." He said this last part slowly, with meaning.

"Is he trying to recruit me?" Max asked the kobold and the dybbuk.

"Maybe?" said Stein.

Just then the beers arrived—tall, thin glasses, carried in a steel canister like bullets in a revolver. The waiter placed one in front of each of them and moved away quickly.

Commander Scheel raised his glass. Max picked up his beer. He had never tasted beer before. They toasted, and then Max took the smallest sip he could.

It was disgusting.

"Come on, Max!" Scheel laughed. "Drink up!" And he stared across the table, waiting.

Max filled his mouth with the beer and swallowed it. It made the insides of his cheeks and throat burn.

Commander Scheel said, "I have known, from my earliest days, Max, that I was made for greatness. I'm sure you can't imagine that feeling—knowing that you're smarter than everyone else."

"This nudnik has no idea who he's talking to," said Stein.

"I grew up during the war," Scheel went on. "The first one. But the only people who got glory were the men who *fought*—and I was too young." Scheel made a sad face. "I knew I was better than all the other boys. I wanted to *prove* it. I *had* to. And then, one day, I got my chance."

Scheel wriggled his butt in his chair, like he was excited for his own story. "There was a big science fair happening in my town. I had some idea for it—I don't remember what. Something good, but not great. Not good enough to win. But there was a Jew in my class, and as the science fair was approaching, I heard him talking to another boy about his project. It was *brilliant.* It had to do with the movement of electricity through wires submerged in waters of different temperature." Scheel grinned. "So what do you think I did, Max?"

"Something awful?" Berg guessed.

"I'll tell you what I did. I went to the teacher and I told him that the Jew had stolen my idea. Brilliant, right? The teacher was a good German and believed my word over the Jew's, even though the boy wept and begged and swore that it was his idea first. We had the contest, and of course I won." Scheel seemed really pleased with himself. He took a drink of *Kölsch.* Then he gestured at Max. "Come on!" he said cheerfully. "Drink to my cunning!"

Max took another drink. This time it burned everything from his nose to the bottom of his stomach. His head began to feel like someone was filling it with cotton.

"Anyway, I was supposed to get my prize in front of the whole school, the parents, and even our town's mayor! It was going to be my greatest glory yet! But on that day—*my* victory day!—you'll never guess what happened."

Max couldn't guess. The beer felt like it was trying to crawl back up his throat.

"A train arrived in town. Unexpectedly. A whole bunch of soldiers returning from the front. School was dismissed in a hurry, and everyone rushed out to see them. These soldiers—boys just a few years older than me—limped off the train, missing feet and eyes and fingers. It was disgusting. And the whole town spent the next week celebrating *them*. And I never got that prize! Can you believe it?" Scheel reached out and grabbed a different passing waiter. "Another *Kölsch*."

Commander Scheel went on, "I know that I am more ruthless, more intelligent, more cunning than anyone. And yet I never got my due. *Ever*. Until Hitler came along! Suddenly, there was a path to glory! And I'm striding down it with my head held high, aren't I?"

Max stared at Commander Scheel. He was speechless.

"You have no idea how lucky you are, Max, to be growing up in Germany right now!"

"Oh yeah," Stein said. "Germany, 1940. This little Jewish boy couldn't be luckier."

Scheel continued. "So listen to this—"

"Does he have a choice?" asked Berg.

"Do *I*?" asked Stein.

"I went to medical school, because science was my talent—"

"Stealing science," Stein put in.

"—and there was this *beloved* teacher there. Professor Emil Gumbel. Jewish, of course. The universities were *infested* with Jews back then. Even Goebbels's PhD advisor was Jewish!"

"*What?*" Max said, and beer ran up his throat and almost entered his mouth.

Scheel leaned forward conspiratorially. "His girlfriend back then was Jewish, too."

Max's mouth hung open. How was that possible? No Nazi hated Jews more than Goebbels.

"Yeah!" Scheel grinned, enjoying his words' effect on Max. But he quickly brought the subject back to himself. "Of all the Jewish professors, though, Emil Gumbel was the *worst*. He hated Hitler, and he hated the Nazis. He talked about it in every class—and he taught mathematics! This is the early 1930s, when the Nazi Party was beginning to win elections. Our popularity was spreading. I used to ask Gumbel questions. Challenge him. But he was so slippery. He would always turn my questions around to make *me* look like the coward or the fool or the anti-German one. It was *infuriating*!"

The waiter brought the second beer. Scheel lifted it and waited. Max lifted his. They drank.

As soon as the beer went down, Max felt his stomach lurch in revolt.

"I started a campaign against Emil Julius Gumbel," Commander Scheel said. "To get him fired. Pamphlets. Meetings. We burned torches outside of his house on Friday nights, when he was sitting down to his sabbath dinners. Meanwhile, I was helping shut down anti-Nazi newspapers. Any local paper that published a *single* word against the Nazis, we'd head in and rough up the editors. Who were all cowards, of course. You throw just *one* journalist through a window—from the second floor, he didn't even die!—suddenly the newspaper gets *much* more respectful. Do you see how *weak* our enemies are?"

Max nodded and pressed his lips together to keep the puke from spilling out.

"There was one editor, also a Jew, who wouldn't shut up about the Nazis. Said awful things about Hitler. Just the worst lies. He said that Hitler was crazy. That he would get us all killed. Hogwash like that. So one night, when this editor was walking home late, me and some boys caught him and beat him and then I took out my Walther semiautomatic pistol and I shot him in the head. *That* sent a message."

"I remember that," Berg said. "It was news all over the country."

"It was horrifying," Stein agreed.

The waiter arrived with two plates of lobster.

Max should have been hungry—he hadn't eaten von Roenne's potato salad, or anything other than a slice of bread for breakfast. But he felt so sick from the beer—and from the story Scheel was telling—that the sight of lobster on the plate, garnished with parsley and a wedge of lemon, nearly sent him running from the restaurant.

Scheel tucked his napkin into his shirt and picked up a fork in one fist and a knife in the other. "Well, the campaign against Professor Gumbel was working. It was announced that there was too much chaos on campus, due to his presence." Scheel stopped suddenly. "Do you *hear* me, Max? They said it was *his* presence that was causing all the chaos!" Gustav Scheel threw his head back and laughed, sublimely pleased with himself.

"He gave one more lecture," Scheel remembered, and he suddenly pushed his plate away from him, as if this memory made him lose his appetite. Max knew how he felt. "In the middle of it, Gumbel suddenly points at me. *At me!*" Scheel's face became as gloomy as the gray clouds outside. "And he says to me, 'You are so sure that you are right, Scheel. But if you are right, why do you silence those who disagree with you? Why get us fired? Why kill us? If you were right, your arguments would kill my arguments! So why does Hitler need thugs like you, if his arguments are right?' "

Gustav Scheel shook his head in disgust. "He called us *thugs*. Look at me, sitting here, eating lobster at Horcher right now! Do I look like a thug to you?"

"Of course not!" Max said quickly, as a disgusting, beer-flavored burp escaped his mouth. "You look like a hero!"

He hated himself for saying it. But at least burping had made him feel slightly better.

Scheel nodded vigorously. "Thank you, Max. You understand. So then Gumbel says to me, 'Do you know that you admit, every day, that you are wrong? Whenever you beat someone up, or get them fired, or shoot them, you are admitting that your arguments cannot beat our arguments. Why do you silence us with *bullets*, instead of beating us with your *brains*? Because you are not only afraid that you are *wrong*. You are afraid, Herr Scheel, that you are *stupid*. And do you know what? You are.' "

As Gustav Adolf Scheel stared into the street, the gray light on his lined cheeks, Max realized at last why Scheel had brought him here.

"He *is* recruiting me," Max told Stein and Berg, "to his fan club. He needs me to admire him because it quiets his fear that Gumbel was right. That he really is stupid."

"Those were his words exactly, Max," Scheel went on. "I'll never forget them as long as I live. That very afternoon, he fled to France. Which was clever, because if he hadn't, by nightfall we would have burned down his house while he slept."

Gustav Scheel lifted his glass. Thankfully, he didn't order Max to raise his.

"After graduating as a medical doctor, I joined the SD. When the war began, I asked to be assigned to France so I could hunt Gumbel down and hold him accountable for his words against Hitler."

And against you, Max thought.

"I was part of an *Einsatzgruppe*, what they call the death squads. I rounded up plenty of Jews and sent them to camps. Some never made it to camps, actually. We killed them right there. But I never got Gumbel. He escaped to New York, the coward." Scheel stared gloomily at the passersby on the side-walk. Then he shook himself from his gray reverie. "I got lots of them, though," he added, grinning at Max. He pulled his lobster back in front of him. Then he saw that Max had not touched his food. "Eat up! It's not every day you get lobster with a commander of the SD, I bet!"

And Max said to Berg and Stein, "Thank God."

Outside the restaurant, Commander Scheel shook Max's hand firmly. "So it's settled, Max. You are under my wing now. If von Roenne or anyone else bothers you again, you come to me. Understood?"

"Yes, Herr Doctor Commander. Thank you."

"Oh! Incidentally, I located those Jews you were looking for!"

Suddenly, Max's heart stopped beating. His lungs stopped working.

"You did?"

"I did. They were deported. To a concentration camp." Commander Scheel winked. "We know how to take care of parasites like that."

Then he turned for his waiting Mercedes.

It took all of Max's strength to hold himself together until Scheel's car had driven out of sight.

Then he vomited lobster and beer all over the sidewalk.

As Max was making his way home, Berg tried to comfort him. "I'm sorry, Max. Truly, I am." Then he added, "Do you think it's time to go back to England now?"

Max didn't reply.

"Hello? Max?" Berg called into his ear.

"Quiet, you cretin!" Stein snapped. "Can't you see he's grieving?"

But Max wasn't grieving.

He was planning.

CHAPTER Thirty-Six

Max returned to the Funkhaus the next day, and the day after that, and the day after that.

He had dropped a note in the dead letter box, informing Ewen and Chumley of his new job there. Until he received further instructions, he would gather as much information as he could.

Meanwhile, Max anxiously awaited contact from von Roenne so he could tell him that his parents were in a camp somewhere and beg him to do something about it. Max would have tried to make contact himself, but he couldn't just waltz into the headquarters of the Reich Security Main Office.

So he waited.

Some days were better than others. When he got to work on the transmitter, he could almost quiet his fear for his parents. When Diewerge and Melita laughed at Berndt for his shamelessness, the pain almost went away for a moment. Almost.

Wednesdays were bad, though. That was when Max and Freddie's Hitler Youth group met for "Home Nights."

After work, Max would walk home with Herr Fritzsche, and Freddie would be waiting on the front steps of the house, obviously wrestling with a mix of intense jealousy that Max was getting to spend time with his father and intense excitement that *he* was going to get to spend time with Max.

It was December now, and the sun had been down for hours, so Freddie and Max would set off through the dark, leafy streets of Steglitz. Freddie would beg Max to tell him about everything he'd seen at the Funkhaus, and then he'd moan about how stupid and boring school was ever since the Nazi party had banned nearly all books, including textbooks, from the classrooms. "Not that I'm saying anything against the Nazi Party!" Freddie would add hurriedly.

"If only he would," Stein said once, "maybe he wouldn't be so unbearable."

But Max didn't find Freddie unbearable anymore. When Freddie wasn't acting desperate, he was actually pretty smart and very observant.

The Hitler Youth Home Nights, though, were awful.

They met in a dingy basement apartment owned by the Nazi Party. It was unbearably hot from the coal stove that was kept burning all the time, and the boys were restless and bored. Peter, with the rabbit teeth, was particularly nasty. He couldn't sit still, so he was always needling everyone, trying to pick a fight. Even Rolph told Peter to shut up on more than one occasion. Max always felt like Home Nights were just a disaster waiting to happen.

And then one did.

One Wednesday evening, Rudi, the troop leader, brought forth a box he'd received from the Hitler Youth headquarters. The boys gathered round. Rudi reached inside and pulled out a little booklet.

And a frightening object with two pointy, curved arms.

"What is that?" Peter asked.

"These are calipers," said Rudi, studying the cover of the booklet. "It says here that they're for measuring heads."

"We're going to measure each others' heads?" said Rolph. "That's weird."

"It says," Rudi relayed, "that this is the most scientifically accurate way to determine someone's race."

Max, sitting on a low, threadbare couch on one side of the room, became very still.

"Jews, Blacks, Slavs, Asiatics, Aryans," said Rudi, reading from the booklet, "all have different physical features and different shaped skulls."

"Because every race has different sized brains," Freddie volunteered, from next to Max on the couch.

Max glanced at him from the corner of his eye.

"Jews," Rudi was reading, "have low brows, because their brains are the most primitive of all the races." Then Rudi read the rest of the list. Of course, at the top of the hierarchy was the Aryan race.

"This is us," Rudi said, pointing to an illustration of a pyramid. "Germans and other Nordic people have the biggest brains. It's all science. Completely proven." He held up the calipers. "You measure with these."

Quickly, Max said to Stein and Berg, "Is this true?"

"We don't go around measuring people's skulls," said Berg. "But Germans aren't smarter than other people, if that's what you're asking."

"Yeah, look at them," said Stein, gesturing at the boys in the basement room.

"What I'm asking," said Max, "is—what's going to happen when they measure *my* head? Are they going to be able to tell that I'm Jewish?"

Stein and Berg . . . didn't know.

Rudi held the calipers while a boy named Horst read from the instruction booklet. Once Horst was done, Rudi asked, "Who wants to go first?"

No one volunteered.

"Come on," said Rudi. "There's nothing to be afraid of."

This was not true, and they all knew it. Even though they'd all been born and raised in Germany, if the calipers said they weren't *racially* German . . . what would the consequences be?

The only sound in the room was the coal crackling in the stove.

"How about it, Max?" said Rudi. "Show the boys there's nothing to worry about."

Max hesitated for a moment. Then he said, "Come on, Rudi. This is stupid."

Rudi looked surprised. "Stupid? This is *science*, Max."

Max looked around at the boys. He looked at the small door, leading up to the street. There was no way he could make it out of this place, if they tried to stop him.

"What, are you *scared*?" said Rolph.

They were *all* scared. But here it was, the classic Nazi tactic: accuse someone else of being afraid when, really, *you're* afraid.

Also, yes. Max was terrified.

"Maybe it's because he *is* a Jew," Peter said.

They had dropped that line of teasing after Max had almost killed Peter on the camping trip.

But Max still wasn't moving.

Rudi waited with the calipers.

Max stood up, walked over to Rudi, and sat down on a wooden stool. Rudi placed the calipers around Max's head.

Rudi read out a number. Horst scribbled it down.

Rudi rotated the calipers. "Why are you sweating, Max?" Rudi asked. Max didn't answer.

Rudi read out another number. Horst wrote it down.

The calipers rotated one more time. Rudi read out a final number, and then Horst started studying a chart in the booklet. Horst's finger came to rest on a number. His eyebrows crawled up his forehead. Then, very slowly, Horst handed the book to Rudi, pointing at a place on the chart.

The boys watched, spellbound by the ritual.

Rudi looked. A grim grin spread across the group leader's face.

"*You . . .*" he said to Max.

The boys all held their breath.

". . . are a true Aryan!" Rudi announced.

Freddie broke into wild applause. Other boys cheered. Rolph and Peter looked crestfallen.

"A perfect score!" Rudi was saying. "Not a trace of Jewish blood in you!" He slapped Max on the back and said, "Who wants to go next?"

Rolph got onto the stool and Max walked shakily back to the couch.

"I don't understand," he said to Berg and Stein, collapsing onto the threadbare cushions. "Why didn't it say I was Jewish?"

Berg said, "Max. I thought you were a smart boy. This Nazi 'science' isn't science at all. It's *hokum.*"

Max sat back and rested his head on the couch's moldy pillows and stared at the ceiling. "I thought they were going to tear me apart," he said.

But, it seemed, he said this aloud.

Freddie looked at him. "Why? You're as pure as they come, Max! Anyone can see that!"

Max sat up. "Huh? What? I didn't say anything!"

"Yes you did! You said you thought they'd tear you apart!"

Max stared at Freddie. Luckily, the other boys were all focused on Rolph and Rudi and the calipers. "Sorry, Freddie. I . . . I'll tell you later."

"Promise?"

"Uh . . . yeah," said Max. "Promise."

Stein whistled. "Wow, Max. You need to be more careful."

Clearly.

Living in the lion's den for this long, it was only a matter of time before you got eaten.

"Hey!" Rudi cried. "Rolph is Jewish!"

"What?" Rolph cried. "No I'm not!"

"He's definitely not," Stein said.

Rolph stood up and pushed Rudi. Even though he was the group leader, he was only a few years older, and he wasn't much bigger than Rolph. But Rudi wasn't going to take that, so he pushed Rolph back. Then Peter pushed Rudi. Rudi turned around and punched Peter in the stomach. Rolph jumped on Rudi. Horst jumped on Peter. Suddenly, the boys were all fighting each other.

"Hey," Max hissed at Freddie. "You wanna get out of here?"

He didn't have to ask twice. They hustled out the door and into the night.

Max and Freddie ran through the dark streets, past closed-up shops and office buildings—and they were laughing. Max wasn't sure why. Maybe it was relief, having escaped that sweltering basement and those stupid bullies. Maybe it was the feeling of freedom. Maybe it was having a friend. Max hadn't had a friend his age for a long, long time.

Freddie was breathing hard, so they stopped running

and leaned against the stone wall of an office building, in a streetlamp's cone of light.

They stood, side by side, panting, grinning. Freddie said, "Snow!"

Indeed, snowflakes had started to fall through the night sky. They lit up like they were on fire as they entered the yellow beams of the streetlamp and then dissolved into tiny puddles on the sidewalk.

"You know, I feel like that sometimes," Freddie said.

"Like what? The snowflakes?" Max replied. Every once in a while, Freddie got philosophical. Max . . . kinda liked it.

"Well, before we're born, we can't experience anything, right? And after we die, there's nothing."

Max said: "We don't know for that sure."

"I'm pretty sure," said Freddie. "And if there's nothing before we're born and nothing after we die, that means life is a vacation from nothingness. Just a short break from *oblivion*."

"Huh," said Max.

"So we might as well *enjoy* it." Freddie grinned.

Max smiled in the darkness. Then his smile faded. "Can I ask you a question, Freddie?"

Freddie said, "You can ask me anything."

Max swallowed hard. "What if the calipers had said *I* was a Jew, and not Rolph?"

Freddie laughed. "I would have said the calipers were broken." Then he added, "I *still* say that."

Max tried to smile, then asked, "But what if they had been telling the truth?"

Stein said, "Max, what are you doing?"

Freddie gazed at Max. After a while he said, "I still wouldn't care."

Max put his arm around Freddie's shoulders. Freddie put an arm around Max's waist.

And Max thought about those curving calipers, and Freddie's curving arm, and how, in a certain way, they were opposites. The calipers were a Big Lie—an untruth spread to millions. And Freddie's arm was . . . what?

A small truth?

Yes, Max thought. A small truth. Private, emotional, undeniable.

The beginning of an idea was taking form. Max couldn't see what the moves were, not quite yet. But the pieces of the clockwork were arranging themselves on the black velvet table of his mind.

Max and Freddie looked up into the sky. It also looked like black velvet, alight with spinning flakes of snow. One arm around each other. Enjoying their vacation from oblivion.

CHAPTER Thirty-Seven

And then, the next day, everything changed.

Max emerged from the Kaiserdamm stop of the U-Bahn into a cold, sunny morning and turned onto the main boulevard. Cars rumbled past.

And then one didn't.

Max sensed it without seeing it. A car was driving unnaturally slowly down the wide street, just behind him and to his left.

"Hey, someone's following you," Stein said.

Max didn't turn to look. He just picked up his pace.

"Still following you," Berg told him.

Max went faster.

So did the car.

He saw a small side street up ahead. Suddenly, Max was running. When he got to the corner, he turned sharply down the side street and then ducked behind a parked mail truck, big and red and pulled up on the curb.

The car that had been following him turned down the side street a moment later. The driver put on the brakes, scanning the sidewalks for Max. Not seeing him, the driver sped ahead.

Past Max's hiding place.

Which is when Max recognized the car.

He jumped up, ran into the street, and started waving his arms.

The little black Opel stopped suddenly. Max ran up to the passenger side, opened the door, and got in.

"Good morning," said Baron Alexis von Roenne. "That was an impressive bit of hide-and-seek."

Max would pass the compliment along to Chumley when he saw him again.

If he saw him again.

Von Roenne was gazing at Max, and the smile he'd worn for a moment slid off of his face. He said, "I found them."

Max's heart nearly leaped out of his throat.

"Can you go tomorrow?"

"Of course," said Max. "Whenever, wherever."

"Meet me at Moritzplatz. Five in the morning."

Max got out of the car without another word.

Wolfie Diewerge was walking around the office like he'd just won the war himself.

"Oh lads!" he announced to whoever was listening, "Wait until you hear the *Heard Around the Reich* segment today! It's on the Kaufman Pamphlet! We're going to set the nation on fire! You're going to be astounded!"

Berndt was sitting on the edge of Melita's desk. "I doubt it," he replied. "I haven't listened to that segment since . . . ever. I don't think I've ever listened to it."

Herr Fritzsche was drinking coffee. "Marvelous, Herr Berndt. Your devotion to our programming is admirable. I'm so glad you're in charge."

"I'm in charge?" Berndt asked. "Then why don't any of you let me make any decisions?"

"Because you're a shameless moocher," said Fritzsche.

"And you do no work," said Diewerge.

"And you don't actually know anything," said Melita.

Berndt squinted at them all. Then he asked, "Is it that obvious?"

"Yes!" Melita and Diewerge and Fritzsche all said at the same time.

Max loved this office banter. Yes, he knew that they were a bunch of Nazis. But when they carried on like this, he always ended up laughing.

Max had been flipping through the installations report for the air-raid alarm system. The chief technician had handed it to Hadamovsky, upon completion of the project, and Hadamovsky had glanced at it with a shudder and immediately thrust it into Max's eager hands.

Diewerge looked up at the clock. "Dammit! It's nine already! Who's meeting Dr. Goebbels in the lobby this morning?"

Hans Fritzsche put his cup down in a hurry. "Melita, rush down there, would you? I have to get my notes from my office."

But Berndt said, "Why not let Max go? Dr. Goebbels seems to have taken a shine to our little *Funkmeister*."

"He seems *actually* busy," Fritzsche said, gesturing at the schematics Max was poring over. "Unlike the rest of you."

But Max had already stood up. "I'd be honored!" He took one last, long look at the paths of the electrical lines on the alarm system's schematic plan, made sure they were committed to memory, and then sprinted for the stairs.

"You see?" said Berndt. "Maybe you should let me make the decisions around here! Maybe I know what I'm talking about!"

Fritzsche, Diewerge, and Melita all hesitated . . . and then, in unison, said, "Nope."

Max arrived breathlessly in the lobby just in time to greet Joseph Goebbels as he passed through the revolving door.

"Ah! Look who it is! The *Funkmeister*!" Dr. Goebbels exclaimed.

"It is an honor to see you again, Herr Doctor," Max replied. "Shall we proceed to the small auditorium?"

But Goebbels was grinning from his ratlike face as if he had a surprise for him.

Which suddenly made Max *very* nervous. "Um, yes, Herr Doctor?"

"You know," Goebbels mused, "I have just been informed that we have a very exciting opportunity."

Max swallowed. "Oh?"

"Our Supreme Leader has asked me to invite a few of the Funkhaus's finest to one of his famous luncheons. There would be about a dozen guests in all."

Max's mouth opened, but no sound came out.

"I was thinking," Goebbels went on, "that he would be *thrilled* to meet a young prodigy like you."

Max tried to speak, but he was completely mute.

Just then, Hans Fritzsche stepped off the elevator, holding his notes. Goebbels was laughing. "Look at him, Fritzsche! Dumbstruck! Oh, that's priceless! Then it's settled?"

"What's settled, Herr Doctor?" Fritzsche asked, amused, as he came up behind Max.

"We'll be having lunch with the Supreme Leader!"

Fritzsche blinked very rapidly. "We?"

"You, me, and Max! Three of the ProMi's finest!"

Hans Fritzsche was as stupefied as Max. Goebbels went on. "Next week, right after our Monday-morning meeting. Speaking of which, I've got a packed schedule today, so let's get on with it!"

Goebbels pushed past Max and hobbled toward the elevator. Hans Fritzsche hurried after him.

The bustling lobby of the Haus des Rundfunks swirled around Max.

Berg said, "You're having lunch with Adolf Hitler?!"

Stein said, "You're having lunch with Adolf Hitler?!"

He was having lunch with Adolf Hitler.

Max found Hadamovsky in his office and informed him that he might be out for a few days, because his father in Falkensee had fallen ill. Then he took the U-Bahn back to Kreuzberg.

Behind the red brick church, Max removed a piece of paper and a short pencil from his pocket and wrote: *Lunch with AH next Monday. Permission to assassinate.*

Berg read it and exclaimed, "Max, you're joking!"

"You know, I've noticed," said Stein, "this kid doesn't joke a whole lot."

Max folded the note, put it behind the brick, and made his way out to the street. Then he went to the building across from his apartment, where the red sign was displayed whenever there was a message for him.

He rang the bell for apartment 2B four times.

The emergency signal.

"They're not going to let him try to kill Hitler," Berg said matter-of-factly, as Max climbed the stairs to Pastor Andreas's apartment.

"Why wouldn't they *let* him?" Stein retorted. "How could they say no?"

"Because if he tried to kill Hitler, he probably wouldn't succeed, and then he would *certainly* be executed!"

"I don't know," mused Stein. "Has he failed at anything yet?"

CHAPTER
Thirty-Eight

Just before five the next morning, Max was waiting under a streetlamp on Moritzplatz.

Stein was shivering, even though it was impossible for him to feel cold. "You know, Berg, Max is definitely going to need our help for this next thing."

Berg frowned so hard his whole ugly face became wrinkles. "I know. There is a force, binding me to him. Stronger than ever. What do you think it is?"

Stein's teeth were chattering when he replied, "I think it's our purpose."

At five o'clock sharp, Baron Alexis von Roenne's car pulled up. Max got in, and they drove off into the darkness.

CHAPTER
Thirty-Nine

Three days later, Max returned to Berlin. But as he opened his apartment building's front door, he glanced over his shoulder across the street.

A red sign, in the second-floor window.

He turned around immediately and started for the canal. Someone emerged from the building and watched him hurry away.

Down in the churchyard, there was something different about the dead letter box. The mortar around the neighboring bricks was missing. He examined them closely, trying to detect some sign of a trap—a silent alarm, perhaps. Or an explosive device.

But he saw nothing.

So he removed the central brick and those on either side of it.

In the new, expanded dead letter box was a wide, flat brown envelope. About the size of a record.

On top of the brown envelope was a note, which read:

Permission denied.

Max turned to his right shoulder, to see what Berg would say—and then he remembered that Berg wasn't with him anymore. He turned to his left. Stein was gone, too.

So often, he had hated having them on his shoulders, kibitzing, heckling, questioning everything he did.

He hadn't imagined he would miss them so much.

Max crushed the note in his fist.

And then he noticed that there were words on the record-sized brown envelope.

Grand Finale.

This was the Grand Finale? A *record*?

He was so angry, so sad, so overwhelmed by everything happening all at once, that he marched back to his apartment building with tears streaming down his face.

Which was probably why he did not see the shape crouching in the bushes of the churchyard.

CHAPTER Forty

The Osteria Savasta was nestled into a leafy block north of the Tiergarten, Berlin's grand park.

Max drove there with Hans Fritzsche in silence. Fritzsche had dined with Hitler before. Max probably should have asked him some questions, to prepare.

But all he could think about was that, in a few minutes, he would be sitting down with the most evil man on earth.

And then he was going to kill him.

They waited for Joseph Goebbels on the curb outside the restaurant, and when he arrived, the restaurant's proprietor, Signora Savasta, beckoned them inside with an upside-down hand. It was the same motion you'd use to shoo pigeons away, but in reverse.

Goebbels went in first, followed by Hans Fritzsche. Max tagged along behind.

The restaurant was completely empty. "I closed the place for you, Herr Goebbels," Signora Savasta told him. "I have a regular, he is pleading with me to just drink wine at the bar, have a little ragu. To him I said, 'When they go, you can come. Not a minute before.'"

Dr. Goebbels smiled indulgently. "You are always very kind to us, Signora."

She led them into a flagstone garden in the back, where there was a large round table with a red-checked tablecloth and ten place settings. Other tables had been pushed away, up against the garden walls. It was a warm day for mid-December, and the birds were chattering like spring had come already.

One man was sitting at the table. He had a notebook out and was sketching in it.

"Ah, Herr Speer!" Goebbels said, with obviously feigned enthusiasm. They shook hands.

Hans Fritzsche shook the man's hand next, and then introduced Max. "Herr Speer, this is Max—a *Funkmeister* I've brought on. Max, this is Albert Speer, the Supreme Leader's favorite architect. As two technical men, I am sure you'll get along swimmingly."

"Max," said Albert Speer, bowing his head a little as they shook hands. "Please, sit beside me." Herr Speer pulled out a chair for Max and then sat down himself. "I hope you don't mind if I doodle. I like to keep my hands moving." He turned his attention back to the notebook and picked up his very sharp pencil. Max couldn't see what Speer was drawing. The architect asked, "Have you met the Supreme Leader before?"

"No, I haven't," said Max. His legs were bouncing like they had motors in them. "What's it like?"

"Oh!" said Herr Speer. "It is the greatest possible thrill! You are meeting a world-historical figure. One of the very few across all the ages of man. Alexander the Great, Caesar, Genghis Khan, Napoleon . . . that's about it. And Adolf Hitler. And you're going to have lunch with him!"

Speer placed the end of his pencil carefully between his teeth, studying his sketch—whatever it was—and then he said, "The first time I met him, it changed my life."

"Oh?" Max asked dutifully, as he kept a vigilant watch on the door that led into the garden from the Osteria.

"When I first met Hitler," Herr Speer went on, "I was a young architect with a firm on the verge of failing. But he saw something in me, and soon I was designing grand halls and great buildings. It was the only reason I joined the Nazi party, really. It gave me a chance to live out my architectural dreams."

Max looked around, because Herr Speer said this at full voice, as if he wasn't afraid of being overheard. Speer noticed.

"Oh, the Supreme Leader knows that. We all have our own reasons for coming to Nazism. But we all get here eventually. Everyone will."

"Or we'll be dead in a concentration camp," Max said. But only to himself.

"Here he comes!" Speer exclaimed, and stood up so quickly that his water glass toppled over. He cursed and threw a napkin on top of the puddle he'd made. Then he thrust out his chest and smiled as wide as the Brandenburg Gate.

Max turned, and he nearly lost control of his bladder.

Even though he saw exactly who he'd been expecting.

Adolf Hitler had walked into the courtyard of the Osteria Savasta.

CHAPTER
Forty-One

Adolf Hitler was the most average-looking man Max had ever seen.

He wasn't tall, or short.

He wasn't fat, or thin.

He wasn't handsome—but he wasn't so ugly that if you saw him on the street you'd stop and stare.

He was just . . . a guy.

Max was so stunned by this fact that he forgot to salute and shout "Heil Hitler!"

Which was good, because no one else was saluting or shouting, either.

Hitler was wearing his simple brown suit, which Max had seen a hundred times in newsreels and on posters. The suit was meant to signify that Hitler was still a man of the people, still the person he had always been. And seeing him here in the courtyard of the Osteria Savasta, Max had no trouble believing that. Adolf Hitler looked like one of the men who stood around outside the bars in Kreuzberg on warm nights, smoking cigarettes and telling inappropriate jokes, laughing into their mustaches.

Hitler shook Goebbels's hand, and then Hans Fritzsche's, and then he turned and gave Albert Speer a hearty handshake and a slap on the shoulder.

And then he turned to Max.

"And who do we have here?"

The Supreme Leader's voice was different in person. Not the pinched, nasal bray that came through on the newsreels or radio. It was deeper, and folksier.

Max had no idea how to answer Hitler's question. Nor did he have any confidence that he could speak at all.

Luckily, Goebbels spoke for him. "This, my Supreme Leader, is Max Maas. He is a radio genius who has come to work at the Funkhaus with us. Very promising. And a very good Nazi, if the reports from his Hitler Youth troop are to be believed."

"Excellent, excellent," said Hitler, sitting down. He had come in with an entourage of five or six other men—a personal secretary and a few Nazi officials Max did not recognize. Everyone took their seats.

Suddenly, Max saw the whole thing from a bird's-eye view. The way an angel might see it. Or the way Berg and Stein would.

Adolf Hitler, Supreme Leader of Nazi Germany, was sitting at the same table as Max.

Max Bretzfeld. Alias Max Maas. British spy. Jewish. Thirteen years old.

The absurdity of it, the surreality, the terror, threatened to fall on Max from above and crush him, like a train car dropped from the sky.

He had barely noticed that Hitler was speaking. And he was speaking about Max. Or, at least, about the "youth." He was quoting himself. "I always say that we old Germans are used up. We're just a bunch of windbags and hypocrites. We were raised on *weakness*! On old-fashioned Judeo-Christian morals. Speer!"

Albert Speer, sitting next to Max, had gone back to his sketching, so when Hitler barked his name, Speer was so startled he dropped his pencil to the ground. "Yes, my Supreme Leader?"

"Do you really believe the masses will ever be Christian again?" He didn't give Speer a chance to reply. "Nonsense! Never again. That tale is finished. They will betray their God to us. They will betray anything for the sake of their miserable little jobs and incomes." Adolf Hitler sat back in his chair with a small, satisfied grin on his face.

Every man there was shifting uncomfortably, or smiling and nodding a little too vigorously.

And Max wondered if Hitler hadn't just told the truth about them all—a truth they did not want to hear.

Max tried to collect himself and size up the situation. If he was going to assassinate Adolf Hitler, the best way would be to grab a knife from the table and stab it into his throat. He hadn't brought a weapon—not even a screwdriver—for fear of being searched before lunch by Hitler's bodyguards, who were probably waiting just inside the restaurant. Could Max pick up a table knife and get to Hitler's neck before someone grabbed him? Max thought he could. Maybe.

"Right!" Hitler clapped his hands. "Let's eat!"

Signora Savasta emerged from the restaurant with menus, but Hitler waved them away. "I'm too hungry to wait for everyone to study the menu. Spaghetti with marinara for me."

The signora went around to the rest of the table, quickly collecting everyone else's orders.

"So," Hitler began, looking at Max, but then he turned to address Goebbels. "What was his name?"

"Max, my Supreme Leader."

"Yes. Max, do you hope to rise through the Nazi ranks?"

Max said, "Yes, my Supreme Leader."

Max had decided that saying as little as possible, and always agreeing with Hitler, was the safest path. He put a napkin on top of his knife.

"Well, Max, would you like to know how *I* rose through the ranks? I was not always a Nazi, you know."

"Yes, my Supreme Leader. I would like to know very much," said Max. And he was not entirely lying.

Hitler took a sip of water, and everyone around the table

moved at the same moment. Max's eyes darted around. Everyone had assumed more comfortable positions. As if they knew that the Supreme Leader was going to start talking, and probably would not stop for a very, very long while. Hans Fritzsche put his hands in his lap and began to study them. Speer turned a page in his notebook and started a new sketch. Goebbels put his elbow on the table and his chin on his fist, his face frozen in a *How interesting!* expression.

The Supreme Leader was, Max suddenly realized, a man who loved the sound of his own voice.

And his luncheon guests were all men who, Hitler believed, loved it, too.

Max took this opportunity to move his napkin into his lap. With the knife hidden beneath it.

"Well, Max," said Hitler, "it all started because I was a spy."

And the Supreme Leader looked Max dead in the eyes.

CHAPTER
Forty-Two

Max didn't move.

Adolf Hitler, the Supreme Leader, was gazing at him, curiously. *Into* him.

Or maybe . . . *through* him?

And then, Max realized, Hitler wasn't looking at him at all. He was looking beyond him. To the past.

"The World War . . ." Hitler began, and then he instantly stopped and added, with a hint of glee, "the *first* one . . ." Because he had, after all, started the second one pretty much single-handedly. And he was winning it, too. Adolf Hitler savored that briefly, like it was a delicious morsel of food.

"The *first* World War had just ended, and I was a man without any direction. Any purpose. I think many of us felt that way in those dark days." He looked around the table, and all the men nodded obediently. "I was still working for the army. And there was a group in Munich that the army was worried about. A group of angry men, meeting in beer halls. They would get drunk and make speeches about the good old days, when Germany was great. They also liked collecting *guns*. Which is why the army was worried. So I was sent to listen to their speeches, and report back to my commanding officers if there was any threat from them to the German republic." Hitler snorted. All the men laughed dutifully. "Well, there *wasn't*. These beer hall men were pathetic and disorganized."

He leaned forward, putting an elbow on the table and tapping his chin. "*But* . . . I was surprised by some of the things they said. They said that Germany's defeat in the war wasn't Germany's fault. That it was the fault of a grand Jewish conspiracy, based in Russia and in London, to subjugate the whole globe to Jewish rule. I'll be honest, Max. I had never thought about any of this before. I had Jewish friends in the army. Well, not *friends*. One can't really be *friends* with a Jew."

Or, Max thought, *one can't really be friends with* you, *Adolf Hitler. Certainly none of these men here are. Laughing when you tell them to. That's not friendship.* He gripped the knife handle under the napkin.

Hitler was still talking: "But this idea, that we German soldiers hadn't lost the war—that the Jews had stabbed us in the back—this was a powerful idea! This was something! Another thing they talked about: Why was our government paralyzed by a state of futile bickering, instead of helping the German people? It was a Jewish plot to turn Germany communist! Led by the Jews in Russia and aided by those in London and New York! Yes! How satisfying! How clearly true!"

It was not clearly true, Max thought. *It wasn't true at all. It didn't even make sense: Why would Jews in London want Germany to be communist?*

"But here was the problem, Max." Now Hitler lowered his voice and put both of his hands flat on the table.

Max recognized this move from the newsreels of Hitler's speeches. And he realized, with a little bit of wonder, that Hitler was giving a speech. In the restaurant. While they waited for their spaghetti.

"Their ideas were good, and strong, and useful, Max. But the speakers? They were piss! They had a weapon that could mobilize all of Germany, if only they knew how to use it! So, even though I was supposed to be there as a spy, I asked, one evening, to speak. And I got up on that stage and I repeated everything I had been hearing, but in my own words. I don't think I added a single new idea that first evening in the beer hall. And yet my speech was met with rapturous, thunderous applause! There were only twenty or so men there, but they sounded like a *thousand* that night, Max!"

Hitler leaned back in his chair. It looked like he was remembering his first kiss. It was vaguely obscene. Max was actually embarrassed for him.

Also, as he leaned back, Hitler's neck was completely exposed.

But Max waited.

"Soon I was asked to speak again, and more men came, and posters were put up around town, and week after week I spoke, until hundreds and hundreds of men—and even a few women!—were packed into the Hofbrauhaus and were *chanting* my name. Oh, Max, you should have heard it." Hitler put the back of his hand to his forehead, like he was a movie starlet, and he was going to faint. "People have always told me I like to talk too much, Max. It is, perhaps, my little flaw." He smiled sheepishly, looking around the table as if asking for his audience's forgiveness.

Fritzsche and Goebbels and Speer and everyone else quickly said, "Oh, no! No!"

Hitler said, "It's true! From when I was a child they told me I would rather lecture someone than speak to them! But now, on the stage at the beer hall, I had found my calling. Instantly, I knew how to build a relationship with my audience! I knew what they wanted, I gave it to them, they lifted me up in waves of applause, I gave them more of what they wanted! It was ecstasy! The highest form of being, Max. You must understand. The philosopher Nietzsche said that we are to find what we are excellent at and pursue it ruthlessly. Well, Max, I found my talent, my purpose. I am a leader of men."

Hitler collapsed in his chair, letting his arms fling limply to his sides, as if he was utterly spent from this flight of oratory.

Now. Max could do it *now* . . . Except, a new thought was forming in Max's head . . .

Just then, Signora Savasta came out bearing plates and put the first one down in front of Hitler. "Excellent!" Hitler said, rubbing his hands together. He began shoveling forkfuls of spaghetti into his mouth.

An awful, terrifying idea was dawning on Max. Had Hitler built the entire Nazi party, and the whole Third Reich, this war machine, this nation of terror, because it made him *feel good*?

That's certainly what it looked like to Max. The Supreme Leader was sucking up his pasta, using his utensils as a bridge from his plate to his mouth.

Adolf Hitler had transformed Germany—through murder, terror, and lies—into a country where everyone was required to love the sound of his voice as much as he did.

All of these men, eating their spaghetti or lasagna or osso buco, were feeling transcendently good, Max noticed. Hitler had pushed his empty plate away now and was staring into the cloud-studded blue sky, grinning. He had marinara sauce like a red fringe on his mustache.

They had hoodwinked a nation into *serving* them. They had broadcast lies, big lies, grand narratives—not to make Germany great again, but to feed their egos, to line their pockets, to quiet their insecurities.

Max considered the table knife in his lap. Was it sharp enough to puncture the jugular vein in Hitler's throat?

And even if it could, would it stop the lies?

Or would it make Hitler a martyr?

Would the lies spread further, get stronger, grow bigger?

Max realized that a knife was not what he needed.

He needed an *antidote*. An antidote to these lies that Hitler told.

What was the antidote to Big Lies?

It was very simple. Obvious, even.

It had occurred to him standing under a streetlamp, Freddie's arm curved around Max's waist—feeling like the opposite of a caliper's sharp steel arm. The antidote to it, in fact.

The antidote to a big lie was its opposite, its inverse.

A small truth.

So Max knew the antidote.

Now what was he supposed to do with it?

CHAPTER
Forty-Three

Plates were being pushed aside; hands were placed on stuffed bellies. There was quiet murmuring going on around the table.

"You know," said Hitler, calling everyone's attention back to him, "I have made a very exciting decision. It's still top secret! We must put all of the plans in place. But it is definitely decided now."

Dr. Goebbels looked confused. "My Supreme Leader, have you discussed it with me? I'm afraid I don't know what you're referring to—"

"No, Joseph, I have *not* discussed it with you. I'm telling you now!" Hitler retorted. "I have not discussed it with anyone. But it is the only possible course of action. It is the *right* course of action. Strategically *and* morally."

An anxious stillness settled over the table. Albert Speer had put down his sketchbook. Max tried to look over Speer's shoulder to see what he'd been sketching. It appeared to be a series of buildings, with a hexagonal wall around it. Max realized, with a wave of horror, that Speer was sketching designs for a concentration camp.

"Everyone knows the source of the great global Judeo-Bolshevik conspiracy," Hitler announced. "Yes, there are powerful Jews in New York and London, of course. But the *real* threat, as I have always said, is elsewhere! We can conquer London, and neutralize New York, but Germany will never be safe until we have utterly obliterated Moscow!"

Everyone at the table started talking at once.

"But we're not at war with Russia!"

"This is how Napoleon was defeated!"

"We can't fight on the Eastern Front and Western Front at the same time!"

"There's too much terrain to cover!"

Hitler brought his fist down on the table. The silverware rattled and Albert Speer's glass fell over a second time.

"Listen!" Hitler hissed. "I have postponed Operation Sea Lion indefinitely. We will not be invading England anytime soon. The Luftwaffe's embarrassing performance has made that impossible. Our greatest, most evil, and most cunning enemies are in *Russia*! You have all read *The Protocols of the Elders of Zion*!"

Max looked quickly at Hans Fritzsche. *Didn't Hitler know that document was a lie?* Fritzsche's face had turned a ghostly shade of white.

Hitler went on: "We will never be at peace, we will never be the great nation we are destined to be, until we defeat Russia! Our military is superior to theirs by ten times! They have just a handful of tanks. We can wipe out their air force before it's off the ground. We shall attack as soon as the snows have cleared this spring!"

"This spring?! My Supreme Leader—!" Goebbels objected.

But Hitler raised a hand. Goebbels fell silent. "I have made up my mind," Hitler announced.

All color had drained from the faces of the men around the table. The entire German military strategy of the last hundred years had been to avoid fighting in the East and the West at the same time. Yes, Germany's military was superior to Russia's—but Russia was enormous, and had millions and millions of soldiers, and the winters there were brutal. That is what had ended Napoleon. Had Napoleon not invaded Russia, he might never have been defeated. This is what they were all thinking, Max was certain.

But Hitler was staring off into the sky again, and his face was hard as a gun.

Suddenly, Joseph Goebbels shoved his chair back from the table and stood up. And with every ounce of passion he had in his little body, Goebbels shouted, "Heil Hitler!"

Instantly, all the other men around the table stood up, too, and they saluted and shouted, "Heil Hitler! Heil Hitler! Heil Hitler!"

And the sound was so deafening that no one could tell that Max, also standing and saluting, was saying: "Ein Liter! Ein Liter! Ein Liter!"

CHAPTER Forty-Four

Max asked if he might ride back with Herr Fritzsche to his house. After spending three hours listening to Hitler, Max wanted to be with Freddie.

All through the drive, Fritzsche stared through the windshield, murmuring to himself: "*The ferocious panzers of the German army will roll across the Russian fields of wheat, eliminating the Bolshevik threat before it eliminates us all . . .*"

Max had spent enough time with Hans Fritzsche to know exactly what he was doing. He was writing a story to convince the German people to invade Russia. He was creating yet another Big Lie.

The sun had set when they arrived in Steglitz. The evenings were getting colder and longer. The end of the year was approaching. Freddie was thrilled with the surprise visit, and Max suggested they take a walk. He had no agenda, no mission, for once. He had come to love Freddie's company, but he had never *needed* it like he did now.

He had never imagined that his shoulders could feel *empty*.

He had never imagined that, once Stein and Berg were gone, he'd feel so *lonely*.

Max glanced left, then right, as they crossed Steglitzer Damm.

"You're getting good at that," Freddie said quietly.

Max turned his head quickly toward his friend. "What do you mean?"

Freddie smiled and kept walking down the empty sidewalk.

Max pushed Freddie, playfully, from behind. "What are you talking about?"

"When we first started hanging out, you always looked right first, then left."

Max's stomach lurched.

They were passing a small park. Max indicated it with his head, and they went in.

Freddie said, and his voice was not much louder than a breath, "Did you live in England your whole life?"

Max's heart was hammering the insides of his ribs.

"Or did you live in Germany first, and then go to England, and *then* come back?"

They were standing under a lamp, near a park bench. The bushes behind Freddie were tall and looked yellow on top and black underneath, because of the light from the streetlamp.

Max could strangle Freddie right here and leave his body in the bushes.

"I figure you probably lived here first, because your German is totally natural."

Max was nervously clenching and unclenching his hands.

"Max, I don't know what you're doing in Germany . . . but I don't care."

Max caught his breath.

"I won't tell my dad. Or anyone. I promise."

What if Freddie was lying? What if he told? Or let the truth slip accidentally? Max would end up in a torture chamber under the Reich Security Main Office. Or somewhere even worse.

"I don't know if you're a spy, or a saboteur, or an assassin." Freddie chuckled, as if that were a funny idea, Max being an assassin. "But I just don't care."

Max stared at Freddie's round cheeks, his lank blond hair, his freckles, each one of which was clear and light brown in the yellow lamplight.

"Okay, Max?" said Freddie. "I just wanted to tell you I know, Max. So *you'd* know. So you'd know that, between Germany and you, I choose you."

Max raised his hands to Freddie's throat.

And brought them to rest on his shoulders.

"I love you, Max," said Freddie. "As a friend. I love you."

Max replied, "Freddie, I love you, too." And he meant it.

The two boys embraced.

For a few moments, Max's shoulders didn't feel so bare.

CHAPTER Forty-Five

An hour or so later, Max arrived at his building, trudged up the stairs, entered his apartment—and froze.

Liesel was standing in front of him with her hands on her hips. Pastor Andreas was nowhere to be seen.

"What are you doing in here?" Max demanded. "Where is my uncle?"

Liesel's hair was wild and so was her expression. "Why do you get notes, hidden behind bricks, in the backyard of the church down by the canal?"

It was like Max had been swiftly kicked in the stomach.

"And why does this one say 'Prepare for exfiltration, three days' time, instructions to follow'?" She held up a small white square of paper. "What is 'exfiltration'?"

They wanted to exfiltrate him?

"Liesel," said Max slowly. They were standing face-to-face in the foyer of the apartment. "Where is my uncle?"

"Who knows?" she said nastily. "He hasn't come home yet today. But he left the door unlocked. All pacifists are stupid and trusting like that."

Max nodded. Good. They were alone.

Twice today, Max had considered killing someone and then changed his mind.

Liesel would not be so lucky.

"I'll tell you why I get those notes," said Max. "But it's not what you think." He walked to the kitchen area. "Are you hungry?"

"Tell me what 'exfiltration' is," Liesel demanded.

Max opened the refrigerator, as if he had all the time in the world, and took out a circle of cheese. He put it on a cutting board.

Then, from a wooden block, he took out a very large knife.

Liesel's eyes lingered on it. "That's a big knife for that little bit of cheese," she said.

Max was trying very hard to control his breathing. In. Out. He shrugged and gave Liesel a brief smile. He began to slice the cheese, and as he did he spoke. "Liesel," he said, "remember that little man in the green uniform who visited my apartment?"

"Yeah . . ." Liesel said, her body tense, watching Max work with the knife.

"Well, Liesel," Max went on. He had learned, during his time back here in Berlin, that using someone's name was a great way to control their attention. And to creep them out. "He works for the Abwehr. The military's spies. And I work for him. The place where I get notes behind bricks is a dead letter box. It's spy stuff. A hiding place for secret messages."

Liesel mulled this over. Then she demanded, "Why would you need a secret hiding place in Berlin? You could meet with the Abwehr anywhere, anytime!"

She was right. That part of the story made no sense. Max tried to think of a response—but he didn't have time, because Liesel was already on to the next question. "And what is happening in three days? Why won't you tell me what 'exfiltration' is?"

"It's . . . it's ending a mission," Max said quickly. Which was true. Specifically, it meant getting a spy out of enemy territory. But Max wasn't about to tell her that.

"If this is your secret way of communicating with the Abwehr," Liesel said, "then you won't mind me taking this letter to the Gestapo and showing it to them, right?"

Max didn't move. The cheese was all sliced.

"That's what I thought," said Liesel, and suddenly she turned and ran for the door. Max was after her in an instant, the knife in his hand. Liesel saw it, and her eyes went very wide, and she bared her teeth. She was at the door, but if she tried to open it, Max could lunge and drive the knife into her stomach.

So she didn't open the door. Instead, she grabbed the coat rack and shoved it at Max.

Max raised his arms and it bounced off of him—and Liesel was out the door and pelting down the stairs. Max ran out onto the landing. He thought, for a moment, about pursuing her and trying to stab her before she made it out onto the street. But she was too fast. And maybe . . . maybe he couldn't actually have stabbed her.

Maybe he wasn't a monster after all.

For a moment, Max stood there, listening to her feet slap the worn stone stairs: the beginning of a cascade of events that would lead to every member of the Gestapo, SS, SD, and Grüne Polizei searching for him. The end of his mission. Very likely the end of his life.

And then he thought: My mission.

Max ran back into the apartment, threw the knife on the kitchen counter, ran to the living room, and, with shaking hands, opened the cover of a sofa cushion. He removed a brown envelope with the words *Grand Finale* written on it in pencil.

What was on this record?

Cradling it carefully in one arm, he ran quickly down the stairs, across the street, and pressed the bell for apartment 2B four times.

Next, Max ran to the brick church, slipped behind it, scribbled a note on a piece of paper, and shoved it in the dead letter box.

It said, *EMERGENCY. EXFILTRATE. 9 P.M.*

That would give Max just enough time.

He started for the Funkhaus.

CHAPTER
Forty-Six

Max walked beneath the looming Funkhaus facade, toward the entrance. He tried to calm his breathing. The sky was already dark, but the birds were chirping loudly in the sycamore trees that lined the wide boulevard of Masurenallee. Max wondered if he would ever hear these birds again.

He wondered if he would ever hear any birds again.

When he arrived at the Funkhaus, he joined a steady stream of people passing the SS guards. It wasn't strange to arrive at this hour—the Funkhaus ran all night. Herr Fritzsche's program—*This Is Hans Fritzsche*—didn't even go on until 8 p.m.

Max glanced at the clock in the echoey, linoleum-floored lobby.

Seven thirty.

He took the stairs down to the basement, where, stretching to the left, was the corridor with the transmission room and the recording studios. Max went the opposite way. There was only a closet with cleaning supplies in this direction, and the technical supply room.

Max went into the supply room. It was a warren of tall

shelves and small wooden drawers. Max rummaged through a few different drawers until he found what he was looking for: a wire cutter, some screws, a screwdriver, and a dead bolt.

Then he hurried back into the hallway and walked toward Studio 4—the smallest recording studio, which was always empty at this hour. Studio 2 was only two doors away. In a few minutes, Hans Fritzsche would walk into Studio 2. At eight o'clock sharp the red broadcasting sign would light up and all of Germany would hear a smooth voice say, "This is Hans Fritzsche."

Except, not tonight.

Max slipped into Studio 4 and closed himself inside. It was dark in there, empty. He began to screw the dead bolt into the wood of the door.

It was hard work because his hands were sweating, and the screwdriver kept slipping and falling to the ground. He glanced up at the clock. Seven forty-two. He worked as fast as he could, but he didn't finish installing the dead bolt until nearly seven forty-eight. He turned the bolt, and then yanked on the door. It didn't budge. He yanked it harder. Just a rattle, and nothing more.

He hoped it would be strong enough.

Then he unlocked the door, turned off the lights, and slipped back into the hallway.

Max went to the transmitter room, closing the door behind him. He walked up to the humming bank of machines. He knelt, and then he unscrewed a panel just below a switch marked *Studio 4*. He unplugged a wire, and replugged it into another port. He replaced the panel.

Seven fifty-one.

Next, Max went to the opposite wall and lay down on the floor by a foot-long gray metal panel. He unscrewed it to reveal more wires—including a brand-new wire, wrapped in red fibers. Just where the air-raid siren schematic said it would be.

With the wire cutters, Max scraped away some of the red fibers. Then he scraped some black fiber off an electrical wire that passed nearby.

Finally, Max twisted the electrical wire and the air-raid siren wire together . . .

A *deafening* wail erupted from a speaker high up on the wall. The noise was sudden, violent, and it pummeled Max's eardrums, again and again and again. Max dumped his tools inside the wall and hastily shoved the panel back into place. He didn't bother replacing the screws.

He jumped up and ran into the hallway. The air-raid siren was even louder here, if that was possible. Max saw Hadamovksy screaming "Hurry!" against the deafening wail. People were running down the corridor, toward the stairwell, covering their ears. The air-raid shelter for the building was one level below this one, dug deep into the earth.

Max ran the opposite way. No one seemed to care. They were all too panicked, too disoriented by the siren, too determined to get to the shelter.

Max slipped back into Studio 4. He closed the door. The wailing was suddenly very distant. There were no air-raid sirens in the recording studios, of course, and the walls were soundproofed.

Max threw the dead bolt and turned on the lights.

There were no windows to the hallway. Windows ruin soundproofing. No one would know he was in here.

At least, not until the red broadcasting sign in the hallway lit up.

Max removed the square envelope from the small of his back. It was wet with sweat.

He opened the glass lid of the record player that was connected to the broadcasting console.

"Let's see what you are," he breathed.

Max placed the record on the record player. On the console was a large red switch covered by a plastic shield. He made sure that the switch was *not* in the broadcasting position. Not yet.

Seven fifty-five.

Max powered up the turntable and lowered the needle to the smooth edge of the record.

From the monitor speaker on the wall above Max's head, Max heard a hiss, and then a voice he knew very well. Winston Churchill. After every few sentences, someone translated his words to German.

Max listened:

What tragedies, what horrors, what crimes has Hitler committed in Europe and around the world! Consider the misery of the conquered peoples!

We see them hounded, terrorized, exploited. They are forced to work under slave-like conditions. Their goods are stolen. Their homes, their daily life are pried into and spied upon by the secret police, which, having reduced the Germans themselves to obedience, now stalk the streets of a dozen lands. Their religious faiths, their traditions, their culture, their laws, are persecuted and oppressed in the interest of a fanatic paganism devised to perpetuate the worship of a monster.

The brave people of Britain stand side by side with the British dominions beyond the seas: Canada, Australia, New Zealand, South Africa, the Empire of India, Burma, and our colonies in every quarter of the globe! We have drawn our swords in this cause and will never let them fall till life is gone or victory is won. We shall aid and stir the people of every conquered country to resistance and revolt! Together—

Max switched it off.

Ridiculous.

This was the Grand Finale?

Did they understand *nothing*?

Max knew instantly what Hans Fritzsche would say about it. How ironic, how hypocritical, for Churchill to criticize the Nazis for persecuting and oppressing other nations, destroying their traditions and religions, and then in the very next breath mention the colonies where the British had done exactly that!

The hypocrisy aside—this was *not* the way to change the minds of the German people. Perhaps changing their minds was impossible. But if there was an antidote to the Nazis' Big Lies, this wasn't it.

Max took the record off the turntable.

Seven fifty-nine.

He had one minute to collect his thoughts.

Forty-five seconds later, Max was lifting the plastic shield, flipping the red broadcast switch, and walking to the microphone.

CHAPTER
Forty-Seven

"Good evening, Germany," said Max.

It was embarrassing, hearing himself like this. He sounded like a *child*.

What would the seventy million people, all across Germany, be thinking right now? Would they be adjusting their sets? Turning them off?

Or would they be calling their families closer—because they could tell that something strange was happening?

Were they listening in that hotel on the Thames?

Was Hans Fritzsche? Was he listening down in the basement, sheltering from the supposed air raid? Or had he ignored the siren and gone into Studio 2 as scheduled? Did Hans Fritzsche think that *he* was broadcasting to his usual audience of seventy million Germans, plus the millions all over Europe who tuned in each night to hear the most urbane and intelligent of all Nazis explain the war to them?

Well, tonight, *Max* would be doing the explaining.

If he could manage to get a word out.

The microphone stood, like a giant eye, peering at him. Waiting.

"Usually," Max said, "my fellow Germans, you tune in at eight o'clock sharp to hear the voice of Hans Fritzsche. You expect him to inform you, to amuse you, and to tell you the truth. Well, you won't be hearing Herr Fritzsche's voice this evening. You'll be hearing mine. My name is Max. I work at the Haus des Rundfunks, helping broadcast your news and entertainment. I am only thirteen years old, as you can probably tell.

"Why does a thirteen-year-old work in the Haus des Rundfunks? Well, they say I am a *Funkmeister*. But I think the real reason is that the esteemed Herr Fritzsche is a kind man, a good man, and he took pity on this poor boy. I am deeply grateful to him for all he has done for me."

There. Now the listeners would be relaxing, settling in. This wasn't so strange. A special guest, praising their beloved Hans Fritzsche.

"I have the opportunity to tell you a story this evening. A true story that I witnessed with my own eyes, and that I will now relate to you without changing a single detail. It is a story about the German Reich, and the heroism of a German mother. A mother who can, through her strength, teach us all an important lesson."

Max took a step away from the microphone. His mouth was dry already. Speaking on the radio was harder than he'd thought. He found himself wanting to take big slurping breaths in the middle of sentences. Also, his legs were shaking.

He wondered where the Gestapo was now. Where the SS was. Where Commander Scheel was.

He wondered if the employees of the Funkhaus were listening to his broadcast in the bomb shelter right below his feet. If they were running upstairs to stop him. If, once they got here, the dead bolt would hold.

He stepped back to the microphonc.

"This German mother lives in a modest apartment, like so many of you. Her husband works on fine machine parts, until his hands ache and his eyes water. Her son is going to school, and this heroic German mother does everything she can to give him what he needs to be a success. During the day she takes in mending, to make a few extra pfennigs. She cooks at all hours, so there is always something warm for her husband and son to eat before they leave in the morning and when they come home in the evening. She is a model German woman. You all know someone like her. She may be your mother, she may be your sister, she may be you."

Max swallowed hard.

"One day, the son must leave home, to protect his people. Now this mother has a hole in her heart the size of her son. Many of you know *just* how this feels, don't you? Don't we all? But she continues, this strong German mother, to care for her husband and to work for Germany. She does her duty. She is the home-front hero we all must emulate!"

Max was doing his very best to imitate Hans Fritzsche: his cadences, his rhetorical questions, his invitation to the listener to imagine themselves in someone else's shoes.

"And then, my dear German friends, then one day, her husband goes off to work . . . and he does not come back. She does not know why, and she does not know where he has gone. She goes to his factory, but all they can tell her is that an SS truck came and picked him up. Why? What had he done? He is a good German! The workers at the factory don't know why he was arrested.

"This German mother goes to the police, but they will not help her. Her panic rises. Where is her husband? She goes to the SS office—they will not help her either. What has happened to him? Every day she returns to the SS office, begging to see her good German husband, begging to know what has happened to him, this desperate German mother. She will not give up. She has already lost her son. She cannot lose her husband, too!"

Max turned his head away from the microphone. Collected himself.

"Finally, after weeks of visits to the SS office, the good German mother breaks through. The SS officer on duty says, 'Fine! You want to see your husband?'

"Of course she does. So she gets into a car, and they drive.

They drive north. As they drive, she asks, 'Will I see my husband now?' 'Soon,' says the SS officer. And soon indeed they have arrived, just outside of Berlin, at a place with high concrete walls topped with barbed wire. The German mother asks, 'Will I see my husband now?' 'Soon,' the SS officer says again. She is taken through the wrought iron gates. 'Will I see my husband now?' He says, 'Take off your clothes and you can see him.' This German mother is afraid. What? Take off her clothes, in front of this stranger? But she has come this far. She must see her husband. So the proud German mother *strips off her clothes*. The SS officer won't turn away. She tries to keep her courage. 'Will I see my husband now?' she asks. He gives her the clothes of a prisoner and says, 'Put these on, and you'll see him.' So she puts them on. The SS officer takes her across a dusty field, where a large ditch has been dug into the ground. She is pleading with him: 'Will I see my husband? Will I see him now?' And finally, when they are standing just over the ditch, the officer says, 'Look! Don't you see him?' And he points down.

"The German mother looks down into the ditch. She sees a dozen corpses. And on top of the pile, she sees her husband, his eyes open, his mouth open. Dead. The German mother wails and says, 'What did he do? Why did you kill my husband?' The SS officer just hands her a shovel. 'Cover him up,' says the officer, 'unless you want to join him down there.' The German mother sticks her spade into the earth, says a silent prayer to God, and begins to bury him."

Max stopped. He wiped his cheeks with both palms. His nose was running, but he didn't dare blow it.

"Why am I telling you this, my fellow Germans? Why would I come on the radio, instead of your beloved Hans Fritzsche, to tell you such a *terrible* story? Because, my dear friends, this story is true. And that good German mother *is my mother.*"

When Max said this, his voice broke.

"She is my mother," he made himself go on. "And do you know, while she was shoveling dirt on her own husband, on *my father*, she turned to that SS officer and she asked him again, 'Why? What have we done? What have we done to deserve this?'

"And do you know what that officer said, my fellow Germans? My countrymen? My brothers and sisters? Do you know what he said? He said, 'You are Jewish.'

"And that was all he said.

"Listen, my friends, my fellow Germans. We all know someone who has ended up in one of these camps. We all have a friend who was forced to flee Germany, to become a penniless refugee in some nation across the sea. We all have a neighbor who had his shopwindows smashed. We all have a colleague who was put into the back of a truck and never seen again.

"Where are your friends? Your neighbors? Your colleagues? Why are they gone?

"You know why. Because the Nazis have laid a foundation of lies and built upon it a house of evil. And we, my fellow Germans, have built it with them.

"You have. And I have, too.

"Hans Fritzsche is not speaking tonight, but I am sure he will speak tomorrow. And he will tell you comfortable lies, to distract you, to enrage you, to quiet the doubts inside of you. All day long, you will hear such lies on this station, you will read them in the newspapers, you will see them on posters lining your street, you will hear from the mouths of your neighbors.

"But underneath all the lies, you *know* the truth: That a lie told often is still a lie. That a house built on lies cannot stand for long. And that we are all brothers and sisters of one race—the human race."

Max turned away from the microphone.

He took the headphones off.

Which is when he finally heard the banging on the studio door.

CHAPTER
Forty-Eight

He recognized the sound instantly. It was the way they always knocked.

BomBomBom

When they came for you.

BomBomBom

Three blasts in quick succession, like antiaircraft fire.

BomBomBom

And then he heard, "Max! Max, give it up! Come out now!" It was Commander Scheel.

Max walked to the door. His heart had taken up the beat of Scheel's pounding.

BomBomBom

As swiftly and quietly as he could, during the next burst of pounding, Max unlocked the bolt on the door.

BomBomBom

Scheel didn't notice.

BomBomBom

"It's open!" Max shouted.

BomBom—

The doorknob turned.

The door swung inward.

Looming in the doorframe was Commander Scheel, his two gray eyes glowering over his boxer's nose, his large body poised to leap.

But Max didn't see that.

He saw a dummy, stuffed with straw, with dozens of swastikas all over it.

And Max had already started to swing his foot forward with every ounce of strength he possessed, aiming right for the big red swastika between the Nazi's legs.

When Max's foot connected with Scheel's groin, the SD commander's mouth opened in a great O, and each of his eyes did, too, and his face became suddenly scarlet. Had he been the dummy in Lord Rothschild's workshop, Max was certain that his head would have exploded, confetti floating down around him.

Instead, Commander Scheel dropped to the ground, gripping his private parts with both hands.

Max stepped over Scheel's prostrate form and ran into the corridor. He looked left.

At that end of the corridor, two soldiers with rifles were waiting for him.

Max looked right. Two soldiers, rifles gripped in their white-knuckled hands, were waiting there, too.

Rifles, thought Max. *That was a mistake.*

He charged the two soldiers to the left, who were closer.

They raised their weapons, but neither fired because of the difficulty of aiming a rifle at close range—they were more likely to miss Max and strike one of their fellow guards at the other end of the hall. And clearly they had not expected a small boy to run directly at two armed soldiers. Max was already between them when they finally tried to turn their bulky weapons on him. But it was too late. Max looked up at the soldier, but he didn't see the man's face or the surprise in his eyes. He just saw lots of tiny swastikas. Max punched the swastika in the middle of the soldier's throat. He gurgled and fell to the ground.

Suddenly the other solider grabbed Max from behind. Max gripped one of the man's thick hands and dug his sharp thumbnail into the fleshy space between the soldier's thumb and forefinger. At first, all that happened was that the soldier started to choke Max. But Max kept working until he found the exact spot where Lord Rothschild had drawn the small swastika, and he applied all the pressure he could.

The soldier screamed in pain and let go of Max immediately. Max turned around and punched this soldier—a young, skinny man—in his large, protruding Adam's apple.

One of the soldiers from the far end of the hall was helping Commander Scheel get up, but the other was running down the hall at Max, shouting "Stop! Stop!"

Max did not stop. The elevator was in front of him. It briefly came to rest before reversing direction and beginning to rise again. Max ran toward it—and then took a sharp right at the stairs. He was not going to mess with that elevator. Not now.

The first floor was deserted because everyone was in the air-raid shelter, waiting for the British bombs to start falling.

Max flew through the lobby, out the unguarded doors of the Funkhaus, and into the dark street.

People on the sidewalk were staring. They *had* been staring at the building, wailing with air-raid sirens even though the public address speakers in the streets were silent. Now, though, they were staring at Max.

He saw Scheel's black Mercedes pulled up on the curb. Scheel's driver, wearing an SS uniform, was leaning against it. When the driver saw Max, he shouted and started for him.

Max sprinted away, down the block.

The driver shouted, "Stop him! Traitor! Stop the traitor!"

More voices joined the driver's shouts. The soldiers—and maybe Scheel himself—had made it outside.

Max wanted to turn a corner and try to get lost in the streets, but the Funkhaus was as wide as the whole block, and there were no alleys or side streets to duck into.

BANG!

A shot was fired into the air.

At least, Max *hoped* it was into the air.

"Stop that traitor!"

Scheel's voice. Not far behind.

He would be on top of Max in moments.

BANG!

"Stop, Max! Stop!" Scheel shouted, his voice hoarse and vicious. "I will shoot you in the back!"

Max stopped.

"Good, Max! Now, turn around . . . slowly!"

Slowly, Max turned around.

Scheel's face was crimson, sweat plastered his thin, blond hair to his forehead, his eyes were crazed—and he was grinning. He snarled. "Got you."

"No," said Max. "You didn't."

And he stepped off the curb, into the zooming traffic of Masurenallee.

"No! Max!" Scheel screamed.

A truck was barreling down the street. It wouldn't have time to stop. Its horn blasted, its brakes screeched, and Max went down.

Into the darkness.

CHAPTER Forty-Nine

Max landed on his butt with a wet slap.

The sewers were dark and stank of mold and human waste.

Max looked up at the large storm drain he had slipped through. The truck came to a shuddering halt above.

He heard Scheel's voice, calling down into the darkness. "Max? MAX!"

The space between the sidewalk and the top of the sewer grate was far too small for Scheel to get through, even if he managed to crawl under the truck. Max had scraped his stomach and neck and cheek sliding in. Scheel would never fit.

Max ran down the narrow walkway that bordered the sewer stream as Scheel's screams of "MAX!" echoed through the tunnels.

After a few minutes, Max came to an intersection where the sewer branched in three directions—one passageway angling off to the left, one straight ahead, and another to the right. Right would be approximately east. Max went that way.

His entire body hurt from the fall. And the stench made

it hard to breathe. He wished Stein and Berg were with him, to make jokes about it. But where they were now didn't smell much better. So he stopped feeling sorry for himself and tried to focus on orienteering through the sewers.

Every time Max came to a fork in the path, he tried to go east, or as close to east as possible. He tried to keep track of time in his head. Twenty minutes, forty minutes, an hour.

When he'd walked for an hour and a half, roughly due east, he stopped in front of a set of iron rungs that jutted out from the sewer wall and led up to a manhole cover. He began to climb.

Moving the manhole cover from below was brutally hard. It was very heavy, and Max needed to hold on to the iron rungs with one hand so he didn't fall. Eventually, he put one shoulder and the side of his head against the huge iron disc, and pushed as hard as he could with his right hand.

The manhole cover lifted, but scarcely an inch. Max pushed harder. Then he slid the iron disc sideways with a juddering sound, until a crescent of streetlight filtered into the sewer. He kept sliding it, until the crescent was large enough that Max could slip through.

It was night on a quiet street. He looked around.

Someone was staring at him. A woman holding two large shopping bags who had been about to enter her apartment building. When Max looked at her, she dropped them and ran inside. To call the police, Max was sure.

He walked away from the open sewer as quickly as he could, leaving the manhole cover where it was, to not draw any more attention to himself. He stayed close to the shopfronts and facades of apartment buildings.

He came to the corner of Rauchstrasse and Friedrich-Wilhelm-Strasse.

Max was impressed with himself. He was only a short walk from his intended destination.

He exhaled.

Which was when he heard the sirens.

Not air-raid sirens this time. Police sirens. And they were nearby.

Max started down Rauchstrasse, trying to stay in the shadows without *looking* like he was trying to stay in the shadows. It was not easy.

The sirens were swirling just a few streets away.

Max came to a broad, dark boulevard—Drakestrasse—with imposing buildings guarded by black iron fences.

A soldier was standing in the middle of the block.

Max hesitated—and then walked up to him fearlessly.

The soldier was not wearing a German uniform. He was wearing an Irish one. He looked down at Max and said, in German distorted by a heavy Irish accent, "Can I help you?"

Max replied, in barely accented English, "I caught this morning morning's minion."

The soldier looked very surprised for a very short instant,

and then he stepped aside, and Max walked into the grounds of the Irish Diplomatic Mission. The soldier locked the iron gate and hurried after him.

Another soldier wearing the tall steel helmet of the Irish army stood blocking the doorway. But the solider from the gate said, "Ultra urgent. Open the door *now*."

Max was let into the fine lobby of the Irish Mission as his soldier sprinted up a curving staircase, and the soldier who'd been guarding the front door locked it behind them.

A minute later, a very short man with bleary eyes hustled down the stairs. "Who are you?" he asked.

Max repeated the passcode, a line written by Gerard Manley Hopkins, the great English poet who had lived and died in Ireland: "I caught this morning morning's minion."

"Yes, I know what you said. Who *are* you?"

"My name is Max Bretzfeld." The taste of his own, real name in his mouth was both strange and unutterably sweet. "I work for Ewen Montagu."

The man shoved his arm out and shook Max's hand quickly and vigorously. "William Warnock," he said. "Come on, let's get you to the safe room."

Max was taken up the stairs to a beautiful little library. William Warnock pulled the spine of a book on one of the bookcases, and Max heard a *click*. The bookcase swung open. An actual false wall, hiding a secret room. Like something in a movie.

Max had to smile.

Inside was a small cot, a table, and a radio transmitter with a Morse code key. Warnock sat down at the radio, put on headphones, and began hammering out a message.

Once he'd finished, he turned to Max. "It's not usually safe to use this—the Germans have vans that circle Berlin, looking for illegal radio transmissions." Max knew that. They were called the Funkabwehr, the radio spies, and they were the reason Chumley and Montagu hadn't let Max communicate with them via radio. Warnock went on: "But this time, I had to risk it." Then he held up a warning hand. Someone was responding to his transmission. He wrote down the letters as they came through.

S-E-N-D—V-I-A—A-M-L-A-U-N-D-R-Y—O-V-E-R

Warnock nodded and put down his pencil. "Just as I figured. We'll put you in the bottom of our laundry van tomorrow morning."

Max sighed deeply.

He was getting out.

That night, Max ate beef stew with soda bread at the table in the safe room of the Irish diplomatic mission, while William Warnock perched on the edge of the cot. "So," asked the Irishman, "I know I'm not supposed to ask you anything about your mission, but I can't resist . . . Was that *you* on the radio tonight?"

Max put down his spoon. “You heard it?”

“Indeed I did. All of Germany heard it.”

Despite Max’s exhaustion, and all of the death-defying things he had done in just the last few hours, he nevertheless felt nervous when he asked, “So . . . how was it?”

William Warnock said, “Max. It was *brilliant.* There’s nothing so intimate as radio, I always say. The sound of your voice, jiggling tiny bones and hairs in the ears of every German, sending your message directly into their brain. I think you made a real difference with that broadcast.”

Would it shake Germany free of the Big Lies that were drowning it?

Of course not.

But at least he had done *something.*

“Did they write that in London for you?” William Warnock wanted to know. “Because you delivered it like you really *were* talking about your own mum and dad.”

Suddenly, Max’s eyes were flooded with tears. Tears he had held back for so long.

“Couldn’t you tell? I was.”

They didn’t speak much after that. But William Warnock didn’t leave the room until Max had curled up under the starchy linen of the cot and fallen asleep.

CHAPTER
Fifty

It was before dawn the next morning when Max was taken out with the laundry and loaded into the van. They moved the piles of dirty sheets and bedspreads out of the way and opened up what appeared to be the right wheel well—but was actually a secret compartment. Max climbed in and folded his body into the small space. William Warnock said, "Stay quiet, and good luck, Max. Know that not a single German slept well last night because of what you've done." Max nodded, and the cover to the compartment was closed.

Max spent the next two hours in darkness, as the truck rumbled from one stop to another, picking up linens. He even dozed off, a few minutes at a time. Whenever he did, he had horrible dreams, of barbed wire and high walls and dirt yards and ditches full of bodies.

Finally, the brakes squealed and the engine was cut. Max heard the back of the truck open, and he waited.

And waited.

And waited.

And then, at last, the cover was opened, and a woman Max

had never seen before helped him out of the secret compartment and down from the back of the van.

They were in a garage, and there was a plum-colored Mercedes sedan parked beside the laundry van. The back door was open and the back seat was lifted, revealing another secret compartment. Max got in without a word. The woman handed him a glass bottle of milk and a half loaf of bread. Then she lowered the seat, and Max was once again plunged in darkness.

They drove for hours. Max tried to drink the milk, but he was lying down and the car was moving and it sloshed all over his face, leaving him sticky and smelling. He had a few bites of the bread. Then he closed his eyes and slept and dreamed of a skeletal woman in prisoner's clothes. The same dream he'd been having every night this week.

Max's eyes jerked open. They had stopped, and there were voices outside the car. Men. Shouting. German soldiers.

The engine was cut, and he heard the driver get out. Then he heard all the doors open, and the trunk, too.

They were searching the car.

Max began to pray: *Please, God, let me fulfill my promises. Don't let her down now, when I am so close.*

But God must not have heard his prayers.

Because the back seat was lifted, and the dim light of evening framed the face of a German officer, staring straight down at Max.

CHAPTER
Fifty-One

Max's eyes adjusted to the sudden light and the backlit face.

He saw that the German officer wore glasses that looked like two moons.

And he heard the officer say, very quietly, *"Almost there, Max."*

And then Alexis von Roenne closed the seat again and shouted, "Wrong car! Keep looking! I want *every car* searched, do you hear me? *Every car!*"

Von Roenne had pieced it all together. Where Max would have gone from the Funkhaus. How the Irish would try to get him out. Which highway their car would take to the coast. How he could buy Max more time.

Of course he had.

A minute later, they were moving again, very fast, and the woman who was driving was playing the radio loudly and singing, and the sticky milk on Max's face was being washed away by tears of gratitude and relief.

It was pitch black when his driver pulled up the seat and helped Max up and out. There was a distant light, and the sound of a foghorn, and the smell of the sea. She hurried him down a long dock to a small white fishing boat, and without a word she ushered Max below, into the hold.

Max lay down, and they threw blankets over him. He closed his eyes again. He remembered the last time he'd crossed the channel by boat. He wondered if, when he opened his eyes again, Stein and Berg would be sitting on his shoulders once more.

He hoped not.

He missed them. But he didn't need them anymore.

And she did.

CHAPTER
Fifty-Two

They were waiting for him at the dock.

Two men, one tall and one *very* tall, and one young woman; they were framed by pale blue on the eastern horizon, crowned by a million stars overhead. Max began walking toward them—and then he stopped walking and started to run.

Just before he collided with Uncle Ewen, Max managed to stop himself. Ewen looked down at Max with that same old crooked smile. Max was glad it was so dark because it allowed him to believe that Ewen couldn't see the tears coursing down his cheeks.

After a long, warm handshake with Uncle Ewen, Max turned to Jean. She just smiled at him with her beautiful, crooked teeth and lightly punched his shoulder. And yet, as light as the punch was, his legs wobbled.

Last, Lieutenant Chumley pumped Max's hand up and down while whispering, *"Good on you, Max. Good on you."*

They rode in a car together, Chumley driving, Jean and Ewen in the back, and Max enjoying the view from the front seat. The sun rose, and they stopped for breakfast at an inn and sat outside, despite the frigid December weather. They told Max all about how the war was progressing—badly—and how the Blitz was going—bombs fell on London every night and every day—and how the Montagu family was safely away in the South.

But they had not uttered a word about the mission. Not yet. It wasn't permitted.

Max needed an official debriefing.

Which is why they were heading to Camp 020.

They steered through the South Downs—steep hills that were impossibly green, studded with white sheep. Lieutenant Chumley switched on the radio.

A chorus of voices blasted from the speaker, backed by swelling strings, and then there was an impossibly high female voice, like the scream of a battle angel appearing out of the heavens—and finally, Vera Lynn, "Sweetheart of the British Army," started singing "Land of Hope and Glory" to the tune of "Pomp and Circumstance."

Land of hope and glory . . .
Mother of the free
How should we extol thee
Who are born of thee?

Chumley tapped on the steering wheel and hummed along. The song was plodding like a military march, and goopy-sweet like a mouthful of honey.

Wider still and wider
Shall thy bounds be set
God who made the mighty
Make thee mightier yet!

Max found himself imagining what Hans Fritzsche's commentary would be: "Britain calls *us* aggressors? How much farther can their *bounds be set*? And what people have they not enslaved, in order to make themselves *mightier yet*?" Max began to fidget uncomfortably in his seat as the chorus was repeated:

Wider still and wider
Shall thy bounds be set . . .

Jean leaned forward and tapped Lieutenant Chumley on the shoulder.

"Turn it off, would you?"

As they turned into the drive and passed the guardhouse, Max thought of how nervous he'd felt the last time he'd come here, and how it was only Stein and Berg's constant patter that had distracted him enough to bear the fear. This time, he had nothing to fear. He wasn't a suspected spy, and he wasn't here to face interrogation.

He was a hero.

This was made instantly clear by Admiral Godfrey, who burst through the front door of the central building and shook

Max's hand vigorously. "Well done, you! Bloody well done! Back home, safe and sound! Well, I never would have believed it!"

"You thought I would die?" Max asked wryly.

"Or worse!" Admiral Godfrey laughed. "Absolutely worse!"

Then Max said, "I'm sorry I didn't play the record—"

Godfrey hushed him. "Not now, Max. Not now." But he winked at Max and his face was stretched wide with a smile. He was clearly not concerned about the record.

Tin Eye Roberts was standing behind Admiral Godfrey. He was shorter and uglier than Max remembered. But he, too, was grinning. "Welcome home!" he barked. "Look at this young man! Shake hands, Max! Shake hands!"

So Max shook hands.

"This way, this way!" Tin Eye gushed, leading Max down the hallway, as the other military men followed. Jean hadn't come inside.

They came to the same room they had used before. Max said, "I thought maybe we'd do the debriefing somewhere nicer this time. Now that I'm not a suspect."

"Just procedure! That's all! That's all!" Tin Eye laughed. And he had Max stand just where he'd stood before. There were four chairs now, and Godfrey, Ewen, and Chumley all sat down.

Tin Eye remained standing. "So, Max," he said, grinning and putting his hands on his hips, "tell us *everything*."

CHAPTER Fifty-Three

This time, the room felt more like a stage than an interrogation chamber. A large reel-to-reel tape recorder was running in the corner, and Chumley made an occasional note, but mostly the men grinned and nodded and groaned sympathetically as Max emptied that dark place underneath the stairs, one memory at a time.

He began with the parachute landing—Admiral Godfrey murmured, "Tragic, tragic," at the death of Major Johnny Jameson—and Max proceeded day by day from there, as best he could remember.

And Max remembered *very* well.

Throughout, Tin Eye would say things like "Is that *just* what he said, Max? If you're not sure, no need to invent dialogue for us." But Max usually did remember exactly what everyone had said. At least, the important things.

When Max told them about Melita Maschmann, and how she managed not to think about the Polish and Jewish peasants she was putting on train cars, Tin Eye gritted his teeth and said, "The Germans are *bloody* animals!"

And when Max revealed how Joseph Goebbels had come into the transmitter room while Max was fiddling with the wires, Uncle Ewen banged his thigh with an open hand and said, "Great Scott, Max! That took courage!"

Chumley scribbled ferocious notes and muttered, "Good! Good!" as Max described how the Funkhaus worked, from their policies to the technical details of the transmitter.

But it was the luncheon with Hitler that fascinated them the most. Max had to describe everything twice. And when he told them that Hitler had decided to invade Russia, he had to repeat that *four* times, to be sure he got each detail right. "He said it would take place in *spring*, is that correct? Spring of *1941*? You're sure?" Tin Eye demanded.

"I can't believe it. I just can't," Admiral Godfrey muttered to Uncle Ewen. "Has the man not read a page of history in his life? A two-front war would be catastrophic for them! It's madness!"

Finally, Max got to the end of his story. He was hungry and tired. It must have been past dinnertime now. His legs were aching. He wanted to ask for a chair, but he knew that would be "against procedure."

The men were shifting in their seats, glancing at one another. Tin Eye was paging through a dossier. Finally, he looked up. "You know, Max, there are those here in Britain who wonder *why*. *Why* would the average German collaborate with this gang of murderous lunatics? What you described Melita Maschmann doing, for example. That would require the participation of *hundreds* of German men and women. Maybe *thousands*. And that's just in Poland! *Why* do millions of Germans collaborate with terrorists and murderers?"

Tin Eye added, "Personally, I think the answer is rather obvious. It's the utter moral depravity of the German race!"

Max winced. He was getting *very* tired of people talking about other "races."

"But *some* among us," Tin Eye went on, casting a sidelong glance at Ewen, "seem to think that further explanation is necessary. So tell me, Max. Having made it into the heart of the German propaganda machine, did you gain any insight as to *why*, Max? What did the boy genius discover that can solve *that* riddle?"

Uncle Ewen uncrossed his legs, put his hands on his knees, and leaned toward Max. Lieutenant Chumley put down his pen and raised his long chin. But Admiral Godfrey and Tin Eye regarded Max with skepticism, clearly expecting that he would have no answer.

Max wondered when they would stop underestimating him.

CHAPTER Fifty-Four

Max said, "How many Germans are there?"

Lieutenant Chumley answered immediately. "Just over seventy million in Germany proper."

"Seventy million Germans," Max said. And then he said: "Seventy million reasons to collaborate."

The folds of Admiral Godfrey's skin became a series of concentric frowns, from his hairline down to the bottom of his neck.

Tin Eye said, "Explain."

So Max explained.

He started with Pastor Andreas. "He hates the Nazis, but he has to be very careful. There are Gestapo informants in his apartment building, in his congregation, among the pastors at his church. He resisted the Nazis by helping us—but in every other aspect of his life, he collaborates. He doesn't know what else to do."

He went on to the Persickes. "Frau Persicke loves the Nazis because she believes they have made Germany great again, just as they promised. Also, they hate all the same people she hates. Jews, Black people, the French . . . it's a long list.

"Liesel Persicke is a fanatical Nazi because it gives her power. Over her neighbors, and her family. And especially over her mother, whom she could inform on at any time.

"I don't think Herr Persicke cares much about politics, but he certainly likes the watch repair shop that the Nazis took from a Jew and *gave* him for free.

"Herr Pfeiffer hates the Nazis, but he's too terrified to resist. I think he hopes to escape to Australia one day." Max did not explain why Herr Pfeiffer wanted to go to Australia. He didn't think they would understand.

"Melita Maschmann grew up feeling like a useless rich girl, despised by even the people who worked for her family. Now she feels useful, a part of something greater. She loves the National Community—and works *very hard* to never think about all the people who aren't included in it. Or who are murdered by it.

"Herr Hadamovsky went from being a car mechanic to running the most important radio station in Germany. Albert Speer went from being a nearly broke nobody to a world-famous architect. Herr Berndt is a pathological liar and now he gets paid handsomely for it."

Maybe this was an oversimplification. Maybe they all were. Maybe there were as many reasons *inside of each* German as there were Germans. But Max wasn't about to stop.

"Gustav Adolf Scheel fears, deep down, that he is stupid. He tries to prove that he isn't—to himself and everyone else—by frightening and murdering people.

"Joseph Goebbels was bullied as a child. Now he has a bully of his own, someone who actually believes in him. Even if his family won't speak to him anymore."

Based on the range of their expressions, the men seemed to rate Max's analysis somewhere between amusing and astonishing. Finally, as Max had apparently run out of Germans, Uncle Ewen quietly asked, "And Adolf Hitler? Why is *he* a Nazi? Or is that a stupid question?"

Max said, "It's not a stupid question. I think Hitler first joined the Nazi party because he loves the sound of his own voice, and he finally found some other people who did, too. But now it's more than that. Hitler has convinced millions and millions of people to admire him. To *love* him. If *that* was the reward, wouldn't you be a Nazi?"

Silence hung over the room. At last, Ewen said, "And all it costs is a world war and the deaths of millions."

Max shrugged. "To feel proud, comfortable, and loved, we humans will do and believe *anything*."

Uncle Ewen folded his lips in on themselves.

Lieutenant Chumley was nodding, very slowly.

Admiral Godfrey looked at his hands.

But Tin Eye expostulated, "There is *one* more thing, Max!" As if he'd just remembered a question he forgot to ask. "What is *your* reason?"

Max was momentarily lost. "Uh . . . my reason for what?"

"Well, you explained why all of these people collaborate

with the Nazis . . ." Tin Eye was now peering cruelly at Max. All the other faces in the room had turned to ice.

And suddenly, Max realized that this was *not* a stage. It *was* an interrogation chamber.

"What's *your reason* for collaborating with the Nazis?"

CHAPTER Fifty-Five

Max had no idea what to say.

"Oh, come on, Max," Tin Eye murmured as he strolled around the room. "You don't think we're *quite* that easily fooled, do you? So tell us. Why are *you* helping the Nazis?"

"I . . . I'm not!" Max protested.

"DON'T BLOODY LIE TO ME!" Tin Eye thundered with such sudden ferocity that Max stumbled backward. His exhausted legs momentarily gave out and he had to catch himself against the back wall. In an instant, Tin Eye was next to Max. He grabbed Max's arm and straightened him up again. Then he kept holding on to Max with fingers that seemed to be made of battleship rivets. "There are holes in your story a mile wide! Or perhaps not a *mile* wide. But a few hours here, a few *days* there." Tin Eye now got very close to Max's ear and spoke very quietly and very crisply. "Yes. Perhaps the hole in your story is three days wide, and about five feet, four inches tall."

"I really don't know what you're talking about," said Max.

"I find it *strange*," Tin Eye replied, "that, in *everything* you told us, you never *once* mentioned a certain lieutenant colonel of the Abwehr. This lieutenant colonel's name is Alexis von Roenne. Does that ring a bell, Max?"

Max inhaled very slowly and very quietly and very deeply through his nose.

"You didn't mention Lieutenant Colonel Alexis von Roenne, Max, even though he was interviewed on the radio the *same day* you started work at the Funkhaus. But perhaps you just didn't cross paths?"

Max kept his teeth clenched together.

"You didn't mention *why* you were at the Reich Security Main Office when you bumped unexpectedly into Commander Gustav Scheel. The Reich Security Main Office, which just *happens* to be the same building where Lieutenant Colonel Alexis von Roenne works."

Max tried to make his face as still and blank as a pair of full-moon spectacles.

"You didn't mention that Lieutenant Colonel Alexis von Roenne *visited your apartment building*! *Why* did he do that, Max?"

Max didn't answer. He thought of his interview with von Roenne, in his office.

Tin Eye ground on: "Is it because you are *working* for the Abwehr? For German intelligence?"

Max thought about what von Roenne had said: *I* hate *the Nazis, and* I hate Hitler.

Tin Eye was merciless: "Did von Roenne *turn* you, somehow? For money? For country? For family? *Why*, Max?"

Von Roenne had also said: *Do not tell him my secret.*

So Max wouldn't. He would protect it. He would keep it in the darkest recess of that space under the stairs.

"Or is it what I always suspected, Max? Is it that von Roenne has your parents, and you are working for him, in exchange for their lives? Have you hoodwinked us, while you've been *working for German intelligence all along*?"

And if Tin Eye started rummaging through the cellar, as he was now . . . well, Max would put something in front of von Roenne's secret, and when Tin Eye found that something, he'd think he'd found it all.

Max's eyelids were half shut. Flatly, he said, "No, I don't work for German intelligence."

"NO!?" Tin Eye bellowed. "Well, then let me ask you one more question. And before you answer, I want you to think very carefully. You put an urgent note into your dead letter box, posing the *ludicrous* request for permission to assassinate Hitler. You gave the emergency signal by ringing the bell four times on the building across the street. And then, Max, you did not check the dead letter box for *three days*. *Three days*, Max. During those three days, you did not appear at the Funkhaus. You did not appear on your street. You did not even appear *in Berlin*.

"So, Max, the question I have for you is very simple: *Where did you go for those three days?*"

Max gazed at Tin Eye Roberts.

He glanced at Uncle Ewen, who was chewing his lips and looking worried.

And Max said, “I thought you’d never ask.”

CHAPTER
Fifty-Six

“You’re right about Alexis von Roenne,” Max said.

A sneering grin of victory spread across Tin Eye’s toad-like face. Uncle Ewen put his head in his hands.

“And you’re wrong.”

Ewen looked up.

“I got to know him very well. But I never worked for him, or for the Germans.”

“Why on *earth* should we believe you?” Tin Eye snapped.

Max said, “They call him Hitler’s favorite intelligence officer—and I understand why. He is very clever. He figured out who I was right away. He connected the double harness in the field to the report that a kid—me—was walking through the streets at three in the morning, and figured out the rest himself.”

Chumley let out a little gasp. Admiral Godfrey cursed.

To Uncle Ewen, Max said, “He thinks you’re a worthy adversary.” Slowly, the half-cocked smile appeared on Ewen’s face.

Tin Eye growled, “So did he arrest you? Did he turn you?”

“No,” said Max. “Despite being on the other side of the war, he’s a good man. I confessed that you’d sent me back to

Germany to spy on the Funkhaus, but he didn't seem to care much about that. He wanted to know why I would agree to such a mission. Eventually, I told him. I came to Germany to find my parents. So he took me to them."

"I met him at five in the morning, right after I left the note in the dead letter box. He picked me up near my apartment and we drove north, out of Berlin, headed toward the Sachsenhausen concentration camp. As we drove, he told me our cover story. We were to pretend that I, under my assumed name Max Maas, was an informant for the Abwehr, and that I had information about anti-Nazi activities undertaken by Miriam Bretzfeld.

"We would tell the officials that von Roenne wanted me there when he questioned her so I could expose her lies. She was supposed to have been involved in the distribution of pro-British propaganda pamphlets. Von Roenne claimed he wanted to know her source for these pamphlets, because he was looking for British agents in Berlin. He made the accusation both convoluted and banal, in the hope that the camp officials would not report the interview up the SS chain of command.

"After a few hours of driving, we arrived in the little town of Oranienburg. Von Roenne offered to buy me breakfast at a local cafe, but I couldn't eat. My stomach ached—but not with hunger.

"Just before nine o'clock we got back in his car and drove down a long access road, to the gates of the camp."

"What's it like, Max?" Uncle Ewen asked.

Tin Eye turned furiously on Ewen, and Max knew Ewen had broken protocol by asking a question. So he knew that, for some reason, the question must be very important to Ewen.

"It's huge," said Max. "I couldn't believe how big. It's shaped like a triangle, but each side must be half a mile long."

"Don't exaggerate!" Tin Eye snapped.

"We have aerial photos, Roberts," Ewen said. "Each side is around six hundred yards. Max isn't far off."

Tin Eye glowered at Max.

The child spy continued. "The walls are white and solid and high, and topped with barbed wire. There are three watch-towers on each side. We came to a gatehouse, just beyond the walls, which looked like a big, cream-colored country home. In the center of this gatehouse was a tall gate, and in wrought iron were the words ARBEIT MACHT FREI. Work Will Set You Free."

Ewen shut his eyes and said, "A play on Jesus's maxim: 'The truth will set you free.' "

"Well, that's sinister," Chumley muttered as he chewed on the stem of his unlit pipe.

Max continued. "We were let through the gate, and parked in a grassy lot next to one of the walls. It's weird to think about—a concentration camp having a parking lot. But they do. Then we went inside.

"The first thing you see is a huge open area. Enormous. And I saw hundreds and hundreds—maybe thousands—of prisoners, standing at attention. Some were wearing blue prison uniforms. Others were in brown sackcloth. They looked like they had been standing for a long time, because I saw someone fall down. The people around him tried to pick him up, but I saw soldiers running and shouting at the man who had fallen. Then we were taken inside, and I couldn't see what happened to him."

Max himself had been standing for a very long time. No one remarked on this fact.

"In the office building, there was a small receiving area where an officer sat behind a high desk. Von Roenne did all the talking. He told them exactly what we had discussed as our cover story. He showed his credentials. A higher-ranking officer was brought out, and he and von Roenne talked for a long time. Then the officer went away, and when he came back, he led us down a narrow hallway to a small room." Max looked around. "Very much like this one."

This made Tin Eye shift his weight uncomfortably.

"We sat down on one side of a table, and there was a chair on the other side of the table. They told us to wait. We did. We waited for a very long time. Neither of us spoke. All I could think about was those prisoners in the yard. Were my mother and father among them?

"We sat there for more than an hour. And then the door opened, and the officer walked back in. We stood up. He said, 'We have located your suspect.'

"And my mother walked into the room."

CHAPTER
Fifty-Seven

Max inhaled, and exhaled. Tears were brimming all around his eyes. He felt his nose running.

"She looked like a skeleton."

He heard Ewen suck in his breath.

"They had shaved her head. She wore a shirt and pants with blue stripes, and a number was stitched over her heart. My mother always used to have a soft face—I had never seen her jaw or her cheekbones. But now I could. She used to have gold teeth, in the front on the bottom of her mouth. They were gone. Her gums behind her lower lip were bare, and turning black. And I could see all around her eyeballs. The skin had shrunken away from them. But her eyes were still a beautiful hazel color, and they widened when she saw me.

"I wanted to run to her . . . and also to run away from her. She was my mother, but she looked . . . *ghoulish*. I felt so guilty—I still feel guilty—for my emotions right then. But I didn't run to her and I didn't run away. The SS officer was watching.

"Von Roenne pointed to the chair across from us and said, 'Please.' My mother sat down.

"Finally, the SS officer left us. He closed the door. My mother reached her hand across the table. I glanced at von Roenne. He nodded. I took her hand. It was so dry, and thin. Like sticks wrapped in paper. I won't ever forget how it felt.

"And my mother, staring at me with huge, haunted eyes, said, 'Maxy, for God's sake what are you doing here?'

"I told her I had wanted to see her. But she wanted to know what I was doing back in Germany, when they had worked so hard to get me out. I told her that I couldn't explain, not here, but that I was safe. I was protected by powerful people now, I said. And I wanted to come and see her. I begged her to tell me about Papa. Was he all right?

"She became very quiet. Then she told me the story that I told on the radio."

Tin Eye said, "The German mother? She really *was* your mother?"

"Yes," said Max. "They brought her to Sachsenhausen and made her bury my father." Max sniffed violently, a ripping, phlegmy sound. "Work will not set you free. Not that kind of work."

"Please, tell us more," said Ewen.

So Max told them more. He told them that the Jews were separated from everyone else, in their own barracks, but all the prisoners mustered in the yard every morning and every night. Every prisoner, Jew and non-Jew alike, was starving to death. They were crammed into bunkbeds, two prisoners on top and two below. One morning his mother had woken up to find that the woman lying next to her was dead.

"They are experimenting with different ways to kill us, she told me. There is a room where prisoners were taken for 'measurements,' a room no larger than a closet. You are told to stand straight so they can measure you, and then a rifle is inserted through a hole aimed right at the back of your neck, and you are shot. But the soldiers complained that this took too long, and was a pain to clean up. So they are trying other methods. Having prisoners dig deep ditches, and once they've dug deep enough, they are shot. Then other prisoners bury the bodies in the ditch. This is currently the most effective method, but it's bad for morale. It makes the prisoners refuse to work. So they are trying others. Someone told her they were experimenting with poison gas.

"She also said that there is a crematorium, where the bodies who aren't buried are burned. As the prisoners stand at attention each evening the ashes of dead friends and family members float up from the chimneys and land on their clothes."

"For God's sake," Admiral Godfrey muttered.

"All right," Tin Eye said, "that's enough. We don't need all the details."

"Yes, we bloody well do," Ewen snapped. "Max, is there more?"

Max said, "I didn't tell you about the children."

Chumley murmured, "Dear God."

Max told them how the children had been taken away from their families, and were kept in a basement room, with a thin window at the top. Doctors drove up from Berlin to do experiments on them. And when the experiments were over, the children's bodies were carted out of the basement by the adult prisoners and taken straight to the crematorium.

Admiral Godfrey had crossed his arms in front of his body and was covering his mouth with his hand.

Lieutenant Chumley had chewed his pipe stem so hard he'd broken it. The mouthpiece was lying on the floor under his chair. He was still chewing on what remained of the pipe.

Tin Eye was pacing behind their chairs, as if he could get away from the truth if he just walked fast enough.

And Uncle Ewen . . . well, Max could not interpret the expression on Ewen's face.

"We stayed in a hotel in Oranienburg," Max said. "And we returned the next day, and the next. I got to see my mom for three straight days."

"And then?" Tin Eye demanded. "Did you get her out? Did this kindhearted Nazi von Roenne save your mother?"

Max stared incredulously at Tin Eye. "Of course not."

"No? Why not? Are you telling me that 'Hitler's favorite intelligence officer' and Max the Boy Genius couldn't find a way to save one bloody woman from a concentration camp?"

"This isn't a story I'm making up so you can feel good," Max said quietly. "It doesn't matter how smart von Roenne is, or how lucky I am. No one is escaping from the concentration camps unless it's through a smokestack."

There was not enough air in the room. It was suffocating.

"Is there anything else?" Tin Eye asked wearily. "Anything else you have not told us?"

"No," said Max. "That's all."

But it wasn't, of course. Max had left something else hidden under the stairs, even deeper in the shadows than von Roenne's secret.

They would never have believed it anyway.

CHAPTER Fifty-Eight

Stein and Berg had been there. Of course.

They had been on Max's shoulders through it all. They had raged, and cursed, and wept, and done their weird little best to comfort Max.

Max had gotten to see his mother for three days, and at the end of the third day, Max said to her, "I was mad at you, Mama. I was mad at you for sending me away."

And she held his hands across the table. He wanted to hug her so badly. But he knew that a hug was far too dangerous, for him and for her and for von Roenne—so he held her hands as tightly as he could.

"Why did you?" Max had asked. "Why couldn't we have stayed together? Why should I be out there, in the world, when you're in here, and Papa is . . . Papa is down there?"

His mother replied, "I do not pretend to understand the world, Max."

"Neither do I," Berg sobbed.

"I'm going to ask the Boss, at the end of time," Stein added as he wiped his nose with his dirty little sleeve. "God has some serious explaining to do . . ."

"I'll turn myself in," Max said rashly, as tears spilled down his face. "I want to be here with you. So we can be near each other, help each other . . ."

"Don't you *dare*," his mother snapped. "Don't even *say* that to me. You have to live. That's your only job. Don't come here again. Don't try to save me. I didn't give birth to you so you would protect me, Max. I gave birth to you so you would live. That is all I ask of you. Go. Live."

She stood up.

It was time.

For him to go.

But before they could move to the door, Max felt a very strange sensation.

He couldn't tell what it was at first. But then he saw that Stein had crawled down off his shoulder, down his arm.

"His shoulders aren't so sticky anymore," Stein said, looking back at Berg.

Max felt odd now. Unbalanced.

"Goodbye, Max," Berg said.

"Goodbye?" Max repeated silently.

Stein, now at the end of Max's arm, said, "You've got this, kid. Whatever you face, you're going conquer it. No question about it."

"And don't worry," said Berg. "We're gonna stay on your mother's shoulders right through to the end of this war. You're going to see her on the other side."

"She's gonna make it. We promise," added Stein. "I get it now. It's what we're for."

Max's last words to them were: "You're going to make her *wish* she was dead."

Stein chuckled. "Yeah, we'll miss you, too, kid."

Then they were gone. Max couldn't see them anymore. His shoulders felt strange. Empty. Light. Bereft.

But Max saw his mother's face change. She looked at one shoulder, and then the other. She appeared to be terrified. Von Roenne couldn't see any of that—but Max could. He grinned as his mama glanced back and forth, back and forth, as if she was listening, and talking, to immortal, invisible creatures . . .

Then she turned to Max, with awe and wonder and more than a little fear.

"They'll take good care of you," Max said. "Even if they're complete pains in the neck."

His mother tried to smile. "I love you, Maxy."

And Max said, "I love you too, Mama."

CHAPTER
Fifty-Nine

It was long past midnight as Ewen piloted his blue sports car under the shadowy bare branches of Richmond, away from Camp 020. There had been one last round of handshakes, a sisterly smile from Jean, who had still been waiting outside, and that had been it.

"I want you to know, Max," Uncle Ewen said, "how impressed I am with you. What you accomplished in Germany is more than I had even dreamed of."

Max was exhausted. But he refused to let his head fall back on the headrest. Not quite yet. The English didn't pay compliments very often, and if Uncle Ewen was going to compliment his work, Max was going to stay awake for it.

"We have other spies in German territory. But no one who has risen as high in the ranks as you. Lunch with Hitler? Unimaginable! Really, Max."

This reminded him: he had an urgent question for Uncle Ewen. Suddenly, Max was no longer sleepy. "Why didn't you want me to assassinate Hitler?"

Uncle Ewen smiled ruefully through the windshield.

"I considered giving you a chance. I really did. But I discussed it with Admiral Godfrey. Godfrey and I discussed it with the heads of the British Intelligence. And then we all met with Winston Churchill. It was the middle of the night, actually. Churchill was in his war offices, underground, wearing a nightshirt."

Max pictured the spymasters of Great Britain, standing around Winston Churchill in his nightie. Discussing *him*.

"So why wouldn't Winston Churchill want Hitler dead?" Max asked.

"It wasn't just Churchill who decided it. We all did, Max. Hitler is a lying, psychopathic murderer. He is also his own worst enemy."

Max said, "Huh?"

"Hitler believes his own lies, Max. If someone else were leading the German war effort . . . if the brilliant tactician General Rommel were suddenly in charge, or your friend Alexis von Roenne . . . I don't believe we would ever defeat Germany. Their army is too large, their factories too productive.

"But with Hitler at the helm . . . You told us as much yourself! Hitler is invading Russia! The entire foreign policy of the German nation for the last hundred and thirty years has been devoted to *not* fighting both Russia and the Western powers at the same time! And now Hitler is *choosing* to! Because he believes that he alone knows best, and that the center of the 'global Judeo-Bolshevik conspiracy' is in Moscow." Ewen shook his head in disbelief.

"If we ever beat the Nazis, it will be because of this. Because Hitler believes his own lies." Ewen took his eyes off the road and looked at Max. "That is why we did not let you kill him."

Max had to think about that for a while.

He stared out the window as Ewen piloted the car out of Richmond and into the streets of London. Ewen cleared his throat. "I also wanted to say that I am so sorry about your father and mother," he said.

Max did not reply.

"It must have been awful, seeing your mother that way. Still, I'm grateful that you did. Your report was more than I dared hope for."

Max turned sharply to look at Ewen.

"What do you mean, *dared hope for*?" Max demanded. And then, "You *hoped* I'd see a *concentration camp*?"

"No, no!" Ewen said quickly. "But I hoped you would learn about the camps. As much as you could. I was counting on it, actually."

Max found himself blinking many times as he stared at Ewen.

"Admiral Godfrey and Lieutenant Chumley believed that infiltrating the Funkhaus was your only mission. But we knew better, didn't we, Max? We knew you were going to look for your parents."

Max could not believe it. *"You told me not to!"*

"Reverse psychology," Ewen said apologetically. "Please, let me explain:

"There have been rumors coming out of Germany for over a year that the Nazi concentration camps are *changing*. They were set up to house enemies of the state. This is not strange. We do the same thing in times of war. But through my networks I'd been hearing rumblings of something different. It wasn't just enemies of the state any longer. It was 'degenerates.' The disabled. Romany. Jews. And they weren't just being held there. They were being worked to death. Or *worse*.

"I, and many others, have tried to confirm these rumors, and warn our leaders. But Admiral Godfrey, and Churchill, and even President Roosevelt, have not wanted to believe that such a thing was possible. They did not want to believe that the Germans would round up millions of people in order to *murder* them. And no matter how I howled and wailed in meetings, no matter how many memos I wrote to various offices in Whitehall and in Washington, DC, no one listened. They were all rumors, they said. Just hearsay. Nothing solid. No eyewitness accounts."

Ewen ran his tongue over his thin lips. "Well, now they have an eyewitness account. Yours. Recordings of what you said tonight are being sent to Churchill and Roosevelt as we speak. Maybe now they will believe the truth. Maybe now they will *do something*. *That* was my real mission for you, Max. Whether you knew it or not. I even gave it a name. Just in my head. I called it *Operation Kinderspion*—or, in English, Operation Child Spy."

It had been a lie. His mission had been a lie. Max suddenly realized that von Roenne had guessed from the beginning that Ewen had some ulterior motive. He'd said, *This is not your mission.*

"Why didn't you tell me?" Max asked quietly. They were in Kensington now. Not far from the Montagu house. There were bomb craters where three houses had once been. A light snow had started to fall from the black sky.

"Admiral Godfrey never would have let the mission go forward if he knew its real purpose. And I didn't want to complicate things by having you lie to everyone in British Intelligence any more than you already were, on top of lying to everyone in Germany. It was too much lying. Don't you think, Max? Haven't you had enough lying?"

Max watched the snowflakes appear in the dim yellow headlights of Ewen's car and melt away on the cobblestone streets.

"Now," Uncle Ewen went on, "what do you say about forgetting this whole spying thing, and going back to being a child for a while longer? How about giving up the lying, and *living* a little?"

Max thought back to his mother's final command, as the snowflakes fell.

"Yeah," said Max. "That sounds pretty good."

They pulled up in front of 28 Kensington Court. Max never expected to feel so happy to see that pompous brick facade. Ewen cut the engine. Max climbed out of the car. The front door opened.

Uncle Ivor stood on the top step.

A pit opened at the bottom of Max's stomach. Should he turn and tell Ewen that his brother, and Max's favorite person in England, was a spy for Soviet Russia?

Ivor was beaming at Max, his cheeks as round as his eyeglasses, his smile as wide as a table tennis net. If Max told Ewen the truth, Ivor would be imprisoned for life. Or hanged. Quite likely he would be hanged.

Ivor ran down the steps and stretched out his arms to Max.

Max stretched out his own arms and fell into a bear hug. He felt Ivor's soft coat sleeves around his shoulders and he heard Ivor softly, softly crying.

And Max thought, *Between the truth and this, I choose this.*

Ewen wrapped his arms around them both.

They stood there, for a long time, holding one another in the falling snow.

THE END

HOW MUCH OF THIS STORY IS REAL?

Max Bretzfeld is fictional. But most of the other characters in this book are not. Their attitudes, emotions, motivations, and actions are real. The world—the frightening, complicated, often horrific, occasionally beautiful world that they lived in—existed.

In many ways, it still does.

Adolf Hitler

Let's start with this guy, because everything in Nazi Germany started with the *Führer*—a word which literally means "leader" but which I translated as "Supreme Leader" to capture the spirit of how it was used in reference to Hitler—and to underline how creepy it was that everyone called him that all the time ("Yes, my Supreme Leader!" "Thank you, my Supreme Leader!").

My depiction of Hitler was shaped by many sources, including Hitler's own speeches and writing. I was also influenced by a marvelous walking tour of Munich that vividly traced Hitler's first few years as a Nazi, as well as a class at Brooklyn College with Professor Steven Remy, author of *Adolf Hitler: A Reference Guide to His Life and Works*. But as much research as I did on Hitler, I took some liberties as well: While we do know that he held luncheons very much like the one depicted in this book, and I am confident that his favorite sound in the universe was his own voice, I do not know for a fact that he stared off into the distance with marinara sauce creating a red fringe on his absurd little mustache. (Though I suspect he did.)

Many of Hitler's statements in this book are taken from documented quotes of his, though I occasionally condensed and adapted them to convey his point more succinctly (he was not a master of brevity). There is some dispute as to whether Hitler actually said, "Do you really believe the masses will ever be Christian again? Nonsense! Never again. That tale is finished. They will betray their God to us. They will betray anything for the sake of their miserable little jobs and incomes." The quote was reported secondhand by an early confidante of Hitler's—Hermann Rauschning—who later abandoned him, so it may or may not be literally accurate. But it is certainly consistent with my understanding of Hitler and his views.

Adolf Hitler wrote about the Big Lie in his book *Mein Kampf*. He said that people are more willing to believe a big lie than a small one, because they themselves tell small lies every day, but don't believe that someone would have the gall to tell an enormous lie. And even if they don't entirely believe it, he explains, a Big Lie will leave an impression on the mind of those who hear it—and they will give it more credence over time, especially if they hear it over and over again. Hitler never admitted to telling Big Lies himself—in fact, he ascribed the technique to "the Jews." But as with every accomplished liar—including a few who are very active in today's world—he always accused his enemies of what he was actually doing himself.

Joseph Goebbels

From very early in his political career, Hitler relied on Joseph Goebbels to help propagate his Big Lies. My depiction of Goebbels was informed by reading entries from his (deeply disturbing) diary, as well as an introduction to the first English edition of that diary, written by an American journalist who knew Goebbels personally, Louis Lochner. I was startled to discover that Goebbels's long-term girlfriend was Jewish, as was his PhD advisor. I was less startled to discover that the development of his antisemitism was pathetically and transparently tied to failures in his own life: As he quarreled more and more with his girlfriend . . . when his advisor was sharply critical of his dissertation . . . when his plays and novel were rejected again and again by publishers (some of whom were Jewish) . . . when, having failed as a writer, he took an unfulfilling job at a bank (where his bosses happened to be Jewish) . . . each successive failure made the antisemitism of his diary entries more and more virulent.

And then, in the depths of his despair, when he was *begging* the universe for something to believe in and regularly contemplating suicide, he met Adolf Hitler. To the great sorrow of the world.

The Funkhaus

Joseph Goebbels created the Ministry of Propaganda and Public Enlightenment (the ProMi) soon after Hitler took power in 1933. It's a truly dystopian name for a ministry—and I imagine it influenced the names of George Orwell's ministries in *1984*.

Much of the ProMi's work was done at the Haus des

Rundfunks, which was run, in large part, by Hans Fritzsche, Wolfgang Diewergre, Alfred-Ingemar Berndt, and Eugen Hadamovsky. Their jobs were both to invent propaganda and also to report news in ways that made Hitler and the Nazis look good. While their banter is invented, I tried to depict their personalities in accordance with accounts from a highly detailed book called *Hitler's Airwaves* (see annotated bibliography).

Hans Fritzsche was the most trusted voice in Germany, the Walter Cronkite of his time and place, and reading transcripts of Fritzsche's reports is dizzying and disorienting. He was a master wordsmith, and I found myself wondering, after reading a few transcripts, if Hans Fritzsche wasn't correct in asserting that the Allies were the aggressor in World War II, trying to subjugate Germany as just another colonial possession. It's a ludicrous position—Hitler invaded ten countries in less than a year—but Hans Fritzsche was a remarkably convincing propagandist. I don't know to what extent Fritzsche believed his own rhetoric—but I imagine that when he didn't, he used the magic of his own words to convince himself, along with everyone else.

Gustav Adolf Scheel

Scheel was a real person, and while I invented the part of his backstory about stealing a science project from a Jewish student, the rest of his history is real. He did advocate against Emil Julius Gumbel, the mathematician and committed anti-Nazi. And he did join a death squad, deporting and executing Jews in France, the country Gumbel had fled to. I don't know whether Gumbel actually called Scheel stupid, but I'd like to imagine he did.

I invented the scene in which Scheel sees the soldiers returning from World War I, but I was attempting to capture a very real phenomenon. A great many of the most enthusiastic Nazis were of his generation—too young to have fought in WWI and bitter to have missed the chance to distinguish themselves as their older brothers and fathers and uncles had done. Nazism gave them a chance to compensate for a generational inferiority complex.

Alexis von Roenne

Alexis von Roenne was a conservative to his bones—a defender of the monarchy, aristocracy, and the old order. He didn't believe in democracy or people's right to self-determination. And he supported the German military in its ambitions through most of his life. But, unlike the overwhelming majority of Germans who called themselves Christians at that time, Alexis von Roenne saw clearly that Hitler's ideology and actions were contrary to the core tenets of Christianity. So von Roenne stood up for what was right—but sneakily. The espionage historian Ben Macintyre argues convincingly that von Roenne was indeed sabotaging Hitler throughout the war, despite being "Hitler's Favorite Intelligence Officer." Von Roenne may even have aided the Allied invasions of Sicily and Normandy by giving Hitler faulty intelligence assessments.

This theory is supported by how Alexis von Roenne died. He was closely connected to the Operation Valkyrie group, who attempted to assassinate Hitler in 1944. After the attempt, von Roenne was put on trial and found guilty of treason. Before his execution, he wrote to his wife: "In a moment now I shall be going home to our Lord in complete calm and in the certainty of salvation."

The British Characters

Ewen Montagu, Charles Cholmondeley (pronounced *Chumley*), Jean Leslie, and the rest of the cast of British spies are real historical people who are brilliantly documented in the work of Ben Macintyre—particularly in his wonderful book *Operation Mincemeat.* Evidence presented in that book indicates that Ivor Montagu was very likely a Soviet agent, with the code name "Intelligentsia." We don't know if he was passing information to the Soviets about his own brother, or if Ewen ever found out who Ivor worked for. If Ewen did discover his brother's secret identity, he never reported him to the authorities. Love is complicated.

Melita Maschmann

One character I wish I could have featured more is Melita Maschmann. She was a real person who wrote a searching autobiography about her role in the Holocaust. Growing up, Maschmann had been good friends with a Jewish girl—until Melita betrayed her family to the Nazis. Thankfully, the Jewish family managed to escape Germany. Maschmann became a committed Nazi, active in the ethnic cleansing of Poland. The story about a man chasing her through the field of flowers, and her appropriation of the large house for Nazi officers, was told by Maschmann in her book, though it took place in Slovenia, not Poland. And Maschmann never worked at the Funkhaus—that was a liberty I took. After the war, Maschmann wrote her former friend letters, apologizing for her betrayal and trying to explain how she had allowed herself to join the forces of evil. The explanation isn't pretty, and it certainly isn't exculpatory. Far from it. But it is believable and, crucially, comprehensible. She ultimately published these letters as a book called *Account Rendered.* I strongly recommend this book to every class, from seventh grade up, that studies the Holocaust. In all my research, I never found a more enlightening explanation of how an average person could become so committed to Nazism.

Hitler Youth

My account of the Hitler Youth's activities is all based on historical documentation. While none of the boys in Max's troop are real people, the hikes, the home nights, the speeches, the hateful song, and the fist fights all come from historical accounts. The moment with the calipers was something that I invented—I wanted to show that bogus Nazi "science" could have infected the beliefs of even of a smart anti-Nazi like Max. But then I watched *Europa Europa*, based on the amazing memoir of a Jewish boy, Solomon Perel, who survived Nazi Germany by hiding his Jewish identity and joining the Hitler Youth—and this very experience with the calipers, including passing the test, happened to him! As John le Carré once wrote, "We invent everything we write; even if someone else has done it before." In this case, Solomon Perel had literally done it, and survived.

The German People

Most of the Germans Max encounters in this book are not real individuals—but they *are* based on types that appear in historical records. I thought of the Persickes as the average German family—supportive of Hitler, though maybe with one parent more aggressive about that support than the other. And we know that millions of Germans, including young people, informed on their neighbors the way that Liesel does in the book. Pastor Andreas represents the many Christian pastors who were uncomfortable with what Hitler was doing but didn't know how to stand up to him. There were, sadly, many other pastors and priests who were strong supporters of Nazism, and quite vocal and influential in their support. Herr Pfeiffer is also an invention, though his story, including seeing Josephine Baker at the Metropol, could have been the story of many gay men in Nazi Germany—at least, the ones who were lucky enough not to end up in a concentration camp.

Overall, my view of ordinary Germans was deeply influenced by a sentiment expressed by Stanley Hoffmann, who survived the Nazi occupation of France as a child and grew up to write a landmark study of French people who collaborated with the Nazis. He wrote, "A careful historian would have—almost—to write a huge series of case histories; for there seem to have been almost as many collaborationisms as there were proponents or practitioners of collaboration." Or, as Max says, "Seventy million Germans . . . Seventy million reasons to collaborate." Some were motivated by ambition, others by insecurity; some by fear, others by greed; some by racism, others by xenophobia; some because they believed in Nazi propaganda; others because they had a desire for a strong National Community; and some were simply searching for meaning and purpose in their lives—and found it in the most evil place possible.

I imagine there will be readers of this book who object to the way I tried to humanize Nazis and Nazi sympathizers. But I did that very intentionally. Too often, books and films about Nazi Germany portray the Nazis as monsters. I think that's a mistake. I think it's crucial to show that the Nazis were *humans* who acted *monstrously*. This is important to me not because I care to defend the humanity of Nazis (I don't), but because if we think of Nazis as monsters, it becomes hard for us to see how our neighbors, or our friends, or our parents, or we ourselves might find ourselves following in their footsteps.

Sachsenhausen

My description of Sachsenhausen, the concentration camp just north of Berlin, is based on records, photographs, and the accounts of survivors of that camp and others.

I want to mention one small detail: the parking lot. It occurred to me, rather late in the process of writing, that concentration camps must have had parking lots—since SS officers and others would have driven their cars there. Curious, I looked at WWII-era aerial photographs and, indeed, I located the parking lot at Sachsenhausen. I was dumbstruck: *A concentration camp had a parking lot, like any other modern building.* These events are not long ago, they are not far away. These people are modern people, who murdered millions upon millions of other modern people as brutally and quickly as they could. And if they could do it, we could.

If we don't tell stories like this one, and make sure as many young people read them as possible, we *might* do it. It won't look exactly the same. History does not repeat itself. But watch the news, read social media—heck, *listen to the radio* these days—and you can hear it rhyme.

ANNOTATED BIBLIOGRAPHY

Nazi Germany is perhaps the most thoroughly documented time and place in history—which is a little daunting when writing historical fiction about it, because years of research left me feeling like the proverbial bird pecking at the mountaintop of eternity. For both young readers and adults looking to learn more, it can be bewildering to know where to start. Here are a few of the sources that were critical in writing this book, with notes—to help you decide if they might be useful to you, too. (Some of these were already cited in *Max in the House of Spies*, which also includes additional sources particular to Great Britain during World War II.)

Maschmann, Melita. *Account Rendered: A Dossier on my Former Self.* Translated by Geoffrey Strachan. Lexington, Massachusetts: Plunkett Lake Press, 2016.

Maschmann's memoir of her path to and life of Nazism was written as a series of letters to a Jewish former friend who Maschmann informed upon—and then lost touch with. As I said in "How Much of this Story is Real?" I firmly believe that anyone in seventh grade and above who studies this period *must* read this book. There is no clearer or more convincing account of how a normal teenager could commit their life to the evil of Nazism.

Fallada, Hans. *Every Man Dies Alone.* Translated by Michael Hofmann. Melville House: Brooklyn, 2019.

Kästner, Erich. *Emil and the Detectives.* London: Puffin Books, 2015.

Lutes, Jason. *Berlin.* Drawn and Quarterly, 2020.

These three pieces of fiction are excellent entry points to the world of Berlin in the 1920s and the Nazi era. *Emil and the Detectives* is a middle grade novel that was written in 1929! It's sweet and delightful—Emil visits Berlin, has his money stolen, and enlists the children of the city to help him get it back. *Every Man Dies Alone* is far less upbeat—it's a novel depicting daily life in Nazi Berlin written immediately after the fall of the Nazis by a writer who suffered through every second of it—including being imprisoned in an insane asylum while Joseph Goebbels tried to force him to write an antisemitic novel (he refused). Also, Hans Fallada is my favorite pseudonym, as its drawn from Grimm fairy tales: Fallada is the name of the horse whose head still talks after he's decapitated in "The Goose Girl." And *Berlin*—which itself has a fantastic bibliography—is an epic graphic novel about regular people living through the rise of the Nazis.

Harris, Mark Jonathan, and Deborah Oppenheimer. *Into the Arms of Strangers: Stories of the Kindertransport.* London, New York: Bloomsbury, 2000.

Kaplan, Marion A., ed. *Jewish Daily Life in Germany, 1618–1945.* Oxford: Oxford University Press, 2005.

Meyer, Beate, and Hermann Simon, and Chana Schütz, eds. *Jews in Nazi Berlin: From Kristallnacht to Liberation.* Chicago, London: Chicago University Press, 2009.

Pine, Lisa, ed. *Life and Times in Nazi Germany.* London: Bloomsbury Academic, 2016.

These were my primary nonfiction sources for Jewish life in Germany. While *Jews in Nazi Berlin, Jewish Daily Life in Germany,* and *Life and Times in Nazi Germany* are excellent collections of scholarly essays, *Into the Arms of Strangers* should join Melita Maschmann's *Account Rendered* as required reading for young people and adults alike who want to understand what it was like to grow up in Nazi Germany. *Into the Arms of Strangers* is a collection of first-person accounts of life in Nazi Germany and Austria; *Kristallnacht*; the flight to England; and their lives once they got there, as recalled by the children who were part of the *Kindertransport.* It is so rare, in primary sources from this period, to find details this specific to and appropriate for young people. I cannot recommend it highly enough.

Bartoletti, Susan Campbell. *Hitler Youth: Growing Up in Hitler's Shadow*. New York: Scholastic Focus, 2005.

Gratz, Alan. *Projekt 1065: A Novel of World War II*. New York: Scholastic, 2016.

My depictions of the Hitler Youth were drawn from these two works. Bartoletti's Newbery Honored work of non-fiction is an excellent resource for young readers, and Gratz's spy thriller is, like all of his work, excellent both as a work of history and a page-turner. Gratz's novel also inspired me to use the Irish Diplomatic Mission, and its secret room.

Jörgensen, Christer. *Spying for the Führer: Hitler's Espionage Machine*. New York: Chartwell Books, 2014.

An historical account, with lots of excellent photographs, of Nazi espionage before and during World War II.

Bergmeier, Horst, and Rainer Lotz. *Hitler's Airwaves: The Inside Story of Nazi Radio Broadcasting and Propaganda Swing*. New Haven, London: Yale University Press, 1997.

Welch, David. *The Third Reich: Politics and Propaganda*. London, New York: Routledge, 2002.

These two books offer a detailed look into the propaganda program in Nazi Germany, and the use of radio in that program. *The Third Reich* is an excellent overview of how the Nazis thought about and implemented propaganda, and was the very first book I read in the process of creating Max's story. *Hitler's Airwaves* is a remarkably researched deep dive into the *Funkhaus* and the specifics of Nazi radio propaganda—including vivid introductions to Hans Fritzsche, Wolfgang Diewerge, Alfred-Ingemar Berndt, and Eugen Hadamovsky.

Sheinkin, Steve. *Impossible Escape: A True Story of Survival and Heroism in Nazi Germany*. New York: Roaring Brook Press, 2023.

Wiesel, Elie. *Night*. New York: Bantam Books, 1960.

Yolen, Jane. *The Devil's Arithmetic*. New York: Puffin Books, 1988.

If you'd like to understand the experience of the Nazi concentration and death camps, these three books—nonfiction, memoir, and fiction respectively—are excellent places to start. Sheinkin's and Wiesel's are best for ages thirteen and up, while Yolen's works for ten and up.

ACKNOWLEDGMENTS

Since the first days of the pandemic, I have been working on this story. Reading, arguing with myself, arguing with other people, scribbling mad notes in the margins of books, dictating into my phone, and, finally, writing. And rewriting. So much rewriting. Each chapter of this book is a palimpsest of previous iterations, which hover just out of sight. I hope I chose the right ones. I owe thanks to more people than I can remember, but here are just a few:

For over a decade now, Professor Steven Remy has been a friend to me and to my wife, Lauren Mancia, who is his colleague at Brooklyn College. He truly went above and beyond in allowing me to audit his course on the history of Nazi Germany, and then in taking time away from his work on *Adolf Hitler: A Reference Guide to His Life and Works* to consult with me for this series. I am in his debt.

Professor Remy was an early reader of both volumes of Max's story. So was Katherine Locke, the brilliant author of *The Girl with the Red Balloon* and *This Rebel Heart*, among many other books; her thoughtful feedback was instrumental for some key decisions I had to make. Other invaluable early readers were Marissa Honma, Lauren Mancia, and Zachary Gidwitz (you read a book, Z!).

I read this book aloud to my mother, Patricia Lewy. We laughed together, cried together, and puzzled together over passages that weren't quite working. I am grateful to her for just about every aspect of my life—including my life itself!—but most relevantly for my taste, my standards, and my sense of humor, which all come from her.

My father is reading the first volume of the book as I write these acknowledgments, along with Linda Boyd Gidwitz. His feedback is more meaningful than I can say. I love you, Papa.

I would like to thank the people who make Brooklyn Bridge Park the most beautiful outdoor office in the world. They may never read this, nor know who that weird guy with the hat is, sitting on various benches (depending on the sunlight and wind), reading entire novels to himself aloud and laughing at his own jokes. But you bring beauty into the world that I rely on daily. Lucy Goosey appreciates it, too.

An enormous thank-you to John and Linda Mancia, my second parents, whose beautiful home sheltered me and the family during the earliest days of the pandemic, and under whose sugar maples this book was initially conceived. The character named after your family, Signora Savasta, isn't half as warm and welcoming as you are.

I have so many loving friends who have worked through every question in these two books, from the philosophical to the most banal: the Hotel Bar, John and Raquel, Ryan and Jesse, Julian, Yoni and Jane, Tony, and Erica. And Ally Horn, who is both a collaborator and a friend.

Speaking of friends, Brandon Woolf and Tina Petereit are

dear friends who lent me their expertise in the German language, German culture, and their actual apartment on Oranienstrasse—which is Max's. Thank you for guidance, good humor, good food, and love.

Penguin Young Readers Group creates the warmest and most supportive publishing home an author could hope for. Jen Loja, Jocelyn Schmidt, Shanta Newlin, Carmela Iaria, Trevor Ingerson, Emily Romero, Anna Booth, Rob Farren, Natalie Vielkind, Olivia Russo, Jenna Smith, Venessa Carson, Christina Colangelo, Bri Lockhart, and the very best sales team in publishing—I am luckier to work with you than I have any right to be. Thank you.

My agent, Sarah Burnes, has held my hand through the tough times and let me run out ahead when times were good. For those times and everything in between, thank you.

Julie Strauss-Gabel—I said it last time, so you already know. We made this book together. Nothing I do would even exist, much less be what it is, without your wisdom, taste, and painstaking attention to excellence.

And to Lauren and Ellie. I love you infinity times infinity infinity times.